FRACTURED CRYSTALS

FURY FALLS INN · BOOK 4

BETTY BOLTÉ

www.MysticOwlPublishing.com

Copyright © 2021 by Betty Bolté
www.bettybolte.com
Digital ISBN: 978-1-7354669-6-5
Paperback ISBN: 978-1-7354669-7-2

To all my readers everywhere…

Dear Reader,

This story continues the series of six supernatural historical fiction stories set in 1821 northern Alabama. With each of these, I fully expect I'll discover more about the history of this state I call home.

I'd like to thank my beta readers who read a prepublication version of *Fractured Crystals* and provided invaluable feedback. I appreciate your time, observations, and suggestions for improving the story!

I'd also like to thank readers like you who continue to inspire me to write stories with joy and passion. I always enjoy hearing from my readers, so please drop me a line at betty@bettybolte.com any time.

If you enjoy this book, please subscribe to my newsletter via www.bettybolte.com to be informed of the release of the rest of the books in the series. You can also learn more about me, my other books, and read excerpts of each book at my website. You may also enjoy learning more about the behind the scenes research and recipes included in this story at www.bettybolte.net.

Again, thanks for reading! I hope you enjoy *Fractured Crystals!*

Betty

Chapter One

Northern Alabama, September 1821

The time had finally arrived. He'd acted upon his best instincts and business sense. He wouldn't change his mind even if his recent actions might upset the girls. Now all he could do was wait for the desired response. Flint polished the mahogany bar with a soft cloth, the dining room nearly ready for the imminent mid-afternoon dinner rush. He nodded to a pair of men dressed in refined suits relaxing at a table, enjoying some quiet conversation over a drink on the far side of the room. The patrons of the Fury Falls Inn deserved the best service. They'd been loyal and supportive of his efforts over the last several months in improving their experience when they visited. Even if they weren't aware of the hidden magical and spectral qualities of the people who lived in—or rather haunted—and worked at the remote inn.

Cassie sashayed into the room, her stylish uniform gracing her slender form as she approached. The blue skirt and white blouse combined to enhance her features and give her a polished look. She'd done a fine job of taking meal orders and providing what the customers wanted. Her caring nature was one of the reasons he'd fallen in love with her. Her generosity and intelligence all came wrapped up in a pleasing package. Long blonde hair braided but left to hang down her back. Pale blue eyes that twinkled when she looked at him, drawing him into her enchanting realm with ease. Petite and slender, he loved when she smiled with her not quite even teeth. A beautiful young woman he was proud to call his girl. However, with the senator's visit only a couple of months away he'd had to make some more changes to bring the inn up to snuff. He swallowed hard as she neared, dreading revealing to her what he'd committed to without forewarning her.

He snapped the towel and then hung it on the rail behind the bar. Propping his hands on his hips, he surveyed the large room filled with twenty cloth-covered tables. Cassie and Mandy had already laid the tables and arranged the vases of flowers and refreshed the candles on each, ready to light. He knew the kitchen staff were hard at work putting the finishing touches to the menu items. He sniffed the subtle scent of spice and the aroma of baking bread. This afternoon's dinner included one of interim cook Matt Simmon's specialties, curried chicken and rice, which had become popular after the cookery competition the previous month. With Sheridan Drake, the renowned cook of the inn, and Zander off to Savannah to find the cook's wife, Matt had filled the role with ease. Which didn't come as much of a surprise since they'd recently discovered Matt and Zander were actually Sheridan's long-lost sons. But Flint really hoped the older man would return before the senator arrived. Two excellent cooks on staff would be far better than one.

Cassie braced her hands on the edge of the bar top, leaning forward to peer closer at his eyes. "What's on your mind? You look far away."

In some ways, he really wished he were far away. But he'd not turn his back on his girl when she needed him. His right hand gravitated to the flintlock pistol on his hip. He'd not leave her unprotected only perhaps disappointed. "I have something I need to tell you."

"You're worried. What have you done?"

Of course, she could sense his feelings. He'd nearly forgotten her unique ability in the midst of stewing over how she'd take his news. "I placed an ad in the paper, looking to hire men to wait on the customers." There, he'd said it. He studied her reaction as she processed what he'd said. "I think it's time."

"Really?" She mulled over his statement and then gave him a big smile. "When will they start?"

"You're not upset?" He examined her expression, seeing only her lovely features. No hurt or disappointment lingered in her eyes or drooped her tempting lips.

"No, I'm glad to have more time to manage my garden." She clasped her hands together. "And I'll be able to sing more. I really want to be better at singing. Then we'll have more entertainment for the senator you're so worried about."

Relief swept through him at her easy acceptance of what he considered a momentous decision. Until her brother Abram had come to the inn and told him about the expectations of more refined customers, such as the senator, to have male waiters instead of female, he hadn't given it a second thought. But if the higher quality establishments in the nation's capital only hired men to wait on the customers, he had to make the change. Reginald Fairhope had hired him to not only manage the inn but to make the necessary improvements to suitably impress the esteemed official.

"I'm glad you're not offended." He dropped his hands to slide them into his front trouser pockets. "I'd hoped you might appreciate having more time for your other concerns."

"You may want to hire some more people to help Matt, too. At least until Sheridan comes home."

"Is he struggling? He hasn't said anything." What else had the younger man been keeping to himself? Flint would have a talk with him, make sure he had everything he needed.

"I don't think he's struggling, but it would make it easier with a couple more scullery maids."

"I'll think about it." He pulled his hands free and rested them on the bar. "We should have a good crowd this afternoon. It's a nice day and Matt is preparing his curry chicken again."

"That always brings them out. Will you do another competition?" She swept her gaze around the room and then met his eyes. "The first one was a fine time."

"We'll see what your father has to say when he gets back from his trip." He hoped the man would return sooner rather than later and bring the new furniture for the inn with him.

The inn's owner had departed in late June to oversee the building of new beds, tables, chairs, wardrobes, and more. He'd contacted a company in Savannah, Georgia, which he had been told made fine wood furniture suitable for the inn. The expense of the large order prompted Reggie to spontaneously decide he needed to go supervise, to ensure it indeed met his expectations. Reggie had ridden into Huntsville to speak to Flint's father about having Flint fill in for him while Reggie was away. Then Reggie left for Georgia while Flint took up residence at the inn. He'd never forget the fury evident on the face of Cassie's mother, Mercy, when she found Flint in charge after she and Cassie had returned from a shopping trip to Nashville. Things had been rocky between them ever since.

"I want him home, too." Cassie shook her head, the light in her eyes dimming as her blonde braid whipped side to side. "I need to talk to him about so many things."

"Maybe you could write to him…" But honestly how could she possibly share all the revelations and secrets in one letter?

After Mercy's murder, and her ghost subsequently haunting the inn, Cassie had written to her brothers, asking them to come to pay their respects and to help her until their father returned. But then she discovered she could sense emotions in others as well as affect those emotions through her singing. As each of her brothers arrived, they'd discovered a unique ability they hadn't known they possessed. First Giles with his superhuman strength and role as Guardian of the family, in particular of Cassie. Then Abram with his shapeshifting. The other two, Daniel and Silas, hadn't yet arrived so remained mysteries as to their abilities. He imagined receiving a letter from her with the details of their abilities and pressed his lips together. A letter with such information would prove difficult to believe.

She shook her braid harder. "I'd much rather sit down and witness his reaction to everything Ma has told us."

She stilled then, her gaze turning inward for several seconds. He waited, assuming she was sensing something with her psychic abilities. Then she grinned at him.

"What?" He couldn't possibly guess what she had discovered, but it was obviously something good.

"Daniel is getting closer."

Flint blinked at her, struggling to grasp how she could possibly know. "How can you tell?"

"He's emoting a sense of urgency, like he's flustered and anxious. He's nearly here now."

"Great." Another brother of hers that he'd have to win over. Despite his own lack of magical abilities or even anything special about him.

He was a simple man with simple desires. His only supposed ability was being able to speak to ghosts. But most everyone could do so with Mercy's haint so even that didn't prove special. He wished he had some capability which would set him apart, make him seem worth being part of her family. But he found himself striving to measure up with a family filled with witches and warlocks, psychics, shapeshifters, and who knew what else. He faced a tough road ahead competing with magic. What ability would Daniel have? Only time would tell.

The nondescript borrowed nag half trotted, half walked up the long dirt lane leading toward the Fury Falls Inn. No amount of kicking or clucking could convince her to increase her pace despite Daniel's former frantic efforts. He'd given up urging her to go faster because nothing worked to make his desire reality. His sturdy gelding had unfortunately bruised a hoof and he'd been forced to leave him behind in Knoxville. The only other horse available proved to be barely sufficient and slow to boot. At least the mare's slow pace gave him the opportunity to now assess the property where his sister waited for him. Had been waiting for him much longer than he'd prefer. He hated the thought of people waiting for him, especially when he should have already arrived.

The large building dominated the hillside. He passed a lattice-sided gazebo off to the right, covered in flowering vines. An inviting retreat he'd need to investigate. The two-story red brick and stone inn ahead of him was actually two structures joined together with a covered porch between them, a structure also known as a dog-trot house. Glass windows sparkled in the late afternoon sunlight. A pair of chimneys flanked either end of the shake-shingled roof. A welcoming front porch stretched across the entire front of the structure with a table and pair of chairs to the left of the double doors leading inside. A single door provided an entry point on the right side. The dirt lane ended at a circular carriageway with a crushed stone surface. Very clever and progressive idea. Such an enhancement would reduce the mud and dust guests would otherwise encounter upon arrival.

Off to the left a fair-sized barn with fenced pastures boasted not only horses but also cows and hogs. Chickens pecked in the dirt in front of the barn. Four dogs nosed about the several coaches and carriages as well as men mounted on horses. Obviously, the popular inn and its hot springs attracted a steady flow of folks to visit. Clouds drifted across the pale blue sky, hinting at rain later in the day. In the distance the foothills rose in their fall glory. The entire place invited him to ride closer and become part of the hustle and bustle.

He found a spot at one of two hitching rails and dismounted, looping the leather reins over the warm wood. Several men in work clothes and brimmed hats stomped up the few steps to the wood plank floor of the porch and through the open double doors. No point in standing outside when his mission waited inside. He snatched his saddlebags from behind the saddle and hurried after them. Surely Cassie was anxious for his appearance since receiving his letter announcing his impending arrival after so many delays. At least, he hoped for her welcoming greeting.

Pausing a few strides inside the entrance hall, he surveyed his surroundings. Sparingly furnished, the inn was clean and refreshing. A side table beside the door held a large vase of colorful flowers to scent the air. A swinging wood door in front of him across the wide expanse revealed a bustling kitchen as a young brunette woman in a tidy blue skirt and white blouse pushed through with a tray of steaming plates. She hurried around the corner to enter the large dining room replete with cloth-covered tables he could espy through an arched doorway to the left of where he stood. A single door to the right led outside to the covered porch between the buildings. Cassie's home was not fancy but in a rustic sort of way it welcomed nonetheless. He needed to find her and then get the hell out of the inn. His real life, friends, and students all waited for him back in Tennessee. Back where he had the respect and admiration he'd worked so hard to attain in his short life. Unlike in this relatively wild outlying area, one so remote it seemed even worse than he imagined. Voices sounded from the dining room. He started to turn toward them when a pair of tall, black-haired men emerged from inside and then hesitated when they saw him.

"Daniel?"

The somewhat shorter of the two men peered at him as he resumed his progress across the space between them. A burly man, with a powerful stride, indeed. The other man was a couple of inches taller but not as stocky. They resembled each other, both having the same jet-black hair and strong jaws. The taller man also wore a small scar on his chin that looked familiar.

Daniel glanced between the two and suddenly knew them. His older brothers. Despite the years since he'd last seen them, they hadn't changed all that much. Taller and stronger, they had matured into self-confident men. Unlike him. Even his dark blond hair marked him as different. "Giles. Abram."

Giles, the stockier of the two, started to hold out his hand and then switched to pull Daniel into a brief bear hug. "It's good to see you."

The strength of the hug nearly crushed his chest and tipped him forward until he was released. When had Giles become so blazing strong? Regaining his balance with some little difficulty after the unexpected embrace, Daniel glanced at Abram. "Why are you guys here?"

"Cassie asked us to come." Abram shrugged with a smirk

on his lips. "Just like you."

"I'm sorry I'm so late getting here. I hate that it took so long, that I'm late to the game, so to speak, but I had to…"

"Finish business. Yeah, we know," Giles said with a brief chuckle. "Are you still taking on more tasks than you have time for?"

"No, I don't—" He'd had to wait for a substitute professor to arrive to teach his natural science students before he could leave the college. Leaving in the middle of the term felt like abandoning them. They relied on him and he'd let them down. But he agreed with Cassie that he had an obligation to come ensure her safety with their father away and her left alone with strangers. Apparently, Giles didn't want to hear the reasons for his delay. Bristling at the interruption to his explanation, he glared at his brothers. "What do you mean?"

"That's a surprise if so. You used to overcommit all the time." Abram tilted his head as if to examine him from a different perspective. "I remember trying to teach you how to say no to requests, but it didn't take. But I guess it's possible you've changed since then."

"I have changed in many ways since last we were together." Daniel blinked at his brothers, grappling with the implications. He drew in a deep breath and released it slowly, striving to calm his flustered self. Best to do what he came to do and extricate himself from the situation. "Anyway, where is Cassie? I came to see her, not you two."

"She's preparing for the afternoon rush, but I know she's anxious to see you. I'll get her." Abram spun around and went back to the dining room with long strides and disappeared through the arched doorway.

"So, what took you so long to answer her request?" Giles folded his arms over his broad chest. "Playing teacher still?"

"I'm a professor, not just a teacher." A distinction he

would have loved to make to his mother. She'd scoffed at the idea of him becoming an instructor of any kind when he'd declared his intention as a boy. Sadly, her untimely death meant he'd missed any chance of talking to her let alone indulging in a bit of bragging over his success.

"I know. Don't get your drawers in a bunch." Giles chuckled again. "I'm sure you try your best."

"What is your problem? I have only just arrived and you're giving me a hard time." He straightened his spine, looking down slightly at his oldest brother. He may not feel confident all of the time, but he did when it came to his profession. The stellar education he'd received ensured he could teach others about those topics he was most knowledgeable about. Nobody could take that away. "Why?"

"No reason. Just joking with you." Giles dropped his arms to shove his hands into his front jeans pockets. "I'll stop if it's bothering you."

Daniel refrained from rolling his eyes with an effort. "Thank you."

The supposed banter didn't settle well on his tense shoulders. He'd not traveled so far to be insulted by his oldest brother. Nor did the poking at his ego after not seeing his family in so long. How could any of them know how he'd changed from his many challenges and experiences? Giles simply stood there with a steady look, as if assessing him and finding him lacking in some inexplicable way. Or perhaps waiting for him to do or say something worthwhile. But what?

"Daniel!" Cassie's sweet voice called across the entrance hall as she trotted toward him. She flung her arms around him, pulling him close. "I've missed you."

"Hi, Cassie." He hugged her for a moment and then stepped back to look at her more closely. "You're all grown up into a beautiful woman. Look at you."

"I'm so glad you're here." She blushed at his compliment, a smile flashing onto her lips before her expression sobered. "Now that you are, we need to talk."

"If you'd like." Something in his sister's suddenly serious tone set his teeth on edge but he could tell she felt it was an urgent matter. A jolt of concern squared his shoulders. "I assume you mean now?"

"It's important but doesn't need to happen immediately." Cassie regretted the worry in her brother's expression after her declaration, but it couldn't be helped. He needed to be made aware of the situation he'd walked into, but she didn't want to scare him in the process of revealing all of the family secrets. Still, surely he'd expect to visit his mother's grave. "Do you want to pay your respects to Ma's grave out back or settle in first?"

"You mean, she's buried here? I hadn't considered where she might be resting in peace." He blinked his deep green eyes at her several times. Cleared his throat and glanced at his brothers. "I suppose settle in and freshen up before embarking on that personal chore."

"I see you have your bags." She'd not correct him in his assumption that their mother was resting in peace yet. Still, she didn't blame him for delaying the moment when he went out to the family cemetery. He'd not had any dealings with their parents in years and to come to the inn at Cassie's summons was a gift in and of itself. His reluctance and nervousness felt normal as a result. She nodded as she looked to her other brothers. "You two need to determine where he'll sleep."

"I have room in my chamber for now," Giles said. "Until Zander comes back."

"Who do we have here?" Flint approached the group by the front doors. Curiosity blanketed his features as he approached. He wore his auburn and gold hair loose about his shoulders, making her fingers itch as always to run through it. Tall and kind, he glanced at her with his jade green eyes before meeting Daniel's expectant gaze. Flint held out his hand to Daniel when he reached Cassie's side. "Welcome to the Fury Falls Inn. I'm Flint Hamilton the innkeeper."

Daniel clasped Flint's hand and shook once. "Professor Daniel Fairhope."

"My brother." Cassie smiled up at Daniel, tapping his elbow once. "We're only missing Silas now."

"You invited all of us?" Daniel frowned slightly at her. "Why?"

"I can answer that." Giles pulled his hands free and pointed at Cassie. "She was feeling alone and abandoned by our parents and wanted her brothers to come to her. To rebuild the family. Only…"

Cassie held up a hand in front of Giles. "Don't. Let him get settled and then we'll go out to the gazebo to have the real talk with him. It's more private. Will that suffice?"

Giles shrugged his broad shoulders. "Fine."

"It's kind of you to offer to share your chamber, Giles. But why don't Abram and Daniel share a room upstairs in the residence side? Giles is already sharing with Matt and Zander or will when Zander returns." Flint glanced to see Abram's reaction. "Would that suit?"

Cassie sensed confusion streaming from Daniel, acceptance from Giles, and reluctance from Abram. She met Abram's placid eyes with a quirked brow. "Are you in agreement with that idea, Abram?"

He hesitated, resignation in his mind, and then shrugged. "I believe so." Abram motioned for Daniel to follow him. "Come on, brother. I'll show where you can put your things."

Abram led Daniel toward the side door leading out on

the dog-trot porch and closed it behind them. Cassie turned to Flint and Giles, Daniel's concern over the mare flowing through her. "His horse, a brown mare, needs to be taken care of."

"I'm heading out that way anyway to check the area. I'll take care of the horse." Giles flipped his hat onto his head then crossed to the double doors and outside.

She reached out to him, his concerns escalating inside as he departed. The farther apart they were the more he worried about what might happen in his absence. Her Guardian deeply cared for her and wanted to ensure her safety. The connection they shared grew taut, vibrating with tension and uneasiness, so she sent her own calm to him until his disquiet eased. Slightly.

"What are you going to do now?" Flint asked, grasping her shoulders lightly and drawing her regard. "Wait on customers or sing?"

"Probably a little of both, actually. Depending on how many customers we have." She loved the care shining in his eyes and his kind strength. Who was she kidding? She loved everything about the man she'd promised to marry. "I—"

Her ma suddenly appeared behind Flint, the pale blue dress she'd been buried in dancing about her ankles as she hovered a few inches above the floor, a smile on her lips in place of her usual tense expression. Her long ash-blonde hair floated around her as her smiling aqua-blue gaze met Cassie's somewhat startled one. She sniffed and detected a hint of rosemary in the air, denoting the presence of magic.

"Cassie, there you are."

Flint dropped his hands from her shoulders and spun around to face the ghost. "Mercy, you startled me." He glanced quickly around the entrance hall. "You shouldn't be here."

"I can go where I want to, Mr. Hamilton. This is my

home, too." Mercy floated a few inches from the planks of the floor. "Even if I am a haint."

"I don't want the customers to know you're a ghost, and that the inn is haunted by you." Flint ran his hand through his hair.

The loose, flowing hair invited Cassie's fingers, but she resisted. Especially in front of her ma. She needn't stir up that kettle of aggravation. "What do you need, Ma?"

"I'd like to spend some time with you." Mercy turned to face Cassie with another inexplicable smile. "When do you want me to teach you how to use your wand?"

A surge of joy enveloped her core at the offer. Her number one priority was to learn how to use her magic, her unique abilities, to best advantage. Improving control over her voice's unique quality of influencing the mood and compliance of others in ways to make their lives better, more enjoyable, seemed like a worthwhile endeavor. Even more, discovering how she could protect herself, create her own defensive techniques, might ease her Guardian's deep-seated concern for her welfare. But she had some other things she must do first.

"I want to wait until after we talk to Daniel about…everything going on here at the inn. I think that will be a little later this afternoon and then I plan to entertain the guests this evening. So, tomorrow morning before I have to work?"

Ma shifted to one side and then back again. "That's fine with me. I'll be sure to join you for the conversation with Daniel, too. He came all this way to see me, right?"

Cassie stiffened. "Not exactly. He doesn't know about you still being here. Please, Ma. Stay away until we can warn him of everything, give him time to adjust to the situation before he sees you the first time. It's only fair to him. Remember how frightened Abram was when he first saw you?"

Her poor brother had bolted from the gravesite, racing inside the inn and crashing into Mandy before he'd stopped his flight. It had taken both her and Flint to calm him down. She didn't want Daniel to have such an alarming introduction to the news of their mother's ghost and their magical abilities.

"True. But how will Daniel know what his special gift is without me to tell him?" Mercy shimmered and then briefly solidified, her agitation evident in her tight expression. "I should be there."

She held out her hand to her mother, wishing she could really touch her. "You will be, only after we talk to him. Please?"

Flint draped an arm around Cassie's shoulders. "He'll appreciate your graciousness by giving him a chance to adjust to the new realities he'll face, Mrs. Fairhope."

"Said like the haughty whippersnapper you are." Mercy folded her arms over her translucent bosom, her mouth a flat compressed line, as she swung her gaze back to Cassie. "If you insist."

"Thank you, Ma. I appreciate your forbearance." Cassie sighed, unable to stop the expression of relief. "So, I will see you tomorrow morning in the attic for my lesson?"

"Very well." Mercy shifted to one side, hovering over the floor like a low storm cloud.

Footsteps sounded on the covered porch, coming toward the trio in the entrance.

"Mercy, you have to go." Flint flashed his glance around the open space. "Before someone sees you."

"Don't be bossing me, young man." Mercy glared at him for a long moment, the booted steps growing louder. "I won't tolerate it."

Flint opened his mouth, but Mercy shook her finger at him until he closed it again. He looked helplessly at Cassie.

"Please, Ma. For me?" Cassie could only hope her mother would comply. She couldn't control her mother as a ghost any more than she could when living. Once her ma became upset at Flint, there was no telling how long she'd harangue him. The finger in the face motion indicated her annoyance with him. "It's for the best and only for a little while."

"Very well. For Daniel's sake, not Flint's." With a darkening glare, Mercy shimmered and disappeared just as the side door opened.

Cassie glanced sharply at the sound of deep voices bantering. She pasted a smile on her face, her pulse beating in her ears, as Daniel returned with Abram, blissfully unaware of the recent exit of their mother's ghost. She planned to keep it that way for a little while longer, too.

Chapter Two

*T*hank goodness it was the Fairhope brothers and not a customer approaching. Flint darted his gaze at Abram who squinted briefly at him, perhaps guessing the reason for his tension. Flint nodded slightly to him in return. Cassie didn't want to scare Daniel by him seeing his mother's ghost before she'd had the chance to tell him everything he needed to know. So at least one goal had been achieved. For now. "Not entirely, actually. That's why I started humming, but it wasn't enough." Cassie released a long sigh. "I felt his fear building but didn't have a chance to try to explain. To calm him down."

"Did we miss anything?" Abram asked, a quirked brow the only indication of his suspicions.

"Nothing." Cassie crossed the floor to stand in front of her brothers. "Why don't you two go find Giles in the barn and then go on out to the gazebo where it will be more private. Flint and I will meet you there in a minute."

"For the talk? Good idea." Abram looked at Flint and then at Daniel. "Right. Come on, brother."

"Is this really necessary?" Daniel studied Abram and then Cassie. "Just tell me already."

"Not in here." Flint made a shooing motion. "Go on. We're right behind you."

Flint took Cassie's hand and followed the two men through the open front doors. The men trotted down the steps and made their way to the barn. Flint surveyed the carriageway and the slower evening traffic, in particular an elegant red and black coach-and-four stopping in front of the inn, and then drew Cassie to a halt at the top of the steps. A tall man with graying hair under his black beaver top hat along with his slender, blonde curly-haired wife in her pink satin gown emerged from their impressive vehicle and started toward him. Their fine clothing and carriage declared to all their prestige and wealth. But what was Sterling Nelson and his wife doing here so late in the day?

"Hello, Mr. Hamilton. I hope you don't mind an impromptu visit." Sterling escorted Abigail up the steps to stand beside Flint and Cassie on the porch. "It's such a nice evening we thought we'd come have our supper here. Perhaps Miss Fairhope will favor us with a song or two?"

"Of course, sir." Flint spotted another carriage coming up the lane and struggled to stop the frown from weighing down his brows. Not in front of this important customer. Even if the unanticipated arrival raised more inner qualms. This time on a business level. "Go in and Mandy will see to your supper needs."

"Very good." Sterling smiled at Cassie. "I'm looking forward to hearing your lovely voice, Miss Fairhope."

"Yes, sir. I will be in before too long." She dipped a slight curtsy and then straightened. "We first need to properly welcome my brother back into the folds of the family."

John Baker's carriage pulled to a halt at the bend of the stone carriageway. Cassie's brothers came out of the barn and headed toward the gazebo, silent and watchful as they passed the group on the porch. Flint glanced at Cassie when Sterling frowned as he noticed the other carriage and the three brothers peering up at them. Sterling's stern regard of the trio softened after a beat. What was that about?

Sterling recovered first, a soft smile erasing the earlier expression as he regarded Abigail. "Come, my dear, let us go in and find some seats."

Abigail took Sterling's arm and they strolled inside, leaving Flint to wonder what was happening. John stepped out of his dark red carriage pulled by a pair of bay horses and joined Flint and Cassie on the porch. Dressed in his usual type of attire—blue trousers, gold coat over a white shirt and blue necktie, shining black low boots—he appeared tired and ready for a hot meal and cold drink.

"Flint, how are things going with you?" John glanced briefly out to where the men had settled on the white benches in the gazebo. "I'm about to report to Reggie how you're managing."

Of course he was. The ever-present embers of concern flared into a flame every time he remembered Reggie had asked John to keep an eye on his efforts. It would have been preferable to know his boss actually trusted him. He'd been left in charge and Flint was doing his best to make viable enhancements to the property and to the services and menu the inn offered. Reggie had not written to him of any complaints as to those improvements. Perhaps his concerns over John's reports were unfounded and he should relax. If only he could. But he could defend himself.

"Actually, business has increased to the point I have advertised to hire a few male waiters like the fine establishments in the big cities do." Stew on that piece of information for a few minutes. John's eyebrows rose a fraction as he momentarily pressed his lips together. "I have a few other improvements in mind as well."

"I'm sure he'll be happy to hear of your progress." John glanced back to the men in the gazebo. "A new arrival?"

"Yes, my brother Daniel arrived this afternoon." Cassie looked to where her brothers sat talking together. "It's been years since we've all been together."

"Is that all of your brothers?" John asked, meeting her smile with a small one of his own.

"I have one more I hope will arrive soon," Cassie said, her gaze flicking to Flint. "Silas is the youngest and so the closest in age to me. He was my best friend when we were little."

"That's a good-sized family." John's smile wavered. "Well, I merely wanted to check in before I wrote to your father. I'm sure he'll be anxious for an update by now."

"I'm afraid we need to join her brothers for a private conversation." Flint really wanted to walk away from this uncomfortable situation but not without a good reason. His boss couldn't object to him talking to his sons after all the trouble they took to journey to the inn at Cassie's bidding. "If you'll excuse us?"

"Of course. I'll go inside and look around and have a little something before I head home." He tipped his hat to Cassie and then eased past them to go into the dining room.

Cassie peered after him for several beats and then met Flint's gaze. "That was very strange."

"Indeed." Flint clasped her hand, his thoughts and emotions in turmoil. "Let's go have this conversation and then get back to work. Ready?"

He shouldn't be so surprised by her beauty. His little sister had grown into a stunning young woman standing on the front porch with Flint and some other folks. Petite and slender, blonde hair in a thick braid down her back. She still possessed a gentle smile and a way of making one feel she cared and was interested in whatever one said. But even from where he sat half-listening to his brothers' inane lecture in the gazebo, he could see the set of her shoulders and the tension in the angle of her neck. What had her so worried?

"Damn it, Daniel." Giles snapped his fingers in front of Daniel's nose, angry hazel eyes inches from his face. "Listen to me. This is important."

Daniel blinked as he focused on his brother. "You keep going on and on. Why should I listen to you?"

He didn't need a lecture from his brother. Not after all he'd survived since the last time he'd seen him. Daniel had been so young when he struck out on his own to make his way in the world. He'd been very fortunate to eventually meet a college professor, Dr. Paul Jenkins, who recognized his intelligence and encouraged him to read all he could, then to go to college, and then to become a professor himself. He'd been surprised to learn he was some kind of boy genius when it came to book learning, especially natural philosophy which studied the earth and its components. He discovered he remembered everything he read, could practically visualize the page it was written on if he focused hard enough.

If it hadn't been for the guidance and mentorship of the kind gentleman, he wouldn't have found a home at the East Tennessee College as a professor despite his very young age. In fact, the faculty had been impressed by his depth and breadth of knowledge in spite of his being only nineteen years old when hired. The fine education was all due to the tutelage of his savior. The man had saved his life.

Now something hard and unrelenting in Giles' eyes made him sharpen his focus. "What were you saying?"

"You need to listen to him." Abram leaned forward from where he sat on a white metal bench off to one side of the gazebo. His piercing blue eyes seemed to glow with intensity within the shadows. "Because he's our Guardian and knows what the hell he's talking about."

"He's not my guardian. I'm an adult." The very idea made the hair on the back of his neck prickle.

He wasn't a child. Unlike when he'd first been kicked out

and he left home. Terror had weighted every step he'd taken as he walked away from home, heading into the city to find work and some place to live. He had few practical skills to turn into a career path. He'd found some paying jobs at the livery, then the printing office which he despised, and then at the bookstore which he discovered he enjoyed. That was where he'd met Professor Jenkins who was looking for a book or pamphlet, any information at all, on the bones and fossils other paleontologists had found over the years in America. The mammoths, in particular, that Thomas Jefferson was obsessed with understanding.

"Not that kind of guardian, for pity sake." Abram shook his head. "He's the magical Guardian of the family. The Guardian assigned to protect all of us. Listen to what he's saying."

"Very well." Obviously, he'd upset his brother through his woolgathering. Now he was talking nonsense. Upsetting him, though, was not his intent. Daniel pressed his lips together as he turned back to his oldest brother. "I apologize for letting my thoughts distract me. What were you saying?"

Giles huffed and then continued. "I'll start again. Before Cassie and Flint join us, it's important for you to understand the level of danger aimed in her direction from our aunts as well as from an unknown killer."

"Killer?" Daniel frowned when Giles and Abram both nodded. "Someone is trying to kill our sister?"

"And other women in the area," Abram said. "We think they are hunting witches, but we don't know for certain."

"What do witches and aunts have to do with this killer and the threat to our sister?" Daniel glanced between his brothers and then noticed Cassie and Flint start walking toward the gazebo. "Cassie's coming."

"You really weren't listening, were you?" Giles turned to confirm Daniel's observation and then peered at him again as he spoke faster. "Our aunts are witches like Cassie and all of us, in fact. They want Cassie to join forces with them."

Daniel started to nod but then a chill swept through him as he realized what he'd just heard. "We're all witches? Are you insane? That's not possible."

"Surprised?" Abram grinned. "We were all surprised to learn we come from a family that practices magic. On both sides of the family, in fact. All of our aunts and uncles, too."

"Dad has siblings?" He stared at his brothers, struggling to absorb the shock. "Why didn't he tell us about them? And what kind of magic?"

"We don't know why he didn't, but as for magic, all kinds, good and bad." Giles studied him for two beats. "We need to keep Aunt Hope and Aunt Faith from getting hold of Cassie no matter what it takes."

He vaguely remembered the two women who had lived in a big house not far from his childhood home. They'd been kind to him when he was very young, giving him treats when he'd visit with his brothers. Sometimes the families shared a special meal on special days of the year and then the food abounded while someone would play the piano and sing. Good times. They'd take their cousin George and go to the swimming hole down the road on a hot summer day. Until the awful day when George drowned, then swimming in the lake was no longer as much fun. In fact, that sad event seemed to trigger other tragic events. But witches? No hint had he seen of his aunts engaging in witchcraft.

"I had no idea." Daniel gripped his knees with both hands to hide their trembling. "And the killer? Do you have any idea who it might be?"

Giles folded his arms over his stocky chest. "Possibly John Baker, a business colleague of our pa, but we're not certain. There appears to be a group of men who are working with John and Sterling Nelson, a local banker and important customer at the inn. We're not sure what their intentions are though."

A man who worked with his father might be involved in hunting down people. Including his sister. That possibility was bad enough. "You think we're witches?"

Giles shrugged. "I know we are. I assume you are, too."

Daniel frowned. "I don't think I am. How would I…" A chill swept down his back as a vague memory surfaced. He had recently felt something odd happening in his body. A strange kind of vibration buzzing inside when he'd run late getting to class. Or to any appointment. "Why now? And would I feel different?"

Abram relaxed back on the bench. "Maybe. After Ma died her binding spell broke, so that's why now. As to whether you'd feel any different, that would depend on your gift."

"Ma's what?" A distinct buzz started in his chest with each revelation dumped on his head.

"Yes, she's a witch, and yes, she put a binding spell on our powers so they wouldn't be detected by our aunts." Giles moved aside as Cassie put a foot on the bottom step. "Cassie will tell you more about Ma."

"There's more?" Daniel ignored the apprehension swirling in his gut. How much more could he take?

I paused just inside the door of the inn, glowering at the gathering of bloody witches and warlocks lurking and plotting in the gazebo. Their numbers kept growing, increasing and becoming alarmingly dangerous to the good people of the community. The young witch seemed to be gathering men to protect her. She must be very important to their plotting. If she's removed from the scene, the potential danger will be reduced. It has become more urgent than ever to gather the intelligence necessary to defend the god-fearing people of the region. Time to tap the right people to step in and deal with the witches once and for all. Nothing else matters.

Chapter Three

"You haven't told him the best part, have you?" Cassie quirked her brows and then aimed what she hoped was a reassuring smile at Daniel. "I assume he's told you we're all witches, not just Ma."

"Yes." He hesitated, apparently afraid to ask the question on the tip of his tongue.

She saved him the need. "That's not everything." She settled beside him on the bench along the back center wall of the six-sided gazebo. "Brace yourself."

"Should I be afraid?" He tensed beside her, his sudden fear and curiosity washing over her.

"No, but it is rather startling what I'm about to tell you." She didn't blame him for his reluctance to hear the rest, so she laid a comforting hand on his where it gripped one knee. "Our mother is not resting in peace. She's haunting the inn."

He stared at her as his mouth slowly fell open. "There's no such thing as ghosts."

Most people refused to believe in the presence of specters even when confronted with evidence. Given she had no proof, she'd need to convince him. "Yes, there is. I didn't want you to be shocked when you see Ma for the first time. She promised to give me the chance to talk to you before she pops in, but she's anxious to see you again."

"I don't believe for a moment she is a ghost or that you've talked with her." Daniel glared at Cassie, his defensive stance a wall building around him. "And she's definitely not anxious to see me even if she is. She's the reason we all left home in the first place."

Disbelief and shock battled inside him like two armies in hand-to-hand combat. She raised her protective barrier to prevent the intense emotions inside of him from overwhelming her. "I know. She's explained her reasoning for sending us away."

"And that is?"

"Giles, why don't you tell him?" Cassie glanced up at the Guardian.

"All right." The burly man shifted his weight to balance evenly on the balls of his feet. "She hid our powers and abilities and sent us away to protect us from being abused or ensnared by her family and their questionable witchcraft practices."

Daniel merely blinked slowly for a second before his anger burst forth. "She forced me to leave home at fifteen for my *protection*?"

"Calm down." Giles held up a hand, palm facing Daniel's scowl. "I understand. Trust me, I do. Now that our aunts know our abilities are free again, they are intent on having Cassie unite with them to form a trinity of witches."

"They think it will increase the power of the magic," Cassie added. "I'm not interested but they are not listening to my desires. Mainly because Ma refused them years ago, too. They are all the more determined to succeed in convincing me to be part of their trinity."

The more she pondered the intensity with which they demanded she face her destiny, the more she wondered if she had all of the facts. The feeling they withheld something more, something important and life-changing, niggled at the back of her mind. What that something might be worried her.

"All right, for argument's sake, let's say we're witches and I have some…kind of magical ability." Daniel glanced at Abram and then back to Cassie. "And let's say there are threats against you. Isn't it Giles' job as Guardian to protect you? So, what do you expect from me?"

Cassie opened her mouth to answer him, but Abram waved her into silence. Mandy emerged from the front door of the inn and hesitated on the porch, scanning the area with a sweep of her gaze, before skipping down the steps and sauntering across the yard toward the gazebo. Shadows stretched across the grass as the sun sought its bed for the evening. A soaring bird—not a hawk, but some other bird of prey she'd never seen before—cried out above, a high piercing sound in the cooling air. Abram's voice brought her attention back inside the gazebo.

"We need you to stay here until Pa returns next month so we can all use our individual gifts to protect our sister." Abram rose to his feet and paced to the other side of the gazebo floor before turning to look at Daniel. "We believe by doing like our aunts, joining forces, we have a better chance of protecting her and the family at large."

"Next month?" Daniel jumped to his feet and clasped his hips as he looked around the group, including Flint who remained mum. Daniel motioned with his chin at Flint. "Are you staying until Pa comes back, too?"

Flint nodded. "And beyond. I am betrothed to your sister and intend to marry her after your father comes home."

"Marry Cassie?" Daniel started shaking his head. "I can't take any more surprises right now."

Mandy walked up the few steps into the shade of the small building. "I hope I'm not interrupting."

Abram took her hand and led her to a side bench, sitting and drawing her down beside him. "Not at all. You're just in time to help us convince Daniel of his role here."

"It's a lot to take in. I understand." Indeed, Daniel really did need to comprehend how vital his presence was in the fight to protect the family from harm. Cassie stood and walked over to take Daniel's reluctant hand. "We don't have time to sit around and think about it though. Between the senator and his entourage coming next month, our aunts pressuring me to go with them now, the chance that the vow Abram made may kill him, and the mysterious killer on the loose, we must come together and present a united front." She squeezed his fingers and he raised his shocked eyes to meet her steady gaze. "Including you."

"But I don't have anything to ward off magic or killers." His scowl dissolved into an anguished grimace. "I'm only armed with book learning about the earth, not weapons or fighting strategies."

"You must have some special ability. Ma will know what it is." Cassie squeezed his hand again and then released her grip. "We'll find out from her soon, I'm sure."

Mandy made a small sound, drawing everyone's attention to her. "You don't need magic to stand by those you love. We each have a skill or talent we can use to defend the family. The one I hope to be a part of very soon." She slanted a smile at Abram.

"You two?" Daniel huffed a sigh as he darted his gaze around the group. "Anyone else around here betrothed or married or anything?"

Flint chuckled and smirked at Giles. "Not at the moment."

"But soon, with any luck." Giles bounced on the balls of his feet. "If she'll agree."

"I don't know what to say to all of this." Daniel flopped back onto the bench and clutched his knees. "I feel like I've walked into an insane asylum."

"Perhaps in some ways, you have." She chuckled as she studied Daniel, reaching out to sense his true feelings. Like so many others, the surface expression of disbelief and dismay hid his actual instinctive resistance to the changes he sensed coming. "It's not a requirement to fall in love when you come to the inn, Daniel. But if it happens, enjoy it, all right?"

Overwhelmed and shocked, Daniel could only stare at his sister. What she implied, the very idea he'd find a woman here to spend his life with, held less water than a bucket shot with a musket. "I have no intention of waiting upon any woman. I must return to my students post haste as the semester is only half over."

His brothers and sister all seemed to expect him to uproot his life and replant it at the inn. For an indefinite period. Leave behind his work, his studies, his students, and colleagues? Overthrow every single plan he'd made in order to become some kind of witch and defend his beloved sister from several threats. Now to consider possibly finding a woman to marry? Bah. Such an occurrence was preposterous. He stood and stared down at her. Perhaps he should turn around and head for home immediately.

"You can't leave. Not yet. Don't even think that way." Cassie shook her head adamantly. "You've just arrived, for one thing. We don't even know what your gift is yet."

A part of him wondered what it might be. But he really didn't want to find out. What did it matter? He wasn't staying. No matter how much she may want him to. His real purpose lay back in Knoxville, teaching students about the composition of the earth. About the stratification of the fossils and how they could help identify different periods of time in the past and the effects of natural processes like erosion on the landscape and formations surrounding them. The increasing interest in the role geology would play in bolstering the economics of the country made his chosen career important and influential. Geological mapping could point to where valuable minerals and gems lay buried. His contribution to the scientific conversation still lay ahead and he wanted to make sure the time he spent on the planet meant something in the future. Thus, he didn't need the interruption to his carefully laid plans.

"How do you propose we unearth this supposed gift?" He pursed his lips, dreading her next words because she'd already hinted at the method of discovery.

"I can only think of one option. Ma!" Cassie called out. "Come here, please." She shrugged at Daniel and then glanced at Giles and his doubting expression. "It's worth a try anyway."

Daniel cringed at the volume of her raised voice and the implications of her command. A shimmer caught his eye to one side in the shadowy gazebo and he stepped backward. Slowly the shimmer resolved into the figure of a slender woman wearing a pale blue dress, with familiar long blonde hair and aqua eyes, smiling at him. It took every scrap of courage in his body not to hastily put distance between himself and his mother…or rather his mother's ghost.

While he hadn't seen her in years, she really hadn't changed. Well, except she was smiling at him. That was new. She'd worn a serious look, distancing and putting off anyone who dared talk to her. She was still pretty and would forever stay so now that she'd become a specter. What a thought.

"Hello, Daniel. Welcome home." Mercy drifted toward him, hovering a few inches above the wooden floor. "I'm so glad to see you again."

He sucked in air, refraining with an immense effort from stating exactly how he felt about her comment. The nerve. After all she'd done to him, what both his parents had done, how dare she even suggest he'd come 'home'? "Mother."

She cocked a brow at him and then smirked. "Ah, still the same, aren't you, my son?"

"I beg your pardon?" He straightened his spine. He'd grown and matured over the past years he'd been on his own, fending for himself and making a solid reputation among his peers. Thus, he'd changed in many ways. "I do not grasp your meaning."

"Exactly my point. Still defensive and on edge. I had hoped you'd have overcome those tendencies. You don't wear them well."

Giles chuckled at the slight and Daniel shot him a quelling look. Giles merely shrugged and pulled a pocket watch from his front jeans pocket. The gold case with its ring of gems glinted in the evening light, a long chain securing the timepiece to his brother's pocket. Everything around Daniel came to a standstill as he stared at the beautiful, captivating, *entrancing* watch. His brother studied the time and then glanced up at him, his smirk shifting into a puzzled frown.

"What's the matter?" Giles held the watch on his palm, his gaze on Daniel.

"May I see it?" He needed to hold it. His fingers itched to grasp the gold object with a circle of small diamonds around the crystal. "Please?"

Giles regarded him for a long moment and then nodded. "I don't know why, but now that you ask I feel like it's the exact right thing to do."

Giles released the chain's clasp and then dropped the pocket watch lightly on Daniel's outstretched palm. The name Abraham Colomby, the watch's maker, graced the white face of the watch in a flowing script. The metal case warmed to his touch and a sense of peace and rightness filled him. A truly unique sensation. As if the watch had come home to him. He turned it over to stare into the painted coquettish eyes of a young woman in a fancy pink gown and large purple hat with white feathers arching above it on the back. On one side of the watch a nub of a stem bumped the pad of his thumb.

"Where did you get this?" Daniel asked Giles, meeting his brother's surprised expression.

"In the trunks in Ma's attic. At the time, I thought I wanted it for its utility but now I get the impression there was more to it." Giles folded his arms over his massive chest, his eyes serious as he met Daniel's gaze. "You look like you've found your true love, my brother."

No, not his true love. Something more. A deeper connection. Daniel inspected the watch, turning it slowly in his hand. "I… It's mine. I know it is, but I don't remember ever seeing it before." He frowned down at the gleaming gold metal and then glanced at his mother. "Do you know?"

"Well of course it's yours, Daniel. You are a Timeskipper after all. I've kept it safe for you until your return. Or rather, Giles has kept it under his protection as Guardian."

Gripping the watch, Daniel could only stare at his mother. Timeskip? Gibberish. Surely. Right? "What do you mean?"

"It's his job, to protect us and our magical artifacts." Mercy shifted to one side, gesturing toward the eldest brother with a wave of one hand. "I thought you understood."

"No, not about Giles." Although that was another subject he needed to grapple with another day. "What is a Timeskipper?"

Mercy smiled at him tenderly. "Why, you are. Didn't you hear me?"

He contained his frustration with an effort, his thoughts

and emotions whirling inside. "What does being a Timeskipper mean? What can I supposedly do, given I've never known I had any abilities beyond natural ones."

He waited for his mother to continue her banter and refusal to answer directly. Her tendency to cloud her statements until they were practically unintelligible irritated. He wanted answers, clear and concise. Not twisted meanings and allusions to things he wasn't aware existed until moments before.

Cassie leaned forward in her seat and caught Daniel's attention. "Be open to what she's saying, Daniel. Don't resist but try to listen with an open mind and heart. It will be easier that way."

Daniel blinked slowly at her. She spoke as if she could read his mind. Although he hadn't so much as formed the thoughts as felt frustration and annoyance. So how had she known?

"Because I can read your emotions, inside and on your face, especially when they are as strong as yours are now." Cassie settled back on the bench. "Your confusion and denial are particularly prevalent."

His Adam's apple slid roughly in his throat. He'd proceed cautiously so as to not tip his hand, or his emotions. Until he understood what the others' abilities might be, he'd keep his cards close to his chest. "Go on then."

"First, your special gift *is* a natural ability, just one others don't typically possess." Mercy's smile faded and she folded her arms over her chest. "Second, you have the very wonderful ability to bounce, as in move from one place to another instantly, and to timeskip to anywhere and anywhen. Especially with that watch to help you pinpoint the time."

He could do what? A chill swept through him as the ramifications and implications crystalized in his mind. He could travel through time. Could he go back to the beginning of the universe? The origin of the planet he lived on? The time before civilization began so he could see how not only the geographic structures but also geopolitical communities developed? Think of the papers and books he could write. He'd be famous but more than that he'd be adding to the scientific understanding of their world. But what if he tried and couldn't come back to his own time? A shudder rocked his shoulders. Stuck in the past, one he'd love to know better, but unable to return home to share his findings or resume his normal life.

"That's quite a daunting prospect." He pocketed the watch and then rubbed his damp palms on his trousers.

"I can help you learn how to hone your abilities so don't fret, son." Mercy dropped her arms to her sides as she shimmered. "A word of warning. There is one thing you must take care with."

"What is that?" He waited to hear some outlandish restriction as to how he could use his gift. Not to be seen, perhaps. Or not to change the past to his own advantage. What was the point of having such an amazing ability if he couldn't make some changes to improve his life?

"That little stem on the side? There's a small silver button beside it. Those two are what determines the 'when' you're going to. You can go to the past or the future with the watch's guidance." She pointed a stern finger at the pocket where the watch warmed his thigh. "Don't fiddle with them until you know how it works. And do not ever try to take more than two people with you or you'll fracture the time loop. Understood?"

He swallowed the distress rising in his throat like magma from a volcano. Great. Not only could he potentially travel but he could take guests and maybe along the way break everything that would enable him to come back home. With his luck, that's exactly what would happen. He swallowed again and nodded to his mother. "I promise."

Chapter Four

The next morning Cassie hurried to her parents' bedroom, wand gripped and ready. The hints her aunt had provided as to how to use the reddish-brown wood in her hand tantalized her imagination. More than that though. She needed to understand how to wield it to do her bidding. She trotted up the circular stairs to the landing outside of the attic, unlocked the door, and then pushed inside, its dim interior murky in the early morning light.

She crossed the room to light the oil lamp and brighten the atmosphere. "Ma? Are you ready?" She scanned the room as she pivoted in place. "I don't have much time before Flint wants me in the dining room." She wished she didn't need to serve the guests, if only Flint would hurry up and hire a few men to take over like he'd mentioned doing. Then she'd have the time to practice her magic, tend her garden, do her sewing to earn some pin money, and to sing for the customers. "I'm ready."

Mercy shimmered into view by the window, the soft morning light making her hair glow. "You're looking refreshed this morning, Cassie."

"Good morning, Ma." Excitement and curiosity flushed

her cheeks with warmth. "I'm eager to begin. Aunt Hope told me a bit about the wood my wand is made from. Black cherry apparently."

"Hope would start with something benign like that." Mercy inhaled with disdain. "What else did she say?"

"She said I had to have a purpose and intent in mind, then she showed me how to make an object fly."

Mercy frowned at her. "Fly? Why on earth…"

"Actually, she showed me how to make it move in the air at my bidding." The pleasure and pride she'd felt when she'd made the quill from her mother's inkstand write her name in the air with a mere flick of her wrist made her smile again. "I used your quill over there."

Her ma jerked back, her frown turning into a scowl. "You let Hope in here? My private quarters?"

Anger boiled inside of her mother's ghost. The heat washed through Cassie, so she raised her inner barrier to protect herself. "I'm sorry, Ma. She surprised me and then what she told me seemed to make sense. At least, at the time."

Mercy flowed forward with a stern expression on her face. "Now you listen to me and you listen well."

"Yes, ma'am." Cassie stayed in place with an effort against the wave of intense hatred and anger accompanying her mother's haint. While she knew of her mother's distrust and cautionary tales about her sisters, she hadn't been aware of the depth and strength of the antipathy Mercy felt toward them. She swallowed against the rising fear inside her chest as her ma stopped mere inches from her, one forefinger raised and pointed at her.

"Do not ever trust anything those two witches say to you. They will spin their lies and twist the truth around until you won't know up from down." Mercy shook her finger at Cassie and drifted a bit backward. "They care only for their own desires, their own questionable aims. I've seen them do wicked mischief at my father's direction. You mustn't ever fall in with them to do magic, do you hear me? Keep your guard up when you're around them."

"Yes, ma'am." What more could she say in the face of the fury on her ma's features? But why did she feel so strongly about her sisters being so bad? Something bad must have occurred to force the sisters apart. "What happened, Ma?"

"That's history you needn't trouble yourself with. Just promise me you'll be on guard." Mercy waited until Cassie nodded and then gave a nod of acknowledgement. "And one other thing you need to know before we begin your training."

Her ma's tone carried a blend of caution and importance. "What?"

"The real reason why they want you so badly." Mercy shimmered and shifted side to side with agitated jerks. "You have far more power than you realize yet. With the proper training, you will grow into the most powerful witch in the country. That is precisely why my father had demanded my involvement, so he would have control over me and then you."

"Me?" But how? And why her? If she became stronger than her aunts, it would infuriate them. The image of her aunts' ire quaked her nerves. "How do you know?"

"My father once told me as much. He told me of a vision he had, that my daughter would possess the ability to grow into a supreme being." She shuddered and flashed bright before resuming her translucent state. "He scared me with his demands, his intention of using me, finding me a husband of his choosing, to create you and then control you before you could realize your power. I defied his orders and found my own husband, a strong warlock who could protect me from him. I'd do it again, too."

"You defied your father? I can't imagine."

"He did not take it lying down." She shuddered again as her gaze turned inward for several seconds. Mercy focused on Cassie with wide eyes. "After he tried to test you, I knew what needed to be done. I had to do something to make him believe his vision was wrong."

The horror on her mother's face when she said *test* prevented Cassie from asking for details. "That's why you bound my powers? To prove him wrong?"

"I hid your powers so he, and they, couldn't control you. Or me any longer." She trembled as she drifted closer. "It is not your destiny to work with my sisters. That is their wishful thinking. Your destiny is far greater than they can even imagine."

"Will you teach me, Ma?" Her mother understood much more about magic and witchcraft than Cassie had fathomed. "With your tutelage, perhaps I can learn to defeat them."

"Indeed, my dear. I will begin your training, but we'll need your father to complete it." Mercy smiled softly at Cassie. "He comes from stronger stock than even I do. He's the best person to elevate what you know to the heights my father envisioned."

Another reason for her pa to hurry home. She needed his guidance and instruction in order to reach her true potential and realize her destiny. As long as she wasn't killed by the witch hunter or kidnapped by her aunts, she had a chance to become the witch her grandfather actually saw in his vision.

"I hope Pa will come home very soon then." Cassie dragged in a breath and blew it out. "I need him home so much."

"Agreed. In the meantime, let's begin at the beginning. Hold your wand lightly in your hand. No, don't clutch it, but keep it firmly in your fingers. Yes, like that."

Cassie gripped the wand and pointed the tip toward the ceiling. "Can you tell me why my wand is black cherry wood? What does that mean?"

Mercy's features softened as she glanced at the wand with its slow twist handle neatly shaped. "You found that while you were out walking with your pa. He's the one who shaped the handle. He was so proud of you for selecting your first wand at only two years old and a fruitwood at that."

"Is there something special about fruitwood?" Cassie had no recollection of the day she'd chosen a piece of wood for a wand. Her first memories didn't go back to being a toddler. Nor did they even include the fact she owned a wand. She traced the smooth handle with her other finger, wishing she could recall her pa shaping and finishing the wood. At every turn it seemed as if she'd been denied her power as well as her life. But now the future loomed with a far brighter light.

"Fruitwoods are sacred to the Goddess." Mercy bestowed a gentle smile on Cassie. "Cherry wood possesses very positive and harmonious energy. Indeed, a feminine energy useful for healing and love magic. It helps with spells to promote unity and a sense of community, too. And it will help you find other magic around. It's a very powerful and desired wood to have chosen you for its owner."

"I like the idea it chose me." Cassie angled the wand to inspect the fine grain and smooth finish. "What more do I need to know in order to properly use it?"

"The wand is simply a tool for focusing your mind and energy to do your will." Mercy shifted to one side. "Most importantly, you need to remember that you can perform spells and magic without using it."

"I see." Cassie let her gaze drift around the attic until she spied a particular book with a distinctive red cover on the shelf. She pointed her wand at it, concentrated on her desire to possess it, and summoned the heavy tome. After a second or two, the leather-bound book slid off the shelf and floated slowly toward her. She pointed with the wand for the book to float across the room and then come to rest on the table by the window, which it did with a thud and a little puff of dust. "Ha! I did it."

Mercy clapped her hands together once. "Very nicely done, too. But that's simply a parlor trick. You need to learn about how you can use verbal spells to accomplish your goals. Bigger goals than levitation. This is where your special voice will come into its own as well."

"My voice? How?"

"You can infuse your spells with the power of suggestion from your tone and cadence." Mercy floated closer to where Cassie stood. "The emphasis or softening you apply to your voice as you chant your spells will make them far more powerful."

Delight and shock battled in her chest at her ma's confident statement. "Are you sure?"

"Fairly certain."

Her imagination ran wild with possibilities and potential uses for the combination of her special ability with witchcraft. She had already witnessed the effect her singing had on the listeners in the dining room. Perhaps she could strengthen a spell by firming her vocal tone. Or raising her voice might push the magic into higher more powerful realms. But what if she got truly angry and her voice caused harm to someone? That could be very bad. She'd feel awful, no doubt. She took a deep breath and let it out slowly. Well, she simply wouldn't let such an event happen.

"It sounds like my powers are stronger than I realized."

"If only your familiar had made itself known by now. My familiar used to be an owl, but I sent him away when we moved here." Mercy drifted a bit sideways as she shrugged lightly. "Yours will claim you all in good time. But your familiar will aid your abilities in ways we can't predict."

"Tell me more, Ma." She grinned at her mother as she held her wand with both hands, tip to handle. "I hadn't thought about a fam—What's that?"

Tapping sounded at the small window as a shadow appeared on the outside. Mercy frowned as she turned to inspect the noise. She squinted at the dark silhouette for several moments before her brows arched and her mouth fell open. "Open it. It's for you."

"Who is out there?" Cassie eased across the floor, wand at the ready in case the shadow proved some kind of threatening presence.

"Just let him in." Mercy crossed her arms in anticipation of Cassie opening the window.

With a twist of her wrist on the small fastener, Cassie opened the window and peered at the intruder. A buff chested falcon hopped over the sill, stretched its blue-gray wings and flew into the room, making several loops before settling lightly on Cassie's left shoulder. Startled and afraid of what the bird of prey would do next, she held perfectly still and stared into the intelligent eyes intently studying her. It sported a dark and sharp beak with a touch of yellow at the top, and yellow feet with black claws. She swallowed her unease, aware of its calm appraisal. Then she met her mother's amused expression.

"What's so funny?"

"A Merlin, eh? That's your familiar?" Mercy chuckled. "I would have thought a cat was more your speed. But your grandmother would be proud."

"Why?" Confusion and disbelief mingled in her core. A falcon sat on her shoulder, angling its dark gray head at her as if reading her thoughts. Or her emotions. Hmm. And her ma seemed perfectly at ease with the bird's presence, which could only mean she'd seen something similar before. "Which grandmother?"

"Your namesake. Grandmother Cassandra Fairhope, your father's mother." Mercy drifted around to take a closer look at the Merlin. "She also had a falcon for her familiar.

Maybe it's related to your ability to know others' feelings or your siren voice. I'm not sure."

"Grandmother Fairhope was like me?"

"No, she didn't have your siren ability, but she was a very pure and powerful witch." Mercy wore a gentle expression as her gaze turned inward. "She was a lovely woman as well. We were proud to name you after her. It's quite a compliment."

"I wish I could have known her." She'd missed so much by being kept in the dark for so long.

A wash of frustration flooded her gut and the Merlin shook his wings, brushing her hair as he extended them behind her. She lifted her hand toward the bird, tentatively reaching out with her senses as well to calm its agitation along with her own. The bird pressed the top of its head into her outstretched fingers and then peered at her.

"Klee-klee-klee!" the bird called harshly then fell silent.

The cry she'd heard the other evening. The unfamiliar bird in the sky turned out to be her actual familiar. A falcon no less. "I think this little guy feels what I feel." Cassie raised astonished eyes to look at her mother's ghost. "Why do you suppose he came here today?"

Mercy clasped her hands together. "I don't know. I can only guess he felt it was time he introduced himself to you. Perhaps an approaching change prompted him to seek you out at this moment in time."

"Klee!" The falcon bobbed his head twice as he searched her face with his dark eyes.

"You agree?" The bird understood the conversation? At his quick nod, she smiled and shook her head. "Then you probably also know my name is Cassandra, or Cassie. What should I call you?"

He regarded her mutely before launching from her shoulder and zipping around the room, a blur of blue-gray wings until he settled on her shoulder once more.

"You are fast." She stroked his head with her forefinger, the tiny feathers soft and warm. "How about Allegro? I like to play the piano and sing and that means to play music fast."

"I like it." Mercy released her hands to prop them on her translucent hips.

Cassie raised her brows at her mother and then peered at the bird. "What do you think? Allegro?"

"Klee!" The falcon spread his wings and nodded his head, a gleam in his dark eye she took as approval. Then he took off, soaring out the window again. She raced to the window to peer outside, just in time to see him disappear into the trees at the edge of the forest. She searched for several minutes before securing the window and turning with a sigh to face her mother. "He's gone. Why did he leave?"

Mercy shimmered. "You can't expect him to hang around with you all day. He's got to hunt to eat after all. He'll be back. Probably when he feels you need him."

Cassie tucked her wand into her pocket and crossed the room to extinguish the lamp. Then she faced her mother again. "I've got to get to work anyway. Shall we meet again tomorrow so you can show me more about using my wand?"

"Without fail. You have much to learn. See you later, my dear." Mercy dematerialized, leaving the room feeling vastly emptier than when Cassie had first entered the private domain.

She hurried to the door, locking it behind her. Pausing to lean against the wood door, she reviewed the details of the conversation with her ma and the new knowledge about her abilities. A worm of doubt wiggled through her as she contemplated how she might need to call upon her gifts to defend herself and her brothers. Would she be ready when the time came? She pushed away from the door while trying to push away the unease. Still, the thrill of meeting her familiar lingered in her heart as she scurried down the steps.

Late morning on a Monday meant a lull in the number of customers in search of a meal to break their fast. The pause gave Flint a few minutes to take stock of supplies and ensure the tables were ready for the noon luncheon customers and the mid-afternoon dinner rush a few hours later. He scanned the dining room and its remaining handful of guests. Conversation was minimal which allowed the sounds from outside to drift through the open windows. The lowing of cattle and the nicker of a horse punctuated the soft flapping of sheets drying in the sunshine on the lines out back. As he pivoted toward the bar with the intent of checking quantities of bottles and the supply of mugs and glasses, Cassie and Mandy entered the room in quiet discourse together.

He crossed to the mahogany topped bar, pleased yet again with its refined appearance. The polished surface leant a more sophisticated air than the former scarred pine. Over the past several months, he'd methodically worked to improve and refine the inn's presentation and services. He had another month to finish out his plans before the highly anticipated visit by Senator Percy Graham in November. He'd made good progress and had every intention of being ready.

"Hello, Flint." Cassie gripped the wood counter with a welcoming smile on her lips. "You're looking quite pleased. What's up?"

"Just reviewing the upgrades I've made and the ones I intend to make." He grabbed a cloth from the rail behind the bar and quickly wiped down the counter. "Like the men I intend to hire. I put an ad in the paper last week. I'm hoping somebody applies soon."

Mandy's brows lowered as she aimed her light brown eyes at him. "Men to do what exactly?"

He snapped the towel with a crack and then began folding it. "To wait tables. I've told you I was going to, so don't act so surprised."

"Humph." Mandy folded her arms over her slim chest. "You're planning to take away my job, to give it to someone else. Aren't I a good waitress?"

He'd never meant to imply she wasn't. He waved a placating hand over the bar. "You're a fine waitress. It's not about you but about the expectations of our customers."

Cassie tapped a finger on the bar to gain their attention. "Exactly. My brother told Flint the restaurants in bigger cities only employ men to wait on tables."

"So now you're aspiring to compete with city establishments out here in the wilds?" Mandy shook her head. "That's a fool's errand, surely."

"I disagree, Mandy." Flint bristled at the girl's tone of voice. "You have nothing to worry about as you'll always have a job here as long as you want it. You're a great worker and I feel lucky to have you."

She arched her brows and shook her head. "Just not as a waitress. So, what would I be doing? The laundry?"

The umbrage in her voice gave Flint pause as Daniel sauntered into the dining room and took a seat at a table in front of a window. Cassie noticed and headed over to see what he wanted. Flint followed her movements with his eyes but then returned his gaze to meet the frown on Mandy's face. Should he suggest the new role he hoped she'd assume or wait until she'd cooled down a bit? After a moment's consideration he decided to delay that conversation. "For now, you'll continue to wait tables. We'll see what a good fit is for you when the time comes. Deal?"

Mandy cleared her throat as she nodded once. "For now, but I don't like it."

Cassie returned to the bar. "Daniel would like a cider and I'll get him something from the kitchen."

"I'll take it over to him," Mandy said, a meaningful flash in her eyes. "It's my job after all."

Cassie started to walk away and then paused, angling her shoulders to catch Flint's attention. "Flint, we have new arrivals. And they're quite fine to look upon." She winked at him and then smiled toward the arched doorway of the dining room.

Flint followed her interested smile to where two young men hesitated as they talked quietly, peering about the room. They looked to be in their mid-twenties, clean shaven except one had a small mustache, dressed in dark suits and top hats. Flint glanced at Cassie and then Mandy, only somewhat amused by the light in their eyes as they smiled at the two handsome young men. He dropped the towel on the bar and strode over to the strangers.

"Good day, gentlemen. I'm Flint Hamilton, innkeeper." He shook their hands in turn. "How may I help you?"

"You're the very man we came to see. We're here about the job as waiters."

Flint inspected their attire, their carriage, and their appearance in general. The two men seemed to be acceptable if a tad on the young side. "Do you have any experience?"

The man with the mustache nodded, a smile quivering the pale brown hair over his mouth. "We served at a small tavern a ways north of here, up on Sand Mountain."

Sand Mountain was a fair piece away to the northeast of Huntsville. They'd traveled a good way to apply so they must be interested. Still… "And why are you here then? Did they let you go?" He hoped not. He liked what he saw in the pair. If they had the qualifications, he'd be happy to have them. They looked fine and spoke with confidence. They'd both be an asset and would bolster the respectability of the establishment. Hope flared in his chest that he'd found the right men for the opening.

"In a manner of speaking," the other man said. "They had a kitchen fire and the place is ashes. So, we needed to find work elsewhere."

"So here we are." The mustached man bowed to Flint and then resumed his full height with a small grin on his lips. He glanced toward the bar where the girls lingered and the grin bloomed into something else. Something more eager.

Flint tensed at the flirtatious look on the man's face. The hope died. Even if they were stellar at waiting on customers and seeing to their needs, they wouldn't do. He couldn't have such a situation right under his nose. Better to keep looking. And hoping. "I would like to give you a chance, gentlemen, but I'm afraid you would find it tiresome here." Especially since he'd not have the young bucks flirting with his girl nor Abram's. Perhaps he should have specified middle-aged men only. Or married ones. Ones not interested in young pretty girls who already had beaus.

"My apologies, sir, if I said or did something to offend." The smile had fallen from the mustached man's face. "Please, sir, we need the work."

A quick glance at the other man's face confirmed the sudden seriousness in his expression. Flint couldn't have these two making eyes at his girl day in and day out. He would go crazy with jealousy under such circumstances. His gut clenched at the very thought. "I'm sorry, gentlemen. I'm afraid it simply wouldn't work out for either of us. Have a good day."

The pair exchanged glances and restored their hats to their heads. "Thank you for your time." They turned and dejectedly strode away.

Flint swung around to head back to the bar and resume his tasks, suddenly aware of his own limitations when it came to who he'd allow around his woman. Annoyed with himself, he snatched up the towel and snapped it to vent his irritation. Mandy flinched from where she stood beside the bar. Aggravated at himself, he glared at Cassie. "I thought you were getting your brother's meal. Don't make him wait."

She reared her head back at the sharp words. "Who put a bee in your bonnet?"

He drew in a deep breath but couldn't quell the emotions roiling inside. Nor the thought of another man moving in on his girl right before his eyes. Cassie raised a brow at him, mutely telling him she was aware of his jealous reaction. He slowly released the breath. "Please? I'm sure he's waited long enough."

"Very well, for his sake not yours." She darted a glance at him and then flounced out of the room.

He sighed and then spied Mandy watching him with a knowing look. Great, now he'd revealed his feelings to everyone. "Did you need something, Mandy?"

"Not right now." She reached across the bar to pat his cheek lightly. "I'll let you know if I do."

He pulled back and gazed at her, a mix of irritation and curiosity swirling inside his chest. "Go on with you then."

As she sashayed away, he could only wonder—and worry—about what on earth she meant.

Heat and light flowed equally through the open bedchamber window, the delicate curtains breathing in and out with the puffs of breeze. The afternoon was half over but Daniel needed time to think before he ventured out again. While Abram was out and about, he had their shared room to himself. He reclined in a cushioned chair beside the opening, staring at the watch on the table in front of it. Since his arrival at the inn, he'd been assailed with revelations which fundamentally changed how he saw himself and his entire family. Indeed, he felt part of the family in a way never before imagined.

But the very concept of his entire family on both sides being magical in any way overwhelmed him. He couldn't wrap his head around the idea. Then to add the startling possibilities his own special ability opened up. He could not merely move from one place to another in the blink of an eye, but he could travel in time. He could go backward or forward. To where? Or more importantly, to when? Shouldn't he have felt different in some way when his bound powers had been unleashed?

He tapped the clear crystal face of the watch with a finger, then spun it slowly to try to understand its prospects. Light glinted off the circle of small diamonds as it turned. The opportunities and the risks associated with his ability played on his mind. He could go anywhere and at any time. How would doing so impact the other timeline and the people in it? He assumed his presence in the other timeline might have an impact. What if his body didn't really travel there but became some kind of astral projection of himself? Such a situation would be safer. If so, then he needn't worry about being stuck in the past or the future, unable to return to his real life and times. He'd simply have to will himself back to the present day. Ma would know. He hoped.

He revisited the puzzling question of why he didn't feel any different. He should have since he could buzz through time for goodness sake. He sat up straight as a vague memory reasserted itself in his mind. He *had* buzzed. He'd been running late for class and suddenly experienced a tingling throughout his body. Once he arrived in the classroom, it had stopped and he'd forgotten all about it. Until now. Was that the change Cassie had referred to? The moment when his powers awakened and they'd made themselves known to him, muddled as he was about what the sensation meant. Or…had he actually used his powers to transport himself to the classroom far more quickly than his normal locomotion could?

"Well, I'll be." He picked up the watch and turned it over, staring into the lovely eyes of the elegantly attired woman painted on the back. "Just how does this thing work?"

On the top of the case, beside the stem, he brushed the small silver button. The one his mother said enabled his ability to timeskip. But how? He ran his thumb over the case, hesitating to touch the button again as his mother's warning echoed in his brain.

"Let me tell you how it works before you hurt yourself or somebody else." Mercy shimmered into view across the table from him.

Startled by her abrupt appearance, he dropped the watch on the table and grabbed the arms of the chair. He swallowed the rush of fear and let out a shaky breath. "I wish you wouldn't do that, Ma."

"You and Cassie and everybody else, but I think it's fun. You wouldn't deprive me of some amusement from time to time, now would you?" She grinned wickedly at him and then sank onto the matching cushioned chair opposite his. Although, she didn't make a dent in the cushion. "I know, I know, I shouldn't. If it bothers you that much, I guess I won't."

"Thank you." What a relief to know she wouldn't pop in and scare him again. He had enough to worry about. "I'm sure we'd all appreciate a little notice."

"Kill-joy." She folded her hands on the table and studied him. "Now let's get to work. We don't know how much time we have until my sisters make another appearance and another demand. They may even try to accelerate the terms of Abram's promise, made while he was in her form, to go with them. You must be prepared to thwart their efforts any way possible."

There it was again. The supposed threat his aunts posed. He leaned on the table, placing the watch between them. "I know they want to form a trinity, but I don't understand why you're so afraid of them. What worries you so?"

"I've told you all. They are very powerful witches, but they crave even more power." Mercy laid her palms on the white tablecloth. "I don't know what their exact mission might be, but whatever it is can't be good for those around them. Especially your sister."

"So, you think they will kidnap my sister and force her to work with them to do dark magic." He stared at his ma. "You're afraid of losing her for good."

Mercy pressed her lips together as fear simmered in her eyes. "Yes."

"Like you lost us?"

Tears drenched Mercy's ghostly eyes. "Yes."

Another secret revealed. One his parents had kept very well hidden. After they'd insisted the boys go out into the world and fend for themselves, they'd never hinted at caring about what happened to them. What trials and tribulations they might face. Only they apparently had kept Cassie close to hand. Not letting her out of their sight all this time. Why? Because they didn't care about him and his brothers as much as their daughter. Merely thinking the thought made his gut clench.

"I didn't think you cared about your sons, only your daughter." Daniel struggled to get the truth out. To push the words through stiff lips reluctant to share the pain caused by being forced to leave his childhood home. "You only kept her and sent us away."

"Oh, Daniel, don't ever believe that." Mercy swiped at her eyes, drying the tears from her fingers on her dress. "I've missed you all so very much and can only wish your father and I could have found another way to protect you boys. You were each ready and capable of taking care of yourselves. But we had to watch over Cassie."

"It didn't feel like protection being kicked out of our childhood home." He drummed his fingers on the cloth-covered table, the muted thumps vibrating up his arm. Tossed out like refuse more like it. Unwanted by his parents and separated from his brothers. "I almost didn't come here."

"Why did you?" Mercy leaned back in her chair but rested a hand on the table. Almost like she hoped he'd take it in his.

He rhythmically drummed his fingers on the cloth, avoiding touching or trying to touch his mother's hand. "For Cassie. I needed to come for her." He'd felt compelled to find out if she was all right. After all the years apart, he had to know she was in a good situation. "I'm sorry about how you died, Ma. What a terrible thing for everyone. And with Pa being away it must have been very difficult for Cassie. But I'm glad she has Flint."

"Phooey." Mercy waved her hand in the air, shooing away invisible flies. "That man."

"You don't like him?"

"No…" She bit her lip, small white teeth indenting the pink flesh. She sucked in a breath and blew it out. "Actually, he's growing on me. He does seem to care for Cassie."

"Yes, he loves her. And she him." Daniel regarded his ma for a moment, not wanting to discuss his sister's personal business, and then pointed at the watch. "How does this work?"

His mother nodded at the change of subject. "You only need the watch to timeskip."

"Not to bounce?" He drummed his fingers again on the table. "Okay, we'll tackle that subject next. Going back in time is rather a daunting prospect but even more I worry I won't be able to return. Tell me how to use the watch properly and safely."

"It's not difficult. To timeskip, you must set the date using the special stem." She pointed to the silver stem with a ring dangling from its top and a long gold chain attached to it. "You pull it out in stages to set the year, then month, then day."

"How do I change them?" He fingered the stem, lifting the ring and chain away from it.

"Twist the stem slowly to the right to go forward in time and to the left to go back." She pointed to the silver button. "Once you have the date set, you press that."

Daniel angled the gold case and studied the silver stem, then met his mother's gaze. "Should I try it?"

"You can practice setting the date but don't press the silver button until you're ready to go." She held his gaze for several moments. "To return, you simply press the stem in all the way and then press the silver button again. That returns you to the present day."

He pulled on the stem and felt it click once. He looked at the crystal and saw 1821 on the face in glowing numbers. He eased the stem to the left and the years decreased one by one. He swallowed and kept slowly turning the stem until the year read 1800. Then he pulled the stem out another click and read September on the face. Another click and 10 appeared as the day of the month. If he pressed the silver button, he'd go back to this day twenty-one years earlier. Before he was even born.

He looked up at his mother and noted her steady appraisal. "Since I don't want to timeskip right now, how do I reset it?"

"Push the stem back in all the way." She watched him do so and then shrugged. "That's all there is to it. But you must be careful not to take your ability lightly nor to let the watch fall into the wrong hands."

He pressed the stem and the present date, September 10, 1821, glowed on the face for a moment and then faded. He pulled the fob of the chain off the table and passed it through a buttonhole in his waistcoat to anchor it. Then dropped the watch in the waistcoat pocket. "I'll cherish it and protect it with my life."

"Very good." Mercy rose and stood looking down at him. "Take care of your sister, Daniel. She's far more powerful than even she knows."

"I will, Ma." Daniel stood and started to hug his mother before he realized the futility of such a gesture. "What about bouncing? How do I do that?"

"That's far easier." Mercy shifted and began to shimmer. "Use your intent and will to focus on a different place and then quickly snap your fingers twice."

"You mentioned something about I can only take one other person with me?"

"No, two. Be sure they hold on. They must touch you in order to stay with you through the portal."

"Two. Thanks."

"Only up to two. Do not even try to carry more than that. You won't be able to bounce with that much weight and bulk." Mercy regarded him with serious eyes. "That's enough for today. I'm tired. I'll see you later."

Mercy shimmered more and then vanished. Daniel stared at the empty space where she'd stood seconds earlier. After everything he'd learned and experienced since his arrival at the inn, only one thing proved constant. Every time he spoke with his mother, she shared more surprises.

Chapter Five

Cassie awoke early the next morning, excited and eager to learn more about her powers. Knowing men had already applied to work at the inn buoyed her spirits. She'd have more free time to do what she wanted or needed to do. She dressed with care in a simple pale green day dress and wove her hair into a long braid to keep it out of her eyes. Deferring breaking her fast, she went straight to her mother's attic, lighting the lamp with trembling hands. Then she opened the window and peered outside, searching for Allegro in the pale blue sky. Disappointed, she spun back around and laid her wand on the table.

"Ma? I'm ready."

After a few anxious moments, Mercy shimmered into the room and hovered nearby. "You're early."

"I couldn't wait any longer to find out more about what I can do with my powers." She lifted her wand and flicked it left and right. Knowing more about how to wield her power would bolster her confidence in rebutting her aunts' attempts to use magic against her. Of their attempt to persuade her to join them. While she trusted her brothers to do their best, she wanted the confidence which would come with being able to defend herself. At the moment, she doubted she had the magical strength to do so especially in light of her mother's claim she would be the most powerful witch in the country. She sure didn't feel like one. "Where do we start?"

"With you not doing that. It's silly and reckless." Mercy shook her head and crossed the room, stopping at the corner of the flowered carpet on the floor. "Help me pull this up."

"The rug?" Cassie laid the wand on the table and then treaded toward her mother, sensing the emotional battle inside of her. "Why?"

"You'll see." Mercy waited while Cassie struggled to roll the rug up. "I find visuals help me focus."

Cassie stood up from rolling the rug to one side and turned around to see what her ma meant. On the newly exposed wood floor was painted a narrow black line forming a circle with dark green pentagrams spaced around it. In the center of each pentagram there was a triangle, each a different color. Stunned by the unexpected sight, she raised curious eyes to meet her ma's gaze.

"What is it?" Proof of her mother's witching ways. Until then her mother's involvement in magic had been distant, hypothetical even. But the circle proved otherwise, bringing the reality right before her eyes.

"It's where I cast my sacred circle when I need one." Mercy carried a small table with several unfamiliar items on it to the center of the circle. "It's merely a reminder for me. It's by no means necessary to have the circle described this way." She crossed the room to lift a silver goblet and wide candle from a shelf by the books. Mercy set the items on the table and lit the candle with a flick of her fingers toward the wick. "I'll show you how to create one without using anything other than your focus."

Cassie pressed a hand to her stomach at the casual magic her mother had used. She'd never seen her mother perform magic and the sight rattled her nerves. The items on the table would serve what purpose? Along with a dagger and black straight wand, several stoppered bottles and small statues waited.

She swallowed the trepidation inside at the confirmation of her mother's witchy ways. "Why are the triangles different colors and styles?"

She sauntered around the outside of the circle, trepidatious about crossing the line without understanding why. Perhaps merely the sudden concreteness of the idea she descended from powerful witches made her cautious. A power Cassie had only begun to experiment with let alone understand.

"The pentagrams represent the gateways to the Elements. Earth to the north." Mercy walked around the inside of the circle clockwise, pausing at each pentagram. "Air to the east. Then Fire to the south and Water to the west. You only invoke the Elements when you're preparing to do magic with far-reaching consequences." Mercy pinned Cassie with a stern look. "Or when it's dangerous magic."

Cassie followed her mother but on the outside of the circle. Earth's symbol, a black triangle, pointed down with a bar across the middle. Air's pale yellow and pale blue triangle pointed up with another bar. Fire's red triangle was open and pointing up, while Water's was purple and pointing down. She memorized them as her mother halted in the center by the table again. Envisioning the symbols may prove necessary later.

"You can use some of my tools, like the chalice and candles, but we'll need to obtain a few things specifically as yours." She shifted the candle to one side before lifting the dagger, angling it in the glowing light from the lantern. "Some things simply cannot be shared between witches, like your athame and your wand."

"Ath-a-what?" Cassie stared at her mother, intrigued but wary.

"Your athame, your dagger, of course." Mercy contemplated her as she gave a light shrug. "I know this is all new, but I'll teach you everything you need to know. Better me than Hope or Faith."

"Klee!" With a flap of powerful wings, Allegro flew through the window and circled the attic. He landed on Cassie's shoulder and folded his wings, offering his head for her to pet.

"Good morning, Allegro." Her mood lifted with his sudden presence. The falcon aimed his dark eye at her. He seemed to be lending her support for something. After a moment his intent crystallized in her mind. Cassie sucked in a breath and screwed her courage up to ask her mother one more time to share the sisters' history with her. She'd tried several times, but the request had been dismissed or half-answered. She stroked the bird's head in thanks before turning to her ma. "Ma, will you please tell me exactly what happened to drive you apart from your sisters?"

"Hmph. I suppose the time has come when you need to know. In a word, Father." Mercy splayed her hands, palms out for a moment and then folded her arms. Sadness seeped from her very soul as she regarded Cassie. "He had his hopes set on having his three daughters become the most powerful trinity of witches in the country if not the world. He convinced Hope by telling her she had the power to lead such a strong trinity. She convinced Faith but I couldn't go along with it. Not after he shared his vision with me."

"Why didn't he let you make your own way with your magic?" The weight of the falcon was negligible, but she feared it would impair her ability to follow her mother's directions. Cassie sent a silent suggestion to Allegro to perch on the back of the chair so she could work with her mother.

He launched off her shoulder and soon landed on the back of the chair, but close enough to offer his emotional assistance. He flapped his wings a few times before folding them neatly, angling his head left and right as he watched the proceedings.

Mercy inhaled, eyeing the bird, and let it out slowly. "Mother and I both wanted me to use my magic to help others, not control them. She taught me so much about the good that could come from witchcraft even though she wasn't a witch herself. I avoided doing any kind of magic with my sisters as a result. Then I met your father at the Montgomery Coven's summer gathering one year and fell in love. Not only with him but his ideals for the uses of good magic. His family are all such wonderful, happy witches, bringing joy and security to those around them."

"I hope to meet them one day." Cassie struggled to understand the why behind what her parents had done to protect their children. "You and Pa hid our powers from not only us but from your families?"

Indeed, the very idea of parents pushing their young sons out of the house eluded her, especially sending them away without even awareness of their special capabilities. Without any real support or contact from their parents after they'd left. Cassie had fought against her mother's overbearing ways but at least she had her parents' love and protection growing up. She understood now why her mother had been so overly protective. What must it have been like for her brothers out in the world on their own? She could only imagine.

"Yes. It was the only way to ensure my family wouldn't try to ensorcell any of you."

"But why did you move so far away from Pa's family?" She smoothed any appearance of criticism from her features. She merely wanted to understand, not create more anguish for her ma. "Wouldn't they have been welcoming?"

"They would have, but we feared my sisters would discover the truth. We couldn't risk it." Mercy stepped out of the center of the circle and peered at Cassie. "Are you ready to learn how to create a sacred circle?"

"Please." She had a while before she needed to be downstairs, though she should work in her garden to prepare it for the winter ahead. Then she'd change into her waitress uniform and serve and entertain the customers. But first things first. "I'm ready."

Over the next hour she followed her mother's directions for centering herself and then drawing on the earth's energy to make a circle. Since they were only intending to form a simple circle, she didn't need to invoke the Elements to protect her. That lesson would have to wait for a more appropriate time. A time when she'd need the defense the circle could provide. By the end of the hour, she had developed more confidence in her abilities. A sense of power and control flowed through her, leaving her feeling in touch with herself in a new and different way. Her doubts had also lessened as she understood more about her capabilities.

"Now, to dismiss the circle, envision taking it up like a rope laying on the floor. Then be sure to ground the energy again. You don't want to carry it around inside of you."

Cassie walked around the circle counterclockwise, the opposite direction from the one she'd used to create it, and slowly dismissed it. When she finished, she stopped at the beginning point and grinned at her ma. "I'm a real witch now."

"You always have been, my dear." Mercy smiled at her. "There is more to learn but you are well on your way."

Allegro spread his wings and launched toward Cassie, resuming his place on her shoulder. His approval and pride washed through her. Having his esteem made her happy. She'd never thought she'd seek out a falcon's regard, but Allegro was her familiar. A creature attuned to her, loyal to her, and willing to help with her magical endeavors. His sharp eyes and talons could prove very useful. But most of all she recognized her growing attachment to her new friend.

"Thank you for teaching me, Ma." Despite her mother's reluctance to reveal her true nature, at least she'd finally come around to the point of instructing Cassie. The sound of a coach-and-four rumbling up the carriageway startled her. Customers arriving so soon. "Oh my, what time is it? I've got to go."

"Keep your progress to yourself. No one else needs to know the details of what you can and can't do until you need to use your skills. Is that clear?" Mercy shook a finger at her, scowling, then smiled. "Put the rug back and then you can go."

"Yes, ma'am." Cassie rushed to the rolled-up carpeting, Allegro's wings spread open to maintain his position, and quickly unrolled it to hide the painted circle. She straightened and glanced at her ma. "See you later?"

"I'll be around apparently. Cassie, dear, know that I will always love you. I'll always look out for your best interests, too. Now go." Mercy shimmered and vanished.

"Klee!" Allegro spread his wings, gave her a nod of his dark head, and then darted out the window. She closed it, then grabbed up the wand—which she'd never actually used—and raced out of the room to change her clothes.

The late morning sun warmed his face as Daniel paced beside Giles toward the barn. Early September in north Alabama enjoyed warmer temperatures than in the foothills of the Smoky Mountains of Tennessee. He liked not having to wear a heavy coat yet. But before long he'd need to go back.

"So how long have you and Abram been here?" Daniel eyed his brother's alert expression. He seemed to be always on guard.

"I came as soon as I received Cassie's letter, so late July." Giles bumped his brimmed hat back on his head. "Abram came the end of August."

"How long will you stay?"

"I'm not going anywhere, but Abram will have to decide for himself."

"You're staying?" Daniel couldn't imagine anything that would make such a drastic move plausible in his future. "What about your real life—down in the Gulf, right?"

"It was, but now I know my right place and destiny." Giles grinned at Daniel. "You'll find your soon enough."

Daniel kept mum, though he doubted Giles was right. A stocky, pimple-faced boy ambled around the corner of the barn, buckets heavy in his hands. Both his brown hair and the work shirt he wore showed signs of his labor. The boy ducked into the barn, water sloshing over the top of one bucket as he turned.

"Who was that?" Daniel glanced at Giles and the amused expression on his face.

"Jericho Smothers. He helps around the barn and is apprenticing as a blacksmith. He's been a huge asset for the property." Giles chuckled as they drew closer to the barn doors.

"What's so funny?" He hadn't seen anything which would evoke mirth. Surely Giles wasn't laughing at the stable hand.

"Jericho hates having to scrub down the stall walls, but it keeps the barn from descending into olfactory hell." Giles pulled his wide-brimmed hat from his head and dashed it against his leg, a puff of dust settling to the ground. He swiped a hand across his brow and then replaced the hat. "I bet Liam is inside waiting for him."

"Another stable boy?" Interesting. Daniel hadn't seen a need for more than one hand at the small barn.

"Yes, he's apprenticing. He's learning how to handle the horses properly and doing a passable job." Giles grunted as they stopped in front of the barn. "Before long, he'll head back to town to work with the blacksmith."

"His apprenticeship here would help with such an aim." But Daniel remained glad he'd found a less labor-intensive form of employment. He didn't envy the lad. "Since they're inside, perhaps we should go around back of the barn for this?"

"Good idea. Follow me." Giles motioned to the side of the barn where the pigs were kept overnight. The pen stood empty as the swine freely foraged during the day, rooting and snuffling out delicacies in the fields surrounding the inn. "We'll not be seen back there."

"An important consideration." It wouldn't do for anyone to witness his failures. Except for Giles. His reassuring presence might keep Daniel calm and, maybe, prevent any disasters from occurring while he practiced bouncing. He could hope.

They rounded the barn and relief filled his chest at the sight of an empty sand lot shielded from view by the building itself but also by a row of cedar trees arcing from the corner of the barn out toward the creek beyond. Anyone coming down the trail from the springs and waterfall would only see the sentinel trees.

"Now what?" Giles asked, his gaze sweeping the perimeter of the lot.

The details of what he prepared to do flowed through Daniel's mind. So many steps to take in order to make the attempt to bounce from one place to another. He had to make decisions of how much distance to put between the two locations for a first try as well as which locations to choose. All while not drawing attention to himself. First, he had to do one of the more important steps.

"Cassie taught me how to center and ground the other day. So, I need to take a few minutes to do so and then I'll try to bounce." Daniel glanced around, debating on where to go. "What do you think about aiming for the edge of the trees across the way for the first try?"

"I believe it would serve the purpose." Giles folded his arms and braced his legs, assuming a patient stance. "I'll keep watch."

"Here goes." Daniel closed his eyes and held out his arms from his sides. He followed his sister's instructions until he experienced the surge of energy and subsequent calm as he relinquished the extra energy back into the earth. Opening his eyes, he stared at the tree line, concentrating on his intent to be beside it. Raised voices inside the barn distracted his ear but he kept his intent on the trees. A gentle tingling began in his fingers and toes and quickly spread through his body until it became a fine humming buzz. Jericho's voice wafted from inside followed by a sharp retort from Liam. Ignoring the boys, he chanted his desired location silently to himself and closed his eyes to fully focus on his will. Then he snapped his fingers twice.

A whooshing sound filled his ears for a moment before falling silent. Followed quickly by a harsh grunt of surprise. He opened his eyes to find himself not outside by the trees and creek but inside the barn, in a stall, with Flint's buckskin paint and Jericho both staring at him.

"Where'd you pop up from?" The boy's startled eyes peered at Daniel.

"I-I'm sorry." Daniel spun toward the open stall door, mortification burning in his cheeks when he spotted Liam staring at him over the half wall and ducked under the rope barricading the horse inside. He stepped into the recently swept aisle, the rake marks fresh in the fine dirt. "My mistake. I stumbled into the wrong stall. My apologies. I'll just…be on my way then."

"See you mind where you're going." Jericho continued to frown with suspicion at him.

Daniel hurried back outside as fast as his legs would carry him to find Giles searching for him behind the shrubs around the foundation of the barn. "That didn't work as planned."

"Where did you go?" Giles straightened to address him face to face.

"Into a stall along with Jericho. Liam saw me, too." Daniel dragged his fingers through his hair and shook his head. "How embarrassing."

"And risky." Giles glared at him. "Flint will have your hide if you let everyone know about…" He lowered his voice to a whisper as he surveyed their surrounds with his gaze and then continued. "About witches and magic on the property."

"I am aware." Daniel swept his head again with a trembling hand. "I should try once more though. Ma was very clear I need to be prepared."

What she hadn't clarified was how his ability to bounce or skip would defend his sister. He'd lain awake several nights trying to imagine what scenarios might transpire requiring such a skill. Would he perchance be called to rescue her from their aunts' clutches by bouncing her back to the inn? Or to go back in time to try to change the past and thus affect the present? Either eventuality could occur but neither put him at ease.

"She's right. Go on." Giles assumed his watchful position and lifted his chin. "Just focus this time."

"I thought I had last time. Here goes." Daniel gazed at the trees, imprinting the image on his mind.

Closing his eyes, he pictured the arc of trees and willed himself to be standing next to the farthest one. Then snapped his fingers twice. The tingling preceded the quiet whooshing for a moment before silence and stillness filled him. He opened his eyes to find himself standing next to a cedar. He spun around and grinned at Giles from across the expanse of sand and grass. He closed his eyes again and willed himself to stand by his brother, snapped his fingers, and in a flash found himself back where he started.

"That's brilliant." Giles grinned at him. "You just disappeared and reappeared."

"It doesn't even hurt." Daniel grinned back at him with pride in his heart. He really could bounce as his mother had said.

"What about the timeskip?" Giles folded his arms over his chest, tilting his head to one side. "Is that next?"

Daniel's first attempt at bouncing hadn't gone so well. Was he ready to try changing place *and* time? Finding himself beside the boy and horse left him rattled. Perhaps if he took some deep breaths, he'd calm sufficiently to try to timeskip. He inhaled and exhaled slowly several times. He pulled the pocket watch from its home in his waistcoat pocket, trying to ignore the slight tremble in his hand. He stared at the clear crystal face, watching the second hand tick away time. Where and when did he want to go? The choice weighed on him. So many unknowns surrounded the question. Mostly, was he really ready? Or would he end up fracturing the crystal of the watch, breaking time itself? A chilling thought.

"I need to think about this some more." He met his brother's regard with a shrug. "Later I shall try, when I am more certain of myself." He slipped the watch in the small pocket at his waist. "For now, I think a celebratory beverage is required. Will you join me?"

"Indeed, I shall." Giles bowed to his brother, a jesting movement as he assumed a medieval knight's tone. "We shall away to the dining hall and find Flint and his well-stocked bar."

"Indubitably." Daniel gestured for them to proceed with a dramatic sweep of his arm. Chuckling, the two brothers hurried around the barn and toward the inn.

He'd keep to himself his doubts and insecurities. It wouldn't do anyone any good to know how deeply he regretted his failure and cowardice. But he'd put on a good face for the time being.

Grumbling to himself, Flint turned the chair over and inspected the damage. The two men who had neared fisticuffs the prior evening had abused the chair along with the table they'd been sitting at before the argument began. Tarnation, the back leg had splintered. He stared at it, well aware that his limited carpentry skills were outmatched by the task of replacing the leg. In fact, he needn't repair nor replace it since new furniture would arrive in a matter of weeks if Reggie Fairhope's plans held. He surveyed the room full of tables and chairs, seeing them through fresh eyes and noting not only the plebian simplicity of their design but the evident scratches and wear. Replacements couldn't arrive soon enough to suit his taste.

Footfalls at the arched doorway drew his attention. Two nicely attired men, frequent customers to the inn, strode into the dining room. He didn't recall their names, having not been properly introduced to them. He'd seen them with the growing group of men frequenting the dining room, but they seemed to be decent fellows. They spotted him and hurried toward where he squatted by the broken seat.

Flint left the chair upside down on the floor and stood to greet the gentlemen. "Good day. How may I help you?"

"I'm Lawrence Walker and this is Isaac McBroom. We heard about the job opening, for servers?" Lawrence extended his hand.

Lawrence stood a few inches taller than Isaac, which gave him a certain air of authority over the younger man. Both had brown hair beneath their brown beaver hats and wore neatly pressed dark trousers and white shirts with a vest and coat. A bit overdressed to wait on customers but they did present a refined appearance.

Flint shook Lawrence's hand and then Isaac's, pleased with the solid yet controlled strength and confidence each exhibited through the gesture. "I am looking for a couple of good men to assist with serving our customers and guests. I take it you're interested in the position?"

"We are." Lawrence doffed his hat, sliding a look at Isaac who followed suit. "We would appreciate it if you'd give us a chance. We won't let you down."

"Do you have any experience waiting tables?" Flint glanced between the two expectant faces. "I know you've been customers yourselves but working the other side will be different."

"Yes, sir, we're aware. We have no problem serving others." Isaac smiled at Flint, white teeth in a tanned face. "We both enjoy serving our community in any way useful."

Lawrence glanced sharply at Isaac and then nodded, meeting Flint's questioning look. "Well said, Isaac."

Lawrence's reaction rather surprised him, but maybe he was reading more into it than actually existed. Just then, Cassie strolled into the room, chatting amiably with Mandy. They each carried a stack of fresh tablecloths to put out before guests arrived for the luncheon rush. Cassie spied him in conversation with the two men and flashed a smile his way which changed to a question. He slightly raised his brows in response and she shrugged before continuing with her chore. What had she sensed? He'd have to ask her about her reaction later.

He gazed at the two men, considering everything he knew about them. They would suit the job. A bit older and more refined, less likely to be flirting with the young girls from what he'd previously seen of their behavior. Since they associated with the more esteemed gentlemen of the region, he must assume they were held in equally high regard by the others. Perhaps they'd even help to bring more clientele to the inn. "When can you start?"

Mandy frowned at him from where she snapped a cloth over a table.

"I could start tomorrow if that will be all right." Isaac rotated his hat in his hands.

Lawrence motioned for him to stop fidgeting. "Whenever you need me to start, I can."

"Tomorrow morning is soon enough. The girls can cover until then." Mandy made a sound of disgust and stomped to the next table, leaving Flint with no doubt as to her opinion on the matter.

Isaac followed his gaze, seeing the girls in question for the first time since arriving. "Are we replacing them? I wouldn't want to deprive them of their employment."

"Perhaps he's adding to the staff." Lawrence exchanged a silent look with Isaac. "Don't worry about how Mr. Hamilton is managing his employees."

Lawrence's statement confirmed Flint's earlier opinion of his authority over the younger man. "You'll be the primary waiters and the girls will help if the crowd warrants."

"Very good. What time should we arrive on the morrow?" Lawrence asked.

Daniel strode into the dining room and took a seat at the bar. Had he been out practicing his bouncing again like he'd done the previous day? He'd been rather pleased with his ultimate success when he and Giles had toasted with rum after the session. Cassie crossed the room to talk to Daniel in low tones. Curiosity piqued, Flint decided to end the interview with his new employees. "Be here at seven and I'll fill you in on what you need to know and we'll settle on your pay as well."

"Until then." Lawrence donned his hat, tapping it lightly into place. "Ready, Isaac?"

Isaac placed his hat on his head and nodded once to Flint. "Thank you for your trust."

"Don't make me regret giving it to you both. See you tomorrow." Something in Isaac's attitude plucked a nerve but he couldn't quite figure out why. He'd give them a few weeks to prove their worth and then reevaluate his decision. The pair sauntered out of the room as Flint marched over to the bar. "Well, we have our new male servers starting tomorrow."

Cassie settled onto a chair at the counter. "That's grand. Does that mean you won't need me to wait tables any longer?"

"I'd ask you to help tomorrow while they get accustomed to everyone and how I want things done." Imagine letting the men loose to perform their work without any guidance. While he had an idea of what the girls did, he hadn't paid close attention since Cassie routinely waited tables for her father prior to Flint's taking over the management of the inn. It had been lucky for him another girl had covered waiting on the customers. He wouldn't have done nearly as fine a job as she had.

"That's fine." Cassie slid her gaze away to sweep the room, landing on her brother sitting beside her. "You seem happy. What have you done?"

Daniel lifted his tankard in salute. "I've successfully bounced to the falls and back without incident."

"Congratulations." She slanted her head and then met Flint's regard.

"Say, when you first came in you seemed to question their presence. What was that about?" Flint studied the emotions playing across her features, ranging from open smile to hesitance to something else. But what exactly?

"Oh, that." She brushed aside his question with a flick of her hand. "At first I sensed curiosity combined with strong intent, but I realized it was just their desire to get the job." She shrugged. "Sometimes I don't clearly understand what others are feeling, but it usually clarifies over time."

"Time seems to solve a lot of problems, doesn't it?" Daniel lifted the tankard of ale and swallowed a large mouthful.

"In some ways, yes." Cassie tapped the mahogany with a finger. "But some problems require active intervention to solve them."

"In this case, time will tell how well they fit in. Help me keep an eye on how they're doing, will you?" Flint braced his hands on the bar as he noticed the other girl snapping cloths with far more force than necessary. "I need to manage her attitude in the meantime. Mandy, come here, please."

With a long harsh sigh, she approached the bar, a scowl on her face. "Yes?"

"I need to know you won't be upset if I ask you to do something else around here."

"I enjoy helping the customers have a good experience. Is that so wrong?" She crossed her arms and pouted at him.

Understandable but the inn's reputation rested on not only the quality of its menu but on its management and appearance. Besides, he had another opening in need of filling. "I was hoping you'd help out in the kitchen, at least until Sheridan returns. Matt could use some assistance."

"The kitchen?" Mandy barked the words out with a harsh, invective tone.

"Mandy, don't be like that." Cassie reached out a hand to lay on Mandy's stiff arm. "I know you might not enjoy it as much, but so many people come here for the fine food. You'd have a hand in ensuring they continue to receive the best."

"I don't want to work in the bloody kitchen." Mandy scowled at Flint, hugging herself tightly. "I can't."

He frowned at her as he tilted his head to one side, studying the tense, belligerent posture of the young woman. "I promise it won't be for very long. Only until I can find some other women to assist. With the growing number of guests, there's more and more to be done in the kitchen and the laundry for that matter. Please, Mandy?"

A commotion at the doorway halted the tense conversation as they all turned toward the sound of boots and shoes and the rustling of long skirts. A petite, auburn haired young woman in a simple yet elegant dark blue day dress hesitated alongside a slender teenaged boy, a younger version of Flint. Stunned but delighted, Flint dodged around the bar and hurried to take his sister's hands in his.

"Wilma. Julian. What are you doing here?" He squeezed her fingers and then released them to shake his youngest brother's hand.

"We came to see you of course." Wilma clasped her reticule in front of her long skirts. "You've been away from home for ever so long and there is so much to tell you."

"Come, let's not stand in the doorway then." He tucked her hand around his elbow and escorted her to the bar, Julian trailing along. He hid his chagrin as he waited to find out what news she carried. Probably from his father, wanting him to change his plans yet again. "Let me introduce you around."

Chapter Six

The look on Flint's face did not bode well. Cassie reached out with her powers to detect concern emanating from her beau. The cause of his discontent couldn't be his sister and brother arriving since he loved them dearly, so something else must have upset him. She sensed Mandy's anger and dismay simmering behind her. She sensed the happiness from Wilma and the guarded attention from Julian. And surprisingly, she sensed Daniel's potent interest in the young woman the closer they came to the bar. She glanced at him, where he sat beside her, watching the girl greet Flint, with his lips parted. Interesting.

"Wilma, it is a pleasure to see you again." Cassie slid off the chair and stepped forward to greet her before turning to her brother. "And Julian, right? Welcome."

"Thank you." Julian tipped his hat and half-bowed at her. "Are you Cassandra Fairhope? Flint has written to us about you."

"Oh, my apologies. Yes, I am." She observed her future brother-in-law, liking the way he looked at her with an open and honest expression. They'd get along quite well. "Nice to meet you."

Flint grimaced and moved closer to Cassie. "I should have introduced you. I'm sorry for my gaffe."

She sensed his embarrassment but brushed his concern away. "We shall all become fast friends in no time so please do not worry about the lapse."

"Yes, please." Wilma stood quietly beside her brother, her green-eyed gaze drinking in the gathering. "As I understand it, Cassie and I will be sisters before too long. Julian and I decided we should come see how Flint is faring way out here."

"Did Father send you?" Flint's jaw tensed.

Ah, the real reason for his distress. He'd been upset when his mother had visited over the summer with a similar message from his father. Something about his father checking up on the job he was doing. Much like her own pa with John Baker's supervision over Flint. The distrust evident in such oversight rankled in him. Even before discovering she could sense others' emotions and feelings she could tell he objected with regard to such spying.

Wilma shook her head with a wide grin in place. "It was our idea. We wanted a little adventure. So here we are."

"I'm glad you did," Cassie said. "How long can you stay?"

"Mother said we may stay as long as we like if Flint doesn't mind." Wilma turned to her brother and blinked twice. "*Do* you mind?"

"Of course not." Flint kissed her forehead and then smiled fondly at her. "I'm very pleased to see you both."

Daniel shifted in his seat and raised a brow at Cassie.

"Oh, I'm sorry!" She grabbed his elbow and pulled him up from his seat to stand beside her. "Flint, would you do the honors?"

"Certainly." Flint bowed his head toward Daniel. "Daniel Fairhope, may I present my sister Wilma and brother Julian."

"Nice to meet you." Julian briefly shook Daniel's hand.

"It is my pleasure." Daniel turned to peer at Wilma. He clasped her right hand as he bowed over it, lightly kissing the back. Straightening, he smiled at her. "I'm very pleased to make your acquaintance, Miss Hamilton."

Flustered by the uncommon greeting, Wilma pulled her hand free and swallowed as she continued to search his gaze with her eyes. "As am I, I'm sure."

Cassie lightly clapped her hands together as she reached out with her senses to Wilma's excitement. "Now tell us your news. I can tell you're very eager to share something with us."

"Well, the big news is there will be a wedding this November." Wilma met Flint's astonished expression. "Edith has accepted Ambrose Davis' proposal."

"She did?" Flint shook his head. "That's astounding. She's too young to marry at only eighteen."

Cassie arched a brow at him. "Like me?"

"Oh… well…" Flint blushed, his cheeks turning pink.

"Silly goose." Wilma tapped Flint's shoulder with her hand. "Don't be stuffy."

Flint bristled as the pink faded. "I'm not."

"He's just being a good brother." Daniel shot a sideways smile at Flint. "He's in protector mode."

"Always." Cassie sidled over to Flint to grasp his hand. "He's looking out for those he loves."

Flint squeezed her hand. "I'm glad you understand."

"You think I don't?" Wilma asked, her chin raising as she studied his somber features. "I am not a child, you know."

A deep-seated annoyance simmered inside of Flint's sister as she stared at him. Cassie squeezed Flint's hand to try to convey a silent warning. Apparently there was a history between them with regard to how much they trusted each other to know what was going on. Very interesting.

"No one said you are." Flint glanced at Daniel and then Cassie. "Why don't we get them something to eat and drink?"

"A good idea." Cassie gestured toward the nearest table. "Have a seat and perhaps Mandy will be good enough to bring you a plate. Flint, pour them cider, please."

Once she had them settled, Cassie took a moment to assess the emotional balance in the room. Satisfied that everyone was calm and peaceful, except for the still stewing Mandy, she allowed herself to take a seat at the piano and entertain them, infusing her voice with love and hope for the future of them all. Mayhap her singing would calm her friend down from her ire over being asked to work with Matt and the Marple sisters in the kitchen. But she rather doubted it.

Stunned. Intrigued. Enthralled. Daniel could only stare at the beautiful young woman. He wanted to marry her on the spot. To claim her as his. Which of course was ludicrous and not an appropriate thought let alone act. Instead, he simply gazed upon perfection with the name of Wilma. She sat at the white-clothed table across from him, sitting beside Julian, commenting on the appurtenances and furnishings of the large dining room. Mandy returned from a quick visit to the kitchen with a large tray in her capable hands, which she set on a neighboring table.

"Need a hand?" Julian half rose from his chair, his voice threatening to break with each word.

"You're our guest, so please relax." Mandy picked up a steaming pewter bowl and placed it in front of the boy. "Enjoy."

"Very well." Julian did as requested, pulling a cloth napkin onto his lap as he peeked into the bowl. "Smells delicious."

"What is it?" Wilma leaned back as Mandy set a bowl in front of her. "Oh, chicken stew."

"Matt is an excellent cook." Daniel nodded his thanks to Mandy when she placed his meal before him. He lifted a spoon and dipped it into the savory blend of chicken, onions, potatoes, carrots, and parsnips. "I've never tasted better and I've eaten in some fine establishments."

Wilma put a spoonful into her mouth and closed her eyes with an almost inaudible sound of pleasure. When she looked at him again, her smile shot a reaction to his gut.

He flashed her a smile and then concentrated instead on his stew. Despite the red hair and green eyes, which usually sent him strolling the opposite direction, her every movement and shift of her gaze captivated his attention. He'd glimpsed her ire, but she'd demonstrated such a refined annoyance with Flint's comment he was caught. Ensnared by her beauty and her personality. The slight lift of her chin and the dare in her eyes was all it took to have Flint backtracking and apologizing. My, oh my. What a woman.

"Mr. Fairhope."

He looked up at Wilma's inquiring gaze. "Yes, Miss Hamilton?"

"I was asking, how long have you been at the inn?"

"I arrived Sunday, so four days now." Goodness but the time had flown by. Apparently learning about family secrets and hidden abilities made one unaware of the passage of days. Or perhaps it was a matter of wondering what other secrets might be revealed on the morrow or overmorrow.

"Where did you venture from?" Julian asked between bites. "Was it a long journey?"

"I dwell and work in Knoxville, Tennessee, which is a couple hundred miles northeast of here." The ride had been long and difficult but not impassable, although at times it had seemed the roads were nothing more than Indian trails through the woods. "So yes, it took about a week to travel here."

"My, a very long journey indeed." Wilma searched his eyes for a long moment. "Was it worthwhile to make the effort?"

"Yes, Miss Hamilton." He couldn't stop the slow, lopsided grin any more than stop breathing. Indeed, he'd even make the journey again on the slow and frustrating nag if he knew ahead of time she'd be here. He wouldn't voice the reasons behind his feelings on her question. She'd take offense to his sentiments immediately upon the heels of her arrival. As well she should. He must master his emotions until the appropriate junction. "It was most definitely worth the effort."

Flint strolled toward the table, one brow raised in both a question and a warning to Daniel. He stopped by Julian and broke his gaze away from the silent caution to Daniel to address his brother. "Do you have everything you need?"

"After I finish my repast, might you show me to where I'll stay?" Julian gestured to the dark suit and white shirt with a silk cravat at his throat. "I wish to refresh myself and change into something less formal for the afternoon if you don't object."

"A fine idea, brother." Flint cast an affectionate smile on the lad. "I will help get you settled while Cassie sees to Wilma's comfort."

At mention of his sister's name, Daniel glanced over to where she sang along with the ditty she played on the glossy square piano. He'd never seen a finer instrument and could only guess how it came to be at the inn. The rich red of the wood gleamed in the front corner of the large room. The full-bodied sound of the instrument complemented her voice. She played well, and her voice did indeed cast a sort of spell over the growing audience in the room. A crowd that grew by one more as Giles strode briskly in and spotted him.

"Here comes Giles." Daniel motioned to Flint with a lift of his head. "I wonder why he's in such a hurry."

Flint turned to greet the oldest Fairhope brother. "Anything amiss?"

"No, all is well. Just hungry." Giles rubbed his hands together as he peered at the half-eaten bowls of stew on the table. "Any left?"

Mandy appeared at his side as if he'd summoned her. "I can get you a bowl if you'd like."

Giles braced his hands on the back of a chair. "Please and thank you."

Mandy bobbed her head as she spun around and left to retrieve yet another bowl. Daniel watched her until she'd turned the corner toward the kitchen. Flint had his hands full keeping the girl satisfied with her employment if he forced her to confine her efforts to chopping vegetables or kneading bread. She had more fire than a typical scullery maid could handle.

"While Mandy retrieves your food, let me make the introductions." Flint lifted a hand to quiet the chatter. "Giles, I'm pleased to present to you my sister Wilma and my brother Julian. Wilma and Julian, Giles Fairhope is Cassie's oldest brother."

"Nice to meet you both." Giles nodded to each in turn. Then he smiled at Julian. "Say, would you like for me to show you around this afternoon?"

Daniel glanced at his oldest brother, a slight frown of surprise weighing down his brows. When had he developed a mentor mentality? Something he'd never witnessed in his previous interactions with him. But then Giles had tried to teach them how to be good brothers even if it had seemed like heavy-handed instruction more than helping. Perhaps his newly discovered role as Guardian awoke some other qualities in his personality as well. Something to keep an eye out for.

"Yes, sir. I'd like that very much." Julian spooned the last bite into his mouth and then laid the utensil in the empty dish. "I'm ready whenever you are, Giles."

Flint shifted his intense gaze to Daniel. "Why don't you go with them? Get outside for a while?"

Daniel drew in a breath to respond until he noted Flint's cant of his head toward Wilma and then another of those irksome warning brow lifts. So, the brother was protecting his younger sister. From him? How had Flint detected Daniel's interest in her? He'd not said or done anything that should have tipped his hand. Had he? Perhaps he wasn't being as composed as he'd hoped. A little distance may do him some good.

He stood, pushing his chair away with the back of his knees. "Yes, that is a fine idea as well."

Wilma also rose from her seat to stand beside Julian. "I'll see if Cassie can spare a few minutes to do likewise."

She smiled confidently at him, seeming to understand his thinking and feelings far more clearly than she should.

"Miss Hamilton, if you'll excuse us." Daniel bowed slightly to the lovely angel of a woman. "We shall see you at dinner I would imagine."

She batted her lashes at him, a gleam in her green eyes. "Until then."

He swallowed hard. Some fresh air and some time with other men would set everything to rights. With good fortune the time away would give him some perspective and forbearance. Wilma lifted her chin as she continued to regard him with tantalizing eyes. He swallowed hard. Maybe.

Chapter Seven

*T*he room hummed with conversation punctuated with bursts of laughter as well as Cassie's sweet melodies. A fire burned brightly in the large fireplace, adding the pleasing scent of oak burning to the aromas of freshly baked bread and savory meats. Flint rearranged the chairs around a recently vacated table, pushing them in at spaced intervals around the clothed expanse. Lawrence cleared another table as a couple walked out of the room, chatting amicably as they went. Isaac bustled past with a pitcher of cider, striding toward the large group of men gathered at the back of the room by the open windows, an intense discussion underway.

Another meeting led by Sterling and attended by John. But the waiters knew enough to pay special attention and respect to those prominent gentlemen. As well they should given how very important their business remained for the inn's welfare and reputation. Hiring those two fine young men was a good move. He nodded sagely to himself as he made his way back to the bar, feeling utterly smug with his savvy decision and the improvements he'd made.

Giles regarded him with a wry expression. "Do I want to know what's put that grin on your face?"

"Business is good. That's all." No need to brag about his sense of accomplishment. Flint motioned to the half empty mug in front of Giles. "Refill?"

"Please." Giles glanced at Julian sitting beside him. "Did you want anything more?"

"I would enjoy some more cider if it's available." Julian angled his empty mug to peer into its depths. "This time of year it's so refreshing."

Flint studied his younger brother for a moment and then grabbed the mugs and pulled them closer to refill them. When did the boy become so formal in his tone and vocabulary? He needed to spend more time with his brother to help him relax within his own skin. Then perchance he'd not feel it necessary to use such big words to convey small meanings. Assuming Julian stayed around a while, his only brother might have time to help the lad out. He returned the mugs to the two men and then dried the mahogany surface where he'd sloshed some of the apple beverage.

"Cassie sounds pretty good today." Giles gestured to where Cassie sat at the piano, singing a popular tune.

"I think she's happy her mother relented on teaching her how to use her new skills." Flint lowered his voice as he finished his sentence.

"I understand she has a new pet, too." Giles sipped his drink, but kept his gaze on the move around the room. Maintaining his vigilance on Cassie's behalf. The big man stiffened as his sweep of the room paused on the group of men at the back.

"A familiar, not a pet." Flint folded and refolded the towel. "She said it just appeared the other day and then flew away."

Julian held his mug between both hands as he squinted at Flint. "What do you mean?"

Damnation, he forgot his little brother wasn't aware of the Fairhopes' abilities. He may as well tell Julian since he'd find out one way or another, especially after Flint married Cassie. But was it his revelation to share? He met Giles' arched gaze. "Should I tell him?"

Giles peeked at Julian's questioning expression then nodded at Flint. "Go ahead."

"Well, Julian, simply put the Fairhopes are a family of…" He dropped his voice so others wouldn't overhear, glancing around to ensure their privacy in the busy room. "They are a family of witches. It's our job to protect Cassie from harm but especially from her aunts who want her to join them to form a powerful trinity."

Julian took a long swallow of his beverage and then wiped his mouth with the back of his hand. "Witches?"

"Keep your voice down, son." Giles laid a hand on the bar. "We don't share that with everyone."

"I understand your surprise and even disbelief." Flint couldn't blame the shock on the boy's features. He'd been taken aback by the news himself. "But it's true and it's our secret. I'm unsure how our customers would react if they discovered the truth. Promise me you won't tell anyone. Not even Wilma. Not yet."

"Who'd believe me?" Julian sat back in his chair. "Fine. I won't tell anyone. But why not Wilma?"

"Let's give her time to settle in. You know how particular she can be about what she perceives as deception or deceit. I don't think she'll believe it at all."

"You're probably right." Julian rested a hand on the bar. "I'll let you break the news to her."

"I will. Soon." How he'd tell her he had no clue.

"Good choice." Giles patted him on the back. "You're a good kid."

The two had surely bonded in the short time Julian had been at the inn. Having someone to look up to, to encourage a young soul, could make all the difference in the boy's growth and attitude as he matured. He'd looked up to their father to a point, but it might have been useful to have someone as grounded and confident as Giles to serve as mentor.

Giles stared at the group of men for a long moment before slowly turning back to meet Flint's gaze. "I'm seeing the owl again. That's not good."

"The attacking one?" It had been weeks since the Guardian had detected the warning sign only he could see. "Where?"

"The rear table. Someone is posing a threat. But who?" Giles slowly drummed his fingers on the bar. "There are fifteen possibilities."

"John among them. But any of those men might prove dangerous if they're following his orders." Flint glanced at the gathering of respected gentlemen. "Just stay alert. Speaking of trouble…"

Mandy hurried into the dining room and headed straight toward Flint. Anger propelled her stride and he braced himself. She stopped beside Giles and flicked him a look of greeting before pinning Flint with her glare.

"I need to talk to you." She folded her arms over her chest. "I want to work in here, not in the kitchen."

Flint sighed. "We talked about this. It's not forever, but Matt needs help and Isaac and Lawrence have things well under control. If we need you, we'll call you in but not until then."

"Matt has the Marple sisters to help him." Mandy squared her shoulders and glared at him. "Please, Flint, let me interact with the customers again. I enjoyed that far more than standing in the kitchen kneading dough day in and day out."

"I tell you what, when Sheridan returns then you can come back to help in the dining room." Flint held up a finger when Mandy opened her mouth to reply. "The kitchen is where you can do the most good right now. I've put an advertisement in the paper for more help, but nobody has applied yet."

Mandy huffed and dropped her arms to her sides. "You really need me to help Matt?"

"For now."

"As long as it's not forever. You need to know… I'll quit first." Mandy glared at him for a moment and then sighed. "Fine, I need the job. So I'll keep helping in the kitchen for a while longer."

"Thank you, Mandy." Flint smiled at her, happy she'd relented. He couldn't afford for her to quit. Then Matt would be hard-pressed to meet the demands of the increased number of people venturing out to the inn for his fine meals. "I appreciate your help."

With a flip of her hand, Mandy spun around and marched out of the room. He glanced at Cassie and wasn't surprised to see her gazing at him in return. A sudden commotion from the group of men at the back made him look in their direction in time to see a bird fly through the open window and wing its way around the room. Gasps of surprise and awe echoed among the customers as the falcon flew several laps before landing on Cassie's shoulder.

"Is that…?" Julian rose from his seat to stare at Cassie petting the bird's sleek head.

"It is." Flint dropped the towel on the counter. "I'll be right back."

As he dodged between the tables, several agitated guests scraped back their chairs, dropped some coins on the table, and then hurried out of the room. Others cast worried looks at the wild bird perched on Cassie's shoulder, intense whispered conversations surrounding him as he kept walking. Great, already losing business.

He strode across the room to stand beside the piano, a respectful distance from the falcon. While his concern about the business remained high, his bigger concern sat beaming up at him. "Are you all right?"

"I'm fine. Allegro, meet Flint." She stroked a finger down the bird's head. "He's my beau so please be nice to him."

Allegro cocked his eye toward Flint and blinked twice. Then he lowered his beak for a moment and tilted the top of his head toward Flint. Was he nodding his agreement? Flint returned the gesture and then Allegro straightened on her shoulder to peer around the room much like Giles had done earlier. A new member of the guardians of Cassie. Flint followed the bird's steady gaze toward the back of the room.

Sterling and John stood to one side of the large group, engaged in an intense conversation as they kept an eye on the bird and Cassie. Flint's stomach clenched at the worried and fearful expressions they aimed at him. If they'd merely suspected before, now they had evidence if not proof of Cassie's affinity with magic. He scanned the faces of the others in the room and then looked at Cassie. As much as he'd hoped otherwise, it looked like their secret was out.

"Perhaps you should sing something to calm everyone down." Flint shrugged and pointed at the falcon. "Or perhaps see if you can persuade Allegro to fly on out of here."

Having a falcon as a familiar definitely proved a challenge when she was trying to keep her witchiness under wraps. The cat familiar her ma had expected would have been much more readily accepted than a bird of prey. The slight weight and clasping talons on her shoulder didn't make playing easier either. Allegro's glossy wings and intelligent eyes communicated with her in ways she couldn't explain. But Flint had a point. Cassie peered at Allegro, her hands poised over the keyboard as she mentally spoke to him. *You're drawing unwanted attention, Allegro. Come to me later?*

The falcon winked at her and then launched from her shoulder to swoop once around the room to a chorus of startled gasps and then darted out one of the open windows at the back of the room. Cassie met Flint's concerned gaze with one of her own. She didn't dare look around at the expressions aimed their way. Instead, she began playing "In the Garden," one of her favorite hymn's about walking and talking with God. After the chorus, she dared to glance at the murmuring crowd. Most had gone back to their meals and conversations. Not John though. Nor Sterling and the rest of his group. They continued to watch her closely. She played on, keeping her own focus on the familiar words and religious meaning of the next verse of the hymn, and infusing the song with calm and acceptance.

Mandy appeared at the arched doorway, lingering on the verge of entering as she listened to the hymn. She gripped her hands together, tension and annoyance flowing from her. Cassie finished the last chorus and then stood to a smattering of applause. She accepted their praise with a half-smile and a dip of her head before crossing to where Mandy waited.

"Are you all right?" Cassie feared she knew the answer based solely on the woman's irritated countenance.

"No, I'm not." Mandy glanced over Cassie's shoulder to the diners. "And you aren't either from their expressions. What did I miss?"

"They're just surprised." Cassie glanced back at the men continuing to study her, then faced her friend again. "Let's go." She led Mandy into the entrance hall away from the suspicious eyes. "Are you still upset about the change in job?"

Mandy braced her fists on her hips. "Most definitely. I never wanted to be a scullery maid. I don't like working with food all the time. I'm doing it only because I need the money and there's nothing else close by. But this is not what I ever wanted do."

"I understand." Indeed, the anger simmering inside of Mandy made Cassie feel nauseated so she raised her emotional barrier to quell the upset. "It's not for long though. Only a few weeks until Sheridan returns or Flint hires someone else. Whichever happens first."

"You don't understand. I do not want to work in the kitchen." She folded her arms over her chest and glared at Cassie. "It's demeaning."

"What is?" Abram asked as he pushed through the front door, closing it behind him.

"Being a blasted scullery maid."

"It's not all that bad. I help out, too." Cassie had chopped and kneaded right alongside of the others for years without complaining. What was really needling Mandy about it? "Why are you so upset about working in the kitchen?"

"I feel not only demoted but dismissed." She sniffed and lifted her chin, light brown eyes flashing. "It's embarrassing."

"Come on, sweetheart, don't be like that." Abram sidled over to her, wrapping an arm around her waist. "Flint is simply moving his staff where the work is. He's not trying to hurt your feelings."

"Relegating me to the kitchen where I don't get to interact with the customers does hurt my feelings." She tossed her head, her long brown hair rippling across her shoulders and down her back.

"I think it's a fine move to make." He gave her a quick kiss and then a wry grin. "That way you're not working around so many good-looking guys."

A spike of anger flared inside Mandy, bursting through Cassie's internal barrier for a moment. "You're jealous and I should be glad for it? Huh! I don't think so."

"No, honey, I'm not jealous. I'm joking with you." Abram turned her so he could clasp her shoulders. "I'm sorry if I've upset you."

Mandy jerked free from his grasp with a twist of her shoulders. "Nobody cares about how I feel. One day you will. I'm going to my room."

She stomped away, slamming the door leading to the covered passage behind her.

Cassie stared at the door for a moment and then turned to Abram's equally shocked countenance. "I had no idea she harbored such strong feelings about where she worked."

In fact, Mandy had always seemed composed and comported. The friendly kind of mild personality. Cassie hadn't witnessed her anger to such an extent. Rather, she tended to calm others with her meek attitude. She glanced at the door again, half expecting her friend to return and apologize for her outburst. A heart-to-heart talk seemed a very good idea.

"She once told me of something that happened when she was at the orphanage." He shook his head, pressing his lips together for a time. "I don't recall exactly what she said, but it had to do with being forced to learn to cook."

The situation triggered an extreme response in her friend. She obviously stewed over the enforced duties in a way that may prove unhealthy in the long run. The veiled threat in her last statement was out of character for her. Time to probe a little deeper into the previous experiences which led to Mandy's reaction. Something Flint needed to know about as well.

"I'll speak to her later about it and see if she'll tell me." Cassie squared her shoulders as she lowered her inner barrier to its normal level. "For now, let's leave her alone to calm down a bit."

Abram nodded. "I came to find you anyway."

"About?" She sensed his intensity before he spoke another word. He had worried himself into a headache and needed her to act.

"I think you should write to Pa and seek his advice on the situation here. Ask him to come home to help us. If you ask him, he's more likely to come home." Abram pressed his temples, massaging them in slow circles. "I can't believe I was so stupid to make that vow with our aunts. What a mess."

"You did what you had to at the time." Vowing to travel to Montgomery to the aunts' home when he'd shifted into Cassie's form had delayed the seemingly inevitable event. Inevitable from their point of view, but not hers. The unsettling question remained whether the deadly magical vow applied to Cassie or Abram. "You bought us some time if nothing else."

"I've bought more trouble." He lowered his hands as he studied her with pain in his eyes.

"We'll figure it out. Besides, I've asked him to come home before and he said no." Despite her longing for his presence and reassurance. If only he'd hurry his business and return. She harbored so many questions only he could answer. Not the least of which was, what more could he teach her about her powers. "Do you really think it would help to ask again?"

"It can't hurt. Make him understand we need his experience and guidance more urgently than ever." Again, the intensity flared in Abram's chest and echoed in his pounding brain.

"Especially after Allegro made an appearance in the dining room a little while ago." The chagrin and concern on Flint's face when the falcon landed on her shoulder in front of John Baker replayed in her mind. "Flint was not happy."

"So the secret is out." He pursed his lips as he regarded her for a beat. "That's not good. You really need to write to Pa. We need him."

"Yes, I think we do." She heaved a sigh. "All right, I will ask again."

But would he come?

What could be better than relaxing on the back porch, staring at the changing colors of the leaves on the trees blanketing the foothills? Except holding the hand of the young miss beside him. Daniel squeezed Wilma's fingers, simply happy to be with her. She'd surprised his entire being when she appeared a few days before. He hadn't been looking for the love of his life, but he may have found her. She sneaked right into his chest and wrapped her smile around his heart. With any luck, she'd never let it go.

"Matthew made a delicious breakfast this morning, didn't he?" Wilma patted her long dark green skirts with her free hand.

"The waffles were indeed fine." Light and crispy but firm enough to drench in maple syrup. Better than he'd had back in the city. "Matt is a fine cook."

"Flint said Sheridan is even better but I haven't had the pleasure of meeting him." She aimed twinkling green eyes at him. "Have you?"

"Not yet. He's away with his son in search of his wife." Daniel hesitated to tell her more, unsure of her reaction.

"Really? Why is she missing?"

"Because his wife is still a slave, somewhere in Georgia."

Her hand tensed in his as she blinked at him. "Was Sheridan one also?"

"He's a free man now, according to all accounts."

She settled back in her seat to let her gaze drift over the foothills in the distance. "I cannot fancy how he must have felt all this time with his wife so far away. What happened?"

"Apparently, the family was separated years ago by the slave master in retribution for something Sheridan did." Daniel viewed the red, gold, and green coloring the hillside before him. "When Giles came to the inn, he brought two friends with him. Turns out the friends are actually Sheridan's sons."

Matt was two years older than Daniel, but had far more world experience. Knowing he'd started his life enslaved and separated from his parents changed how Daniel approached him. Not as an equal but as someone to look up to. The other man deserved his respect for all he'd endured and survived. He hadn't met his older brother, Zander, but anticipated he'd like the man if he turned out to be anything like Matt.

Wilma shifted to stare at him with glistening eyes. "What good fortune for the man to be reunited with his missing sons."

"Indeed. Which prompted him to make the effort to find his wife." Imagine having no idea where someone you loved lived and worked for years on end? He squeezed her hand to reassure himself of her presence. "I do not blame him venturing all the way to the Atlantic coast to seek her out. Especially when my father may have found her already."

He'd journey as far as necessary to track down his missing wife. Especially if Wilma might be the woman in question. He'd grown quite fond of her in a remarkably short period and couldn't conceive being separated for long. Definitely not for years or, worse, decades. Once Sheridan had learned of the possibility his wife had been located he'd left to find her. Good man.

"I see I've missed quite a lot by not paying Flint a visit sooner." She relaxed back in the seat and trailed her gaze over the scene before her.

The row of outbuildings stretched across the back lawn of the inn. A wellhouse to the left, then an outhouse and a laundry where smoke rose steadily from a stone chimney. To the right of the small wooden building stood a smokehouse and henhouse beside Cassie's impressively large garden with a gated fence surrounding it. A very bucolic and peaceful site.

"Did Flint tell you about the fence around the garden?" He chuckled softly as he recalled the tale. "He had quite an ado about it."

"No, I don't believe so. What is so humorous about it?"

"When he first arrived in June he made the error of trying to shoo some deer that had wandered into the garden back outside. Only, he startled them into trying to jump out and they knocked down not only several of the plants but part of the original fence itself. Quite a disaster from all accounts."

"Oh, yes, I remember now." Wilma patted her lap as she chuckled along with him. "That is what Mrs. Fairhope was so upset about when we visited Flint over the summer."

"You were here before?" Why did the thought make him long to have arrived even earlier than he had? If only he'd been able to depart when he first received Cassie's letter. He'd have met the lovely lady earlier and not missed out on the time they would have had together.

"We only stayed a little while." She squeezed his hand as she peered up at the sound of heavy footfalls on the wooden floor. "Flint, what's the matter?"

Daniel looked up to espy Flint's frowning countenance. "Good day."

"What is the meaning of this?" Flint gestured to their joined hands resting on Daniel's leg.

"We are enjoying this fine Saturday morning together." He couldn't possibly object to them merely sitting on the porch having a discourse. Even if they indulged in the guilty pleasure of holding hands. "Is something wrong?"

"This display of affection is beyond acceptable, Mr. Fairhope, and you well know as much."

"We do enjoy each other's company. That is true." Including showing they cared for each other despite being in a public setting. But Flint's frown didn't bode well. Daniel simply needed to make him understand his actions were not inspired by a passing whim. "We are becoming better acquainted as a result. Surely you cannot find offense in such a simple act."

"You both are too young to know your own minds." Flint waved a hand between them. "Wilma, you barely know him. Why would you agree to such a public display?"

Like he'd harm the girl. Resentment flushed hotly through Daniel at the thought. His motives stemmed from the purest source, his affection for the young lady. He'd never intentionally harm or embarrass her by his words or deeds.

"You're quite correct, Flint, but I would like to know him better." She squeezed Daniel's hand instead of releasing it. "Sitting right here where everyone can see."

Good point. They were not secreted away somewhere having a tete-a-tete after all. But he could see Flint's point as well, being the older brother and thus responsible for his sister's behavior and reputation. If he were back in the city, he'd not dare be so bold as to hold her hand or do more than tip his hat to her. The young girl needed guidance and protection from any man who might try to take advantage of her naiveté and innocent trust. She needed someone like him to defend her, to care for her, perhaps even fall in love with her. To be the model of manners. There was only one way he could fill such a role and also be permitted by propriety to demonstrate his affection toward her. He stood, releasing her hand, and faced Flint's wary expression.

"Flint, I would like to formally request permission from you as her older brother to court her. Will you allow me to wait upon your sister?"

The wariness fled as surprise replaced it in Flint's eyes. "You wish to court my sister?"

"I have found her person to be very pleasing in both appearance and personality. I would enjoy spending more time with her to determine our suitability for one another.

With your permission, of course." Daniel searched Flint's face for hints as to what he thought of his declaration. Hesitance and suspicion abounded.

"Daniel has proven to be a fine, decent man in the time I've known him. He's intelligent, educated, and honest." Wilma pushed to her feet to stand beside Daniel, placing a hand on his arm. "I would very much accept Daniel's attentions, Flint, if you'll allow him to court me as he has requested."

Flint's lips parted slightly and then slowly closed as he regarded Wilma. Daniel waited for some reply from Flint, tapping an errant finger against his leg as he did so. The play of emotions across the other man's face nearly made him chuckle but Daniel refrained. No need to antagonize him.

"My dear sister, you know how much I esteem you and want only the best for you." Flint leaned forward from his waist to search Wilma's eyes for several seconds. "I love you dearly. You know as much, right?"

"Yes, Flint."

Daniel glanced sharply at Wilma, the meek tone at odds with the gleam in her eyes.

"Are you very, very certain you wish for me, acting in our father's stead, to accept this man's petition to court you?" He straightened and slipped his hands into his front trouser pockets. "I need for you to confirm your desires before I make my decision."

So doubt lingered as to the outcome of Daniel's application for permission. He held his breath, afraid to influence her choice any more than he'd already done. He sincerely wanted it to be her wish as well or he'd walk away, leave her to find a better man to court and perhaps marry. His gut clenched as his heart stuttered considering the potential calamity. He'd do it though. Walk away from her for her benefit. No matter the torment such an act might cost him.

Wilma moved closer to Daniel, her skirts brushing the top of one of his shoes. "Yes, Flint. Please?"

Flint drew himself up to his full height as his eyes turned to weigh on Daniel. "As it is my sister's choice to allow your request I will give you my permission to court her on one condition."

Joy flooded Daniel's core, setting his heart pounding and his palms to dampen. What sort of restriction might the man have in mind? A time limit? Only allowed to see her for five minutes at a time? Or only for the next week? How would he survive such curtailment of the joy he suspected he'd experience while courting the lovely creature beside him? He swallowed hard. "Which is?"

"You may only court her as long as others are around. I do not have anyone who can act as a proper chaperone all of the time but you must stay in the public areas when you are together. Agreed?"

Sweet relief buoyed his entire being. He stuck out his hand. "Indeed. Thank you, Flint."

Flint shook with him twice and then finally smiled at his sister. "Don't make me regret this, sister."

"I promise you won't." She wrapped her hands around Daniel's elbow, pulling him closer. "We will be on our best behavior so you will have nothing to worry about."

Daniel heard her simple words of acquiescence but the tone with which she professed to act appropriately suggested a quietly stubborn intent to do as she would. Whether Flint liked it or not. Daniel hid the knowing smile lurking at the corners of his mouth. The next few days might prove very interesting.

Chapter Eight

The middle of September brought cooler temperatures and much concern. Three months. Her pa had been gone for over three long months. Cassie stood at her open window, staring at the hills behind the inn. Cloud shadows drifted across the pale gold, rust, and greens of the foothills. Even surrounded by three of her brothers, she sorely missed her pa. She didn't even have the wisdom of Sheridan to turn to for comfort. Lordy, she wanted them all to come home. She pressed her palms to the warm wood of the window sill and closed her eyes, fighting the press of tears forming.

"Klee-klee-klee!"

She opened her eyes in time to duck sideways as Allegro flew past her. He swooped around the room, his wings flapping with powerful strokes, and then alighted on the headboard of her bed. His intelligent eye followed her movements as she approached him on silent feet. His brown-and-white mottled chest gleamed in the late afternoon light streaming through the nearby window. Dark wings folded neatly along his sides for a moment before opening to help him steady his position, his black-tipped claws in sharp contrast to his yellow feet as he sidestepped along the wooden headboard to be closer to her. She sat on the bed and positioned herself to address him.

"Welcome, my friend." She angled her head and he mirrored her actions, so she tilted her head the opposite direction until he matched her again. "I appreciate your company, Allegro. I was feeling alone and down."

The sleek falcon launched from the bed to fly over to the dresser she shared with Mandy, landing on the slick surface. Gaining his balance again, he stalked to the miniature portrait of her parents standing together in front of her childhood home down south in Montgomery. Cassie held fond memories of that house close to her heart. She'd most likely never see it again even if she were to capitulate and join her aunts in the same area as they most desired. The thought made her miss her parents all the more.

"I miss them both so much. Ma is haunting the inn but it's not the same as having her here. And Pa...well, he's so far away and doesn't expect to be home for another...six weeks." She sighed as she stood up beside the bed and smoothed the quilt back into place. "If only he understood just how precarious everything is right now."

"Klee!"

She glanced sharply at the bird. "What is it?"

Allegro flew the short distance to the writing desk and alighted on the back of the chair. He tilted his head toward the quill pen in its stand beside the ink well. "Klee!"

Of course. She'd delayed complying with Abram's suggestion she write to her father once more and plead with him to return posthaste. Although she'd agreed with him at the time, further reflection deemed the idea most likely fruitless. But if she laid out all the facts for her father, the pressing reasons for his immediate return, then perhaps he'd listen. "You're a very smart bird, Allegro. Do you think it will make any difference, though?" She shrugged as he dipped his head twice. "If you think so."

She hurried across the span of boards to sink onto the chair, selected a page of stationery and then dipped the quill into the black ink. Allegro hopped a little to one side on the chair back so he could peek over her shoulder at what she scratched onto the pale pink paper.

Fury Falls Inn, Alabama
Sat., Sept. 15, 1821

Dear Father,

I trust this will find you well. I am writing to you to plead with you to return to the inn as quickly as earthly possible. Much has transpired since you departed in June. But to come to the main point as quickly as possible, I'm afraid. There. I've put it down for the first time. Ma's sisters have forced Abram to make a vow that he or I, we're not sure which, will go to Montgomery after you return home. See, Abram had shapeshifted into appearing like me when he made the magical vow and now one of us must fulfill the spell's demands or face dire consequences. But who must go, him or me?

That's one concern. The other is that someone is killing witches. One by one. Several women have been killed in the past few months but we don't know by whom. The common element is that they are all suspected witches. Giles is highly worried for my safety as a result. The killer seems to be targeting female witches. We suspect…but no, I don't want to put that on paper until we have some kind of evidence. It's someone you know, though.

I had been keeping the fact that I am a witch secret but my familiar, a Merlin falcon I call Allegro, appeared in front of the guests the other day. Flint is worried about the consequences of the falcon visiting me in the dining room while I was entertaining the crowd. Flint's concerned that the growing number of guests may begin to slow or taper off if they know about our powers.

And of course you know Ma is haunting the inn. It's only

a matter of time before the guests catch on to that fact as well. It's one thing to have witches around, but not too many folks want to be around haints.

I also want your blessing on my betrothal to Flint. He's a good man, kind, decent, hardworking, and he loves me. I love him as well, but I've told him I won't proceed with our relationship until your return so you and I may have a conversation together. Ma won't give her blessing to the union because she harbors a grudge against him for running the inn in your absence instead of her. She's not about to change her opinion of him, I fear.

Please, please, please come home! I beg of you as your only daughter. Your sons are all here except for Silas, but I expect to hear from him at any moment. I'm sure they'd enjoy seeing their father again after all these years. Pray do not make us wait any longer than absolutely necessary, Pa. We love and miss you.

Cassie

She reread her plea and sat back in the chair, Allegro hopping onto her shoulder to rub his head against her hair. "I hope this will bring him home."

The bedroom door opened and Mandy strode in, her steps faltering to a halt when she spotted the falcon perched on Cassie's shoulder.

"Who is that?" Mandy snicked the door closed behind her.

"This is Allegro, my familiar I told you about." She didn't need to hide the magical aspect of her person from Mandy. After all, her friend would soon become her sister. How soon was another question. "He flew in for a quick visit. What brings you up here in the middle of the afternoon?"

"A sick headache. Matt let me take a break before we need to start the supper tea." Mandy eased across the room, keeping an eye on the falcon, and sank onto the stuffed mattress on the bed. "Will it stay, do you think?"

"As long as it wants to." Allegro lowered his head and Cassie took the hint and stroked the soft crown. "I have no control over him. He comes and goes as he likes."

"Thus the open window?" Mandy indicated the curtains gently breathing in and out with the breeze.

"Yes. I had hoped to see him again. After he surprised the guests I had to ask him to leave, you see. I hoped I hadn't insulted him or hurt his feelings by doing so."

"I'm going to lie down for a little while. If you and he don't mind."

"How's it going in the kitchen? Are you adjusting to the routine all right?"

Mandy shrugged from her prone position on the quilt. "I'm doing my best but I don't know my best will ever be enough."

"Can I ask...?" Should she though? With the other girl not feeling quite herself, the moment may not have come to probe into her past. But the topic had been raised. "Abram mentioned you had a hard time of it back at the orphanage with regard to cooking. Can I ask if that is why the idea of helping in the kitchen is so repugnant to you?"

Mandy pressed her fingers to her forehead and rubbed gently. "I've tried to put it behind me but it won't stay there."

"Do you want to talk about it?"

"Not really, but it's probably better to get it out in the open." With a sigh, Mandy lowered her hand and jacked herself up on her elbows. "The woman who ran the orphanage demanded every girl take their turn learning how to cook. Something which I hated doing. The act of peeling the skin off of vegetables and animals makes my blood run cold. I just couldn't. But she insisted I help skin rabbits for the stew and I ended up...vomiting into the kettle." Mandy shuddered, her eyes dimming at the memory. "She beat me with a switch until she drew blood on the backs of my legs."

The mortification along with the agony Mandy had endured at the older woman's hands swelled inside Cassie. She let the emotions consume her for a few moments to fully appreciate Mandy's reasons for objecting to her current position. The association between working in a kitchen and her terrible experience doing so left no doubt about why she vociferously balked.

"Oh, Mandy, I am so sorry. I had no idea." No wonder the poor girl hated working in the kitchen. "I'll talk to Flint and get you reassigned back to the dining room as soon as possible. Or at least urge him to find someone else to work in the kitchen as soon as possible. All right?"

Mandy flopped back and closed her eyes. "If you could do so for me, I'd really appreciate it. He isn't listening to me."

"I'll talk to him. I promise." Cassie glanced at Allegro who opened his wings to their full span. His talons clutched her shoulder without piercing, enough to steady himself. She stroked his head again and he nodded to her. Then he pushed off and flew out the window. Turning to regard Mandy's sleeping form, she could only hope Flint and her pa would listen to both of her pleas.

The staccato flash of lightning lit the empty dining room. Flint ambled across the room, in no hurry since he couldn't sleep anyway. The storm outside didn't help, the booming thunder shaking the inn at intervals. Mayhap a bit of whiskey might soothe the disturbance in his gut. He'd been antsy all evening and as the midnight hour approached he simply had to leave his bed and seek out something to alleviate the sense of foreboding inside.

He leaned down behind the bar to lift a small glass and set it on the counter. A flash of light made him glance up, waiting for the roll of thunder to follow. Only instead of hearing the anticipated chest pounding rumble, he saw standing before him a translucent crone in a sweeping black cloak with long black hair and beseeching emerald eyes. He blinked several times, trying to erase the image but to no avail. He'd not heard anyone enter the building nor the room and yet she stood on the other side of the bar. In the middle of the night.

"May I…help you?" he asked, hoping his roiling gut was wrong in its premonitions.

"I want you to exact vengeance against the man who killed me." She glared at him as he straightened.

He swallowed the eruption of fear in his throat. Another ghost. Damnation. His gut was right. "I will try. May I ask your name?"

"I'm Isabella Reese." She lifted her rounded chin and gripped the edges of her cloak. "I've come in search of my friend Mercy Fairhope, who I believe is haunting this inn."

Flint's stomach sank through the floor and on down to the core of the earth. The word was out about the inn being haunted. After all his efforts to prevent disclosure to the public. First Allegro and then the crone's admission. He opened his mouth but no words emerged. He couldn't process the ramifications of her revelation.

"Did I hear my name?" Mercy shimmered into view and then solidified on the other side of the bar from where Flint stood gawping at the pair of haints in his inn. "Isabella? I had no idea. When?"

"Last month. Specifically, midnight on the twenty-second of August." Isabella paced back and forth, her cloak flaring out as she pivoted and went the other direction. "I want that man stopped. He's wreaking havoc across the county. There are others who wanted me to come seek your help, Mercy."

Wait, others? More ghosts of the murdered witches were out there somewhere. But more importantly, the witch knew who killed her. The break they needed. She possessed details as to the method and, with good fortune, hints as to his identity. To begin, she'd confirmed a man was responsible for the recent murders. Also that he'd targeted her since he snuck into her home in the middle of the night. So the killing wasn't an act of opportunity but intention.

Mercy shifted to one side, shooting a sharp glance at Flint. "He will help you. I'll see to it."

Indeed he would do everything in his power to find the man responsible for killing the witches. Even if it meant accusing the trusted acquaintance of his boss. Doing so may mean his job, especially if he were to be proven wrong. If they were right in accusing John, then what would that mean for Haley Baker and her relationship with Giles? Speaking of whom, the Guardian should be alerted.

"Giles should hear this since he's the Guardian." Flint started out from behind the bar but Mercy waved him to a stop.

"I'll get the others. Wait here." Mercy shimmered and disappeared.

He stood staring at the bent old woman, unsure what to say to her. Minutes passed as she continued pacing back and forth, her cloak brushing the floorboards with a slight hissing sound as she slowly tread to and fro. He finished pouring his drink and capped the bottle. The questions in his mind were all ones the others would want to hear answers to, so he held his tongue. The whiskey burned away any vestiges of drowsiness and any hope of sleeping as he swallowed his first mouthful. He'd not known the crone in life. What did one say to an unfamiliar ghost? He wracked his brain for a moment before the most important question popped into his mind.

He leaned on the counter and searched her guarded expression as she passed in front of the bar. "How did you know about Mercy?"

"I felt her presence when I happened by one day. While I was still alive." Isabella slowed her pacing to halt and look at him. "She has a very strong personality, one easy to discern for a sensitive witch like me."

Relief swept through him. So the haunting wasn't common knowledge after all. With good luck he'd still be able to pull off an excellent experience for the highly respected senator and his entourage when they came in November. Only a couple of months away now and still so much Flint planned to improve. Reggie Fairhope needed to arrive with the new furniture he had gone to Georgia to have made prior to the looming event in order to truly impress the senator. If they could focus on what needed doing around the inn rather than trying to catch a killer it would help. The witch's news might advance the effort to end the murders and allow him to do his job without distraction.

Giles stormed into the room in a flowing white nightshirt and an open, dark-gray robe with matching slippers on his feet, his hair still damp and hastily combed. "What is going on?"

"Calm down." Flint motioned to the ghostly witch. "Meet Isabella Reese."

Giles assessed the woman's appearance with a sweep of his gaze as he reached the bar. A sound at the door prevented him from speaking, instead glancing to where Abram and Daniel marched in with Cassie trailing behind them. All were in similar night apparel and looked not only disgruntled but alarmed. Mercy shimmered into view beside Isabella and waited for everyone to gather at the bar.

"I sense how distraught you are." Cassie approached

Isabella, a worried smile on her lips. "I understand you're in need of some help? You needn't fear. We will help you."

"That evil man must pay for his crimes." The crone stopped and aimed her glare at Giles. "You're the one they call The Guardian? You must see to it."

"Yes, ma'am, I intend to." Giles regarded her with steady appraisal. "What can you tell us about him?"

"Klee-klee-klee!" Allegro darted through an open window at the back of the dining room, his wide wings beating hard as he flew straight to Cassie. Alighting on her left shoulder, he kept his wings outstretched for a second to balance and then folded them neatly on his sides.

"I'm surprised to see you so late." She stroked a hand down his head and back before meeting Flint's gaze. "He's never come to me at night before."

"On such a stormy night, too." What had brought the falcon out during the fierce weather? The bird sidled closer to Cassie's head, keeping near to her. Protective.

Thunder rolled across the heavens followed immediately by a series of flashes of light. Rain pelted the building and poured through the open windows at the rear of the room. Abram and Daniel dashed across the floor to slam the windows closed against the onslaught. Then strode quickly back to the group, drying their hands on their robes.

"Wow! That blew up fast. Sounds like it's on top of us." Abram grimaced as he glanced at the ceiling and then addressed Isabella. "Sorry for the interruption. You were saying?"

Isabella nodded curtly at him and then looked at Giles. "He was fairly tall because he came at me from above and behind." She swirled her cloak as she spun about. "He snuck up on me while I was preparing my offering to the Goddess."

"A most unfortunate time to invoke evil." Mercy shifted side to side as her distress appeared on her strained features. "I am truly sorry, sister."

"What more can you tell us about him?" Daniel asked, leaning against the counter.

"I didn't see him, only felt his presence when it was too late." Isabella looked at each of them in turn. "It was a new moon and I had begun chanting the spell I'd written to honor our Goddess when he grabbed me from behind and slit my throat with a knife." She pressed trembling fingers to her throat as her expression turned grim. "Then he stabbed me through the heart and wiped the blade on my cloak after I fell to the floor, dying. I've never hurt anyone in my life. Why would anyone do such a thing to me?"

A very good question. Only someone bearing a grudge against witches in general would stoop to such evil measures. How could he relay such a thought to the distraught woman? In fact, he needn't share such musings. They'd only serve to further upset everyone in the room.

"Miss Reese, how did he grab you? With which hand?" Giles searched the crone's expression, a slight squint around his eyes.

The woman shrugged. "Why does it matter?"

"Humor me." The Guardian inhaled, swelling his already massive chest.

"I'm sure Giles has a very good reason for asking, Miss Reese." Cassie sent the woman an encouraging look, the falcon tilting his head to one side as if also awaiting for her response.

"Well…" Isabella frowned in concentration, her eyes turning inward as she relived the moment of her death. "One hand on my right shoulder and the other he used to slice my throat with a sharp knife." She shuddered and crossed her arms.

Flint didn't possess special abilities like Cassie but his active imagination provided gory details and sensations without them. Lord above, to have to relive ones' own death with such horrific clarity. To have become a ghost in order to seek justice. Is that why Mercy continued to haunt the inn? But her killers had been caught and awaited trial and had no apparent connection to the witch killings. So something more prevented her from moving on. What? Would ending the threats against Cassie finally give Mercy the peace she sought in order to finally rest?

"I'm sorry to make you go through that again, but thank you." Giles relaxed his posture but remained in a ready-to-act stance. "But his being left-handed is a helpful thing to know."

Flint studied the oldest brother with intense interest. Giles was right. Not many people were left-handed, so they now possessed a useful clue as to the identity of the man responsible for murdering witches. Murdering women he *suspected* were witches without any concern for whether or not his theory proved correct.

"We need to tell Deputy Barney what we know." Cassie chewed her lip for a moment, Allegro opening his wings slightly to maintain his balance. "We must catch him."

Another boom of thunder shook the inn, halting the conversation until it faded away. The rain continued to lash at the windows as flashes of lightning added to the glow of the lamplight in the room. Flint could feel the electricity crackling in the air and raising the hair on his arms.

"And how do we tell him the source of our new information?" Abram folded his arms over his chest. "He'll never believe a witch appeared during a thunderstorm to tell us how she was killed."

"There is that…" Flint propped his fists on his hips. "But we must do something. The stakes are too high to ignore this information."

"You must catch the man. If not for me, for all the others he's killed." Isabella aimed angry eyes at Flint. "He's the one who is evil and hurting others. Not those of us he's attacked."

"She's right. Giles, you must tell the Deputy. He's more likely to act than the sheriff in my view." Mercy shifted closer to Isabella as though she'd like to console her but hesitated. "You have to try."

Giles nodded slowly. "I will go Monday morning at first light and tell him what we've learned but not how. See if he'll accept it without questioning the source."

Isabella scowled at him. "Why wait? Why not go tomorrow?"

"We don't have a name, only a description." Giles splayed his hands with a shrug. "If you can tell me who exactly, then it would be worthwhile to disrupt the man's Sunday. Otherwise, I think it can wait until a regular business day. The murders aren't happening every day but every few weeks. We have time."

"It's not like he introduced himself." Isabella spun away and then wrapped her swirling black cloak around her. "I've done what I can to put an end to him. Now it's up to you. I shall trouble you no more. But I cannot vow the same for the others he's murdered in cold blood."

Isabella flared her cloak out and with a last look at Mercy and a growl of dismay she vanished. Lightning flashed several times as thunder boomed, rattling the window panes, and then rolled away. Flint stared at the glass panes, inspecting them from across the room as to their integrity in the assault from the elements. Then he dragged his attention back to the important conversation.

"Her information changes everything." Mercy trailed her gaze over everyone gathered in the room. "Make me proud, children."

"We will do our best, Ma." Cassie took Flint's hand in hers, the falcon shifting his talons on her shoulder. "You don't need worry so."

"We have a plan and I'll make sure Parker acts on what little we can tell him." Giles raked a hand through his still-damp hair. "I give you my word, Ma."

"If you don't, we all fail." Mercy grimaced as she shimmered for a long moment and then disappeared.

Hope and disappointment swirled in Flint's mind as he glanced from one to the other. Hope they had a lead on the killer. The description of tall and furtive fit John but it also fit a slew of other men in the area. Was John left handed? Not a trait Flint had ever noticed in the man. He could suggest to the deputy John Baker was the killer but doing so didn't prove guilt.

On the other hand, disappointment weighed down his hopes as Isabella's presence had confirmed Flint was not the only one who could interact with ghosts. A slim hope now dashed of possessing his own special ability like the others. One which would put him in a favorable light with Cassie's family. Despite his lack of special gifts, he'd do what he could to remove the most immediate threat to his girl.

"I'll go with you, Giles." Flint gripped Cassie's hand harder. "Barney and I have become friends so maybe if I'm there he won't ask too many questions we don't want to answer."

Chapter Nine

C assie followed Daniel into the entrance hall the next morning after a brief but enlightening conversation in the parlor. Her brother shared his feelings for Wilma, and the surprise he continued to feel as a result of actually meeting a woman at the inn like Cassie had jokingly suggested. He'd gone so far as to request Flint's permission to officially court her, but he hadn't told her about his ability to timeskip or bounce. Keeping secrets of his own. A questionable Fairhope family tradition.

"Are you sure you want to try this?" She crossed to the small table by the door to work with the flowers. She shifted a rose to nestle between some cattails before she glanced at him. "You want to try now?"

He stared at the pocket watch secured to his waistcoat and then lifted his gaze to meet hers. "There's not going to be a perfect time." He winked at her. "Get it? Perfect time?"

"Ha-ha." Such a lame joke coming from him given his intent to timeskip. "How far back do you plan to go?"

"It's a test so only a little while to figure out how this whole thing works." He fiddled with the stem. "I want to make sure I know how to come back to the present."

"Indeed." Cassie crossed her arms around her waist. She sensed Mandy's distress before she saw her, the other girl's anger and annoyance washing through her.

"I said I don't like doing so and I've told you why." Mandy practically shouted as she emerged from the kitchen, carrying a tray of clinking clean tankards and mugs. Abram held the door for her until she'd cleared the doorway and then followed her into the entrance hall. "Why won't you believe me?"

Abram shrugged an apology at Cassie as he continued across the room to follow Mandy toward the dining room. "I do believe you, but I think there's more you're not telling me. That's all."

"Well, there's not." Mandy glanced back at him before disappearing into the other room.

"If you say so." Abram shook his head as he also moved out of sight.

"That's interesting." Daniel turned his attention back to Cassie. "What are they arguing about?"

"Why Mandy doesn't like working in the kitchen." Cassie pursed her lips. Arguments upset her every time she witnessed one let alone participated. "She has good reasons. I need to talk to Flint soon about her preferences."

"After we finish here, all right?"

"Fine. Let's do this. I have other things to do today." The list of other tasks was long. Mending. Candle making. Harvesting the produce from her garden to preserve for use over the winter. Singing for the guests later in the afternoon. She had a new song she planned to perform, one she'd written herself. "How far back do you plan to skip?"

"I think a few minutes is enough for a test. We'll be able to see if we have in fact gone back in time that way."

"Wait. Did you say 'we'?" She gulped at the prospect. "I thought I was here for moral support."

He peered at her as a slow grin spread across his mouth. "Don't you want to see what it's like? Besides, it will give me a chance to see if I can indeed take someone with me. Come on, sister mine. You're not scared, are you?"

"I'd be a fool if I wasn't." A knot of fear lodged in her throat. Not only did her brother intend to skip for the first time but with her in tow. What if he failed? If they didn't survive the process for some unknown cause, nobody would know what became of them. They'd simply vanish from their own time. She could only imagine how the others would react in such an event. "We should tell Giles."

"No, he'd either try to stop me or want to go with me." Daniel angled his head as he peered at her for a long moment. "You know I'll take care of you."

"I know you'll try, but this is new for you, too. We don't know what's going to happen." Her vivid imagination sent chills down her back. Images flashed through her mind of finding themselves somewhere and some when unintended, perhaps amidst a natural catastrophe like a tornado or flood, or in the middle of a battle during one of the previous wars. What if he forgot how to return to the present because of some head injury or worse as a result?

"Maybe nothing happens, we don't go anywhere or anywhen, since I'm not exactly sure how this works." He stared at the crystal face of the watch for several beats before grinning at her. "Ma told me how to do it as best as she knows but she's never done it either. It seems simple enough. Come with me back in time."

His eager expression softened her distress. The concept intrigued without any doubt. Did she have the nerve? She should tell Flint or Giles. They demanded to know her location at all times. They'd probably tell her to stay put. Which is what she wanted. Right? Curiosity swelled inside her chest the longer she considered Daniel's request. What would it feel like? Maybe tingling like Abram experienced when he shifted. Or something else. What about sound? What happens if they were to come across themselves in the past? So many questions and only one way to learn the answers.

"All right." She hugged herself harder, curiosity battling inside with the subsiding fear. "Let's try."

"I'm grateful for your trust." He grinned more widely at her. "All right, let me adjust the time on this to five minutes ago, and we'll move over to the corner by the door so we're out of the way when we skip backward. Right?"

"That makes sense." She strolled over to the designated area and turned to face the center of the entrance hall. "Now what?"

He joined her and held out his left arm, the watch in his palm. "Now, take my arm and don't let go."

She tentatively placed her hand on his forearm and clasped it tightly as she drew in a long fortifying breath. "Let's go before I lose my nerve."

"It makes perfect sense for us to be nervous about doing this. But trust me." He pressed his lips together, manipulating the stem as Ma had instructed.

For a second nothing happened and then a low murmur filled Cassie's ears, increasing in volume as the room began to spin. Slowly at first and then faster and faster with flashes of light increasing in frequency. She clutched Daniel's arm with both hands for fear they'd be separated in the rushing vortex forming around them. Then all fell still and quiet. She gasped for air after the shock of the sound and motion ceased. Daniel recovered faster than she did, probably because the ability to timeskip was his gift and not hers. He laid a hand on top of hers with a happy smile on his face.

"We did it." He nodded toward the other side of the entrance hall. "See?"

She blinked, trying to clear the daze from her head.

Then she gasped, but this time because she saw herself and Daniel in conversation by the table. "What if we see us?"

"I don't know, so let's hide." He pointed to the door nearby leading out to the covered passage. "We know nobody came through that door in our time, so we'll use it to hide behind."

Making good on the plan, they peeked around the slightly open door. Watched as Mandy and Abram emerged again from the kitchen and argued their way across to the dining room. Then Daniel straightened and smiled at her.

"Ma was right about how to skip through time." He exuded pride and surprise at his success. "Time to get back to our own time. Ready?"

"What an experience. But yes, we should go back." She nodded, excited about their successful adventure but eager to proceed with her real timeline.

"Here we go." Daniel reset the watch stem and the sound and spinning began again. When it stopped, she struggled for breath as she spotted the kitchen door finish closing and the sound of Abram and Mandy's argument fading. She and Daniel stood by the flowers yet again. She opened her mouth to say something to Daniel when Flint pushed through the front door.

"There you are." He hurried to Cassie's side, a frown forming on his face. "I've been looking for you."

"I've been…right here." Should she tell him what they'd done? Glancing at Daniel, she spied a slight shake of his head, confirming her own opinion. She caught Flint's eye with a lift of her chin. "I'm glad you're here because I need to talk to you about Mandy."

"What about her?" Flint searched her eyes with his as a frown dipped his brows. "Is she all right?"

Cassie's innards continued to swirl as she fought to regain her equilibrium and thus her composure. Flint's sudden presence didn't permit her time to process the trip back in time and subsequent return to the present. Her mind reeled from the sound and the sensations. If it was that momentous going back only a few minutes she could imagine the effect of a longer timeskip.

"I'll let you two talk then." Daniel inclined his head to Flint and shot a cautionary glance at Cassie before addressing Flint again. "Do you know where your sister might be?"

Cassie wasn't surprised when Flint's concern shifted from Mandy to Wilma in a heartbeat. "Why do you want to know?"

"I thought I'd ask her to take a walk with me up to the falls. I haven't seen them yet and that is a very public place, right?"

"I suppose." Flint nodded to himself as he considered Daniel's request. "I think she's reading in the gazebo out front."

"Thank you." Daniel gave Flint a nod and then started whistling as he left through the front doors.

Cassie took the opportunity to regain Flint's attention. "You need to know why Mandy doesn't want to work in the kitchen so you will find someone to do that work. Very soon."

"I'm listening." Flint regarded her with concern emanating from every fiber of his being.

She loved him all the more for his caring attention as she related Mandy's story. How would he feel if she were to reveal to him her little trip back in time without him? She needn't worry since she had no intention of telling him.

Storm tossed leaves littered the lawn in front of the inn. Daniel strutted toward Wilma's bowed head where she was sitting in the shadows of the gazebo. He all but glowed with the pride of his successful timeskip. He wanted to spend a few minutes with her even if he couldn't tell her why his heart soared with happiness. Flint had taken him aside the day before and cautioned him about telling her. Additionally, his promise to keep the magic and witchcraft and haunting quiet meant he'd refrain from letting that particular truth pass his lips. Not yet. At some point she'd learn his reality but now wasn't the right moment. The young lady seemed oblivious to his approach until the crunch of fragrant leaves under his booted feet interrupted her reading. She lifted her head and blinked at him for a moment before a smile eased onto her mouth. She placed the book on her lap as he climbed the steps to join her.

"My dear, I hope I am not an unpleasant interruption." He stood in front of her, sliding his hands into his front pockets to keep from making any nervous gestures.

"No, sir, you most certainly are not." She clasped the book with both hands, her slender fingers wrapped around the dark cloth binding. "What brings you out here on this morning?"

"I came to invite you to take a stroll up to the famous Fury Falls."

"They are very pretty I understand." She set the book on the seat beside her and stood. "I'd be glad to accept your invitation."

He held out a hand, palm up. "May I hold your hand on said stroll?"

She batted her eyelashes at him as she placed her hand on his. "Shall we?"

"We shall." Clasping her fingers, he led her down the steps.

Her ready acceptance of his invitation brought a surge of warmth and happiness through him. They sauntered across the leaf strewn lawn and then the crushed rock carriageway. A trio of dogs loped off the front porch to trot alongside as they left the stone drive to follow the dirt trail up the hill. After a few minutes, the dogs turned back, leaving them to climb the hill to the falls and springs.

All the while, delight filled his heart in finding such a young beauty with spirit and intellect to match his own. Her brother's permission to court her underscored his great fortune. Merely being with her swelled his heart with contentment, but being permitted to hold her fingers in his sent him over the moon with joy.

"I never thought I'd enjoy staying so far away from town, but I find great pleasure here." Wilma searched their surroundings with wide eyes. "Everything is so fresh and green after that horrendous thunderstorm last night. Did you hear it?"

"Indeed." He'd been awake most of the night not only from the storm's intensity but also the ghostly witch's revelations. Though he'd not even hint to her of the events of the previous night. "It was quite a powerful storm."

"But it did wash away a lot of the dust coating the plants." She glanced at him and then away. "I suppose I will need to return home ere long. Mother will wonder about our safety."

"Surely she trusts Flint and Julian to take care of you while you are here." He tipped his hat to an older couple strolling toward them after taking the waters above.

"Well, yes, but this far out from town the presence of law and order is not often felt." She inclined her head to the pair as they passed.

"What do you do in town? Do you attend school or sewing circles?" His spontaneous question gave him pause. He'd never been curious about a woman's pastimes before. He'd never felt a lot of things before meeting the woman beside him. "If I may be so bold."

"You may. I am tutored at home when one is available. Otherwise, I read from my father's extensive library of books. He's a believer in self-education and keeps up with the latest books to be published. I've taken up archery and am a fair shot. And yes, there is a sewing circle I sometimes attend but mostly I spend my days at home. Church on Sunday, of course. I lead a bible study group during the summer months, but that is disbanded now. Thus I am free to pay my brother a visit."

"You like to read, don't you?" He squeezed her fingers. "What were you reading when I interrupted you?"

She shooed away the question with one hand as they continued up the trail. "It's a new novel, truth be told. Father thought I might enjoy the tale as it is set during the Revolution."

"What is it?"

"*The Spy* by a new American novelist, James Cooper. It just came out this year. Have you heard of it?"

A smile bloomed on his face at the name of the author. "I have. Are you enjoying it?" Daniel had the privilege of having met the young author when he'd visited the college.

James Cooper had a unique perspective of American history. He'd told Daniel about his childhood, growing up in his father's namesake community of Cooperstown, New York. For his stories, he drew from his experiences with the lore of the wilderness and its abundant trappers and hunters as well as the tales of the refugees from war-torn Europe. *The Spy* was his first attempt at an historical romance which followed the same scheme Daniel had seen in Sir Walter Scott's historicals. Daniel had enjoyed reading it, especially knowing the intentions of the author.

"It's quite exciting and I do love to learn more about what life was like in the previous century."

"That's not so long ago, my dear." The Revolution had ended less than thirty years ago. Hardly long enough for life to have changed overly much.

"Oh, look!" She stopped and pointed to the sky. "Is that a hawk?"

He shaded his eyes with one hand as he searched for the

bird she indicated. "I believe that is a falcon, based on the coloring and wingspan."

"It's so pretty against the bright blue sky. How thrilling!" She stared up at the circling bird of prey. "Do you know what kind?"

Indeed he did as it was Cassie's familiar. "It's known as a Merlin falcon and it's quite rare in this part of the state." Rather magical, in fact, that it had chosen this area at all since most sightings of the species apparently occurred along the coast. "I'm sure you'll see it again, though."

She dropped her gaze to peer at him. "Why is that?"

The direction in which their conversation veered would lead to some questions he'd rather not answer. She may not react well to the many shocking secrets of the Fairhope family. Best to tread carefully and slowly. He tugged on her hand and resumed their saunter toward the sound of the rushing falls he could now hear in the distance.

"If you remain in this area, I assume he will make another appearance, that's all." He glanced at her charming expression.

The thrill she'd mentioned at seeing the falcon surprised him and stirred his own delight in the wealth of nature surrounding them. His life in Knoxville did not have nearly the same feeling of living among the wild things in the world. The thrum of city life moved at a far greater pace than the stroll they currently enjoyed. A typical day started before dawn and went mostly nonstop until long after the sun had given up and gone to bed. An enjoyable if hectic lifestyle. One he longed to return to posthaste.

Or *had* until his heart became enamored with the green-eyed temptress gazing up at him. He found himself torn between his professional desires and his heart's desires. He couldn't stay in Alabama, not when everything he'd worked so hard to build for himself waited in Tennessee. He'd worked hard to create a life. His role as teacher to young minds for one thing. He had friends and colleagues depending on his return as well. Besides, the girl needed her family. She wouldn't want to leave them to be with him. Not after meeting mere days before. Perhaps it would be better to squash the burgeoning feelings he had for her before it went too far and they both were hurt. But then she smiled at him and his very soul rebelled at the idea of ignoring his growing attachment to her.

"I do plan to linger for another day or so if Flint and Julian don't object." She batted long lashes at him again. "And if you have no objection?"

"None whatsoever." The sound of the waterfall grew louder as they rounded a curve in the trail. "Look, I believe we have arrived."

The scene bested any landscape painting of a waterfall he'd ever seen. The river, full after the rain of the previous night, cascaded down about twenty feet to crash onto a rocky river bed, foaming and splashing its way past them. The spray sparkled like miniature diamonds in the late morning sunshine. On both sides of the river soaring pines and colorful deciduous trees covered the foothills. He enjoyed being out at the base of the Appalachians. A beautiful and refreshing view indeed.

"Oh, it's enchanting." She let go of his hand to step closer to the edge of the river and peer up at the rapidly flowing wall of water. "I'm very glad you asked me to come."

"My pleasure." Enchantments and magic surrounded him. Should he tell her about them? Was she ready to accept the startling reality of his very being? He opened his mouth and then closed it again. Squashing a sigh, he decided to withhold the news for another more appropriate time. If then. Perhaps he should consult with Flint as to when she'd accept his true nature. At what juncture they should reveal the truth. Yes, that was a better path forward.

"Come, I think we should turn back."

She glanced over her shoulder at him, her long hair pulled up in a knot at the base of her neck, her eyes dancing with delight. "So soon?"

He stretched out his hand toward her. "I'm afraid I have some tasks to attend. If you're quite ready?"

"Very well." She pivoted away from the river and strode toward him, the long skirts of her dress brushing the grass and rocks along the path with each step. "But mayhap you'd accompany me on another visit, perhaps with a picnic?"

He snared her hand and held it firmly as they started back down the trail. "Perhaps."

The church bells rang eight times as Flint followed Giles up the rain splattered stairs to the jail Monday morning. Giles pushed inside with Flint close behind to find Sheriff Stephen Neal himself sitting on the chair at the massive wood desk. Flint hadn't seen the man in a very long time, but he'd recognize his refined appearance anywhere. Dark eyes, small mouth, hair at a reasonable length over the tips of his ears. He wore a dark brown vest over a white collared shirt with a black string tie, his tan coat and wide-brimmed hat hanging on pegs on the wall behind him. Steve firmed his lips as Flint shut the door with a thud.

"Good morning, gentlemen." Steve rose to his feet as Giles and Flint came to a halt in front of the desk. "How may I help you?"

The sheriff's tone hinted at his annoyance at being interrupted in his paperwork. He remained somewhat of an unknown entity since Flint had dealings far more often with Deputy Barney Parker. He'd helped the deputy catch a couple of horse thieves a few months back, including his own buckskin paint. Parker was more open-minded and accepting than what he could tell of the good sheriff. However, the man was liked well enough to be re-elected to serve the county so he'd give him a chance.

Flint glanced at Giles and then met Steve's quizzical expression. "We have information about the recent murders."

Involuntarily, he darted a look toward the trio of men held in the two cells at the back of the jail house, waiting for their trial to be held at the county courthouse nearby. The leader, Joe Madison, glared at him as he gripped the bars separating him from freedom. Greg Chalmers lounged on a cot in the right-hand cell, knee bent and wrist resting on his knee. The very man who had shot Mercy in the head, killing her and causing Cassie so much pain and guilt. Young Teddy's dad, Adam Jacobs, stared at Giles with hate and a healthy dose of fear in his eyes. Flint didn't blame him after hearing about how Giles had threatened him. Nearly seriously injuring Barney and Zander accidentally in the process. That was the day the Guardian discovered just how strong he'd become. He met Giles' stern gaze for a moment, recognizing the lingering desire to exact his own vengeance against the prisoners.

"You know those men?"

Flint swung his gaze to the scrutiny of the sheriff. "Somewhat. When's the trial?"

Steve braced his hands on the desk and glanced at the cells. "Next week. Now, I know you didn't come here to talk about those rascals. They'll get their day in court and serve whatever time or face whatever final sentence the judge declares."

"They should hang." Giles folded his arms across his chest in a familiar defensive gesture. "They killed my mother."

"I see. I'm sorry for your loss, sir, but I assure you they will pay for their crimes."

Flint cleared his throat. He didn't want to discuss those men. They needed to locate a particular man before he committed more murders. "About the recent killings."

"The women?" Steve pressed his knuckles onto the desk. "What do you know?"

"We know it's a left-handed man, for one thing." Giles lowered his arms and propped his hands on his hips. "That should help identify him."

Steve nodded. "Perhaps. Unless he's equally able to use either hand."

Flint shot Giles another glance. He'd not considered the possibility the man could be ambidextrous. "Wouldn't that still help to identify him?"

"It may if we can determine how many men in the area have the capability to be equally proficient no matter which hand they used." He shifted a notepad closer to him to make a few notes. "Thank you for the piece of information, but I must ask how you came by it. Care to share who witnessed the killing? I'd like to interview them myself."

Flint swallowed. The reveal would have been easier if Deputy Barney had been present instead of the more self-important sheriff. "Well…"

Lying did not come naturally. Leaving out specific details surely counted as some kind of deception. Flint never lied. He prided himself on that fact. How many times had he told Mercy he always told the truth? Striving to reassure her of his decency and integrity so she'd relent and approve his courting her daughter. He intended to marry Cassie, if she'd have him after finding out how he couldn't claim any special powers. Like everyone in her family could, apparently. His self-confidence wavered each time he considered his ordinary self. He opened his mouth to try to walk a very thin line between the truth and not revealing everything.

Giles gestured with one hand for Flint to hush before addressing the sheriff. "Let's just say someone who saw what happened but is unable to come forward in person."

A slow lift of the sheriff's brow proceeded his next question. "Why would this person come to you but not to me?"

Giles cleared his throat and folded his arms over his chest. "They are scared of the consequences."

Flint shifted his gaze to peer at Giles. The man's tone held a question in it rather than confidence. "Sheriff, we know how this might look but please believe me when I say that we want to help you catch this murderer as much as you do."

One less threat to mitigate would make possible focusing on other pressing matters he needed to manage. A long list of small but important changes waited on his desk. By his calculations, it would take most of the remaining six weeks to enact each of them if he could concentrate on them. But with the worries from the unknown killer and the looming concerns surrounding Hope and Faith and what they'd do next, he'd been highly distracted and many other tasks had to be postponed.

"What more do you know that you're not telling me?" Steve moved around the desk to confront them directly. "I think you know more than you're saying."

"Wh-why would you think that?" Flint asked, struggling to keep his voice even.

"Well, how do you know he's left-handed?" Steve glanced between the two men, searching and evaluating their expressions. "What did this person say to indicate such?"

"Merely that the killer grabbed his victim with his right hand on the woman's right shoulder, then used his left hand to slit her throat." True with only a few pertinent facts left out. "That's really all we know, Sheriff."

"Hm-hm." Steve gave them a skeptical look before stepping behind the desk to jot down some more notes. "I think there's more to this than you're letting on but trust me, I'll find out what it is no matter how long it takes."

Flint pressed his lips together, as much to prevent anything else slipping out as to quell the concern rising inside. If the man discovered they'd learned the truth from a ghost, that the inn was haunted by them, then the business would fail and his career would be finished.

Chapter Ten

The time had come for his big experiment. Tugging his waistcoat into place, Daniel ensured his pocket watch remained securely fastened so he didn't risk losing it. He inspected his appearance in the small looking glass on the dresser. Hair combed neatly into a respectful queue. Eyes clear and steady. Smoothly shaven jaw. Neatly pressed shirt. It would have to do. He lifted the suit coat from its place in the wardrobe and slipped it on. He grabbed his hat from the peg on the wall and tapped it on his head. With good fortune, he'd return before anyone missed him.

He took up a position in the center of the bedchamber he shared with Abram and drew in a steadying breath. Picturing in his mind his private quarters on the East Tennessee College campus, he focused both his will and intent on returning to his home. Envisioned the precisely made bed and the writing table beside it. A pair of shelves on the wall holding his small collection of books on geology, astronomy, and anthropology. An urn and basin on a table beside the door leading to the central hall in the dormitory. A lone window allowing a fresh breeze into the small space. His sanctuary. Home.

Only, did he really want to go there? He pulled his watch out and checked the time. His class started in a few minutes. Instead of home, the lecture hall would let him evaluate the performance of the professor taking over for him while he took a leave of absence. Did his students like the man? How good a job of educating the young minds was he doing? If he popped into the back row of chairs in the hall, nobody would notice him and he'd have the opportunity to find out for himself. He may as well make the exercise worthwhile by utilizing his next test of his bouncing abilities to see.

He cleared his mind and replaced the image of his small apartment with the cavernous image of the auditorium. The chairs on semicircular tiers and arrayed around the podium on the small stage down center in the room. He could fairly hear the echoing of whispers amidst the hearty voice of the professor. Smell the freshly sharpened wood pencil shavings and tang of the indigo ink as the students scribbled down notes from the instructor. Ah, how he missed teaching. He inhaled and exhaled, focusing on the image for several beats of his heart. Then he snapped his fingers twice.

In a flash he found himself standing at the very back of the hall which was only half filled. Quickly, he slipped into the nearest chair and pulled his hat brim lower. The students closest to him were a few levels away, taking notes and listening intently to the booming voice of the older professor. One day he might present such a learned appearance as the tenured gentleman conducting the lecture. His dark brown hair touched with gray leant a maturity to his demeanor. He calmly paced from one side of the stage to the other with an air of quiet confidence, making eye contact with those near him but also occasionally lifting his gaze to encompass the hall in general. An experienced instructor, one Daniel could emulate after his return to campus.

The door below opened and allowed a small cluster of young men to scurry in to find seats, climbing up the levels until they slipped into the row immediately in front of where Daniel tried to hide his face. Those three always seemed to be late to class, a situation he'd need to address when he officially returned to teach the class. They noisily settled into seats and pulled out their notebooks and pencils.

"Gentlemen." The professor addressed the tardy students in a stern, booming voice. "You will kindly come see me after class. For now, you will keep your disruption to a minimum."

The tone brooked no refusal and the men all nodded. Daniel kept his head down as though he was actually setting down notes but in fact he surreptitiously watched. He wanted to see for himself how the knaves responded to the demand for their consideration of the other students by not disrupting the class. After the professor resumed his lecture, the three young men whispered among themselves.

"He's far more strict than Professor Fairhope."

"I want Fairhope back so we don't get yelled at all the time."

"Not that we learn as much from the young prof."

"But Fairhope is supposed to be some kind of genius."

"He can't possibly know what he's talking about when he's only a few years older than I am."

"This prof surely has more to relay to us so we'll do better when we graduate."

"Gentlemen!" the professor boomed, glaring at them. "That is quite enough."

The hall fell silent. Daniel longed to leave, humiliation swarming inside, but didn't dare while the professor stared in his direction. The boys thought he didn't know of what he spoke when he was trying his best to convey all he'd learned about the history and geology of the earth. He'd passed all of his exams with exemplary success and hearty congratulations from his teachers. Granted, there was far more yet to be discovered and explained, but that was the excitement of the field. The quest for greater understanding of the formation of not only the planet on which humans lived but all the other celestial objects one could see through a telescope. He'd studied with the best in order to comprehend the state of knowledge the most studious researchers had pulled together. Even went out into the field for a few months of digging in the dirt to experience unearthing fossils and artifacts. Only to be dismissed as inexperienced and uneducated as well as a pushover professor. His heart sank along with his confidence.

As soon as the professor shifted his gaze away, Daniel closed his eyes and focused on his bedchamber at the inn. He quietly snapped his fingers twice, ignoring the tears smarting in his eyes.

Feeling quite pleased with himself, Flint perused the bustling dining room. The cookery competition a while back had yielded more returning customers as well as new ones. Word had spread about the healing qualities of the mineral springs, too. As a result, more overnight guests had ventured out to the small inn nestled into the foothills. Isaac hustled into the room bearing a heavy tray toward a group of eight men seated at two tables pushed together at the front of the room. Efficiently he handed out the plated meals to the hungry men. Nearby Cassie played the square piano while singing her favorite tunes in a strong and sweet voice, including a new one she'd made up and the crowd enjoyed. The guests had quickly grown accustomed to Allegro's watchful presence on his perch beside the piano, an acceptance for which Flint remained grateful.

Only a few tables stood empty, waiting to be filled by other customers. He'd need to order more spirits and have

Matt make more cider before long. Either that or he'd need to contract with other locals to provide additional beverages in order to keep up with the growing demand. A good problem to have. Indeed doing so would help bolster the local economy as well as the inn's reputation. A reputation still in danger if word leaked out about the presence of ghosts and witches on the property. Not everyone accepted either, let alone both. Better to keep their presence quiet.

Giles appeared at the arched doorway with Sterling Nelson beside him. Lawrence started into the room with a sweating pitcher but paused to say something to Sterling, who beat him on the back in greeting, nearly sloshing the contents of the pitcher. Surprise sparked inside of Flint as he witnessed the two men exchange such a friendly greeting. Then Isaac joined in, the large tray dangling from his fingers at his side as the three talked. Giles listened for a moment before coming across the room toward Flint, a bemused grin on his lips.

Mulling the relationship between the three men, Flint remembered he'd seen his two waiters as part of the group of men Sterling had assembled the day of the cookery competition. Elegantly attired, seeming upstanding members of the community. The same group who had discussed taking care of the troublesome women in the area. Just how close were they? How involved with the aims of the group were the two and yet working at the inn?

"Those guys are something." Giles slid onto a stool at the bar. "Whiskey, please."

Flint nodded and snared a glass and poured in a measure of dark amber liquor. Setting it on the counter in front of Giles, he glanced back to where Sterling made his way toward the group near Cassie. "Another meeting, hm?"

"You'd think they were about to go out on a jaunt instead of a business meeting." Giles sipped from the glass but his gaze continued to rove the room. He stiffened as he glared at the front of the dining area. "Damn owl. Why is it there? It doesn't make sense that it shows up by that entire group of men."

"The group is very friendly." Flint replaced the bottle of whiskey with a thump. The fact Giles could see the warning owl but he couldn't brought home again his lack of any claim to a special ability. But he had to keep his eyes open and his pistol handy to do his part. "Maybe too friendly?"

Giles paused in lifting his glass toward his mouth. "How so?"

Thoughts rattled in his brain like hail on the roof. The waiters ended their conversation with Sterling and resumed their duties. Going from one table to the next for a brief exchange and a smile. They looked like efficient and friendly waiters doing their job. But what if they were doing more than simply their intended functions? What if they were spying on the Fairhopes? On him? The pride he felt earlier shifted to dismay at the possibility he'd made a grave mistake in hiring the men.

He gritted his teeth as he turned his attention to Giles. "I'm probably imagining things. Being overly suspicious."

Giles placed his glass on the counter. "About?"

"Isaac and Lawrence." He glanced up as Isaac approached the bar, his jaw tensing. "Need something?"

"Cognac for the gentlemen at the table by the window." Isaac settled a small tray on the counter while Flint filled the order. "Mr. Fairhope, how fare you this fine afternoon?"

"I'm well, thank you for asking."

Flint turned at the guarded tone of Giles' response and placed the pair of glasses on the tray. "Here you go."

Isaac cast a glance at Giles and then nodded to Flint. "Thanks."

Flint held his tongue until the waiter had delivered the drinks, ensuring he wouldn't be overheard. "What do you think of them?"

"They seem responsible and fit right in here. Why?"

Flint kept his gaze on Isaac as he caught up to Lawrence for a brief exchange. "Might they be doing more than simply waiting on customers?"

Giles wrinkled his brow. "You're being very terse."

"I just hate to think I might be right." Flint drummed his fingers on the polished dark-red wood. "But could they be spies?"

"For whom?"

"John?" Flint moved his chin in the direction of the cluster of men in deep conversation. "Them in general. Keeping an eye on what happens here."

Giles glanced over his shoulder at the group in question then met Flint's concerned look. "You think they're trying to find out more about Cassie and the rest of us? To what end?"

"Eyewitness accounts of your true natures?"

A chill swept through Flint at his own question. Saying the words made it all too possible he would be proven correct. Then what? What if those men plotted to harm not just any witches but *his* witch? Those upstanding citizens in collusion with the killer. Or rather, one of them actually may be the killer. They suspected John, but they had no proof. He hadn't even determined if John might be ambidextrous. How would one test the man? What if it wasn't John? Then who else might have the skills and the lack of human decency to commit murder? The longer he surveyed the group of well-dressed, mannerly gentlemen the more unwarranted his suspicions appeared.

Sterling rose from his chair and sauntered over to the bar with a calm yet inquisitive expression. "Mr. Hamilton, might I trouble you for a fresh glass of cider? I find I am particularly parched this afternoon."

"Of course, sir." Flint reached for the pitcher, dismissing his previous musings as inane. How could anyone of

Sterling's stature be a criminal? Absurd. Criminals didn't dress in such beautiful and expensive clothes. The buttons on the man's vest caught his attention. "Are those whale bone?"

Sterling glanced down to where Flint inspected the off-white gleaming buttons embossed with a rose. "Indeed. They were special ordered from England."

"Might I inquire where I could obtain some? My father would enjoy having something of such fine quality."

A perfect gift for his father might ease any tension between them. Especially after he'd been away for so long and not there to assist in running the downtown hotel as he'd been doing for several years. Appeasing the man's ego would go far in case Flint found himself out of a job and had to return to work for his father. A not unlikely case.

"I will have to check with my wife and let you know." Sterling quirked his brows. "The cider, please?"

'Of course. I'm sorry for the delay." Flint poured the beverage and handed him the glass. "I hope you find it refreshing."

Sterling nodded and spun on one heel to return to his table. Flint watched him go, concern about what the group was really planning building in his chest. But he remained more convinced than ever of the error in wrongly accusing them of any heinous crimes.

A soft nicker greeted Daniel as he strode into the barn in search of his oldest brother. He'd lain awake the night before mulling his options given his recent eye-opening experience at the college. The comments he'd overheard rankled in his mind, plaguing his every moment. Something needed to change, but what? He kept moving without pausing to let his eyes adjust, eager to locate Giles. The rustle and swish of dry straw amidst a series of grunts drew his attention to the last stall on the left. What on earth?

"Giles? Is that you?" He hurried the last few steps to peer over the half wall.

Giles and Julian engaged in a good old-fashioned straw fight. Flinging flakes of straw at each other, yellow strands flying up into the air and landing on their heads and shoulders. The two laughed and grunted as they bent to grab more and shake it out at each other. After a minute, Giles brushed off his hands as he chuckled.

"What are you doing?" Daniel asked, shaking his head slowly at the comical pair.

"Bedding the stall obviously." Julian piped up, his young voice breaking with suppressed laughter.

Giles emerged from the stall to lean against the wall. "No harm in having a bit of fun while we finished the last one."

His oldest brother willing to play? Daniel hadn't witnessed Giles goofing around since they'd been in their single-digit years. Back then they'd often wrestled in the hayloft or played tag in the backyard. Once he'd entered his teens, though, Giles had taken life far too seriously for anyone's comfort. He'd begun trying to lead and teach his younger brothers despite their protests. A sudden thought struck him. Giles had displayed his Guardian tendency at puberty. His superhuman gift had subtly revealed itself. The brother he remembered from their youth had been far more mature than a typical teen. Thus, this side of Giles, the laughing and playing side, surprised him.

Daniel pointed to his brother's head. "You've still got some up there."

Chuckling, Giles brushed the offending bits of straw from his hair. "Thanks. Did you need me?"

"If you have a second." Where to start? Not with young ears around to begin with. "Julian, might I have a few minutes with Giles? Alone?"

Julian ran his fingers through his hair and then rubbed them on his jeans. "Oh, certainly. We're done here. I'll see you later."

The slender youth sauntered away down the wide dirt aisle of the barn as the orange tabby cat trotted across and jumped up on a stall wall to lick its paws. Then Daniel addressed Giles with the weight of a frown on his forehead.

"I need some advice."

"I have a few minutes before I need to leave." Giles folded his arms and propped himself against the stall wall more comfortably. "Advice about what?"

"I've been working on my timeskipping skills. Which is going well. Surprisingly."

The speed with which he'd mastered the new ability really did surprise him. Perhaps he'd instinctively known he could bounce or timeskip, maybe even had done so without realizing what had happened. Those times recently when he'd thought he'd arrived earlier than expected. Or figured he'd been so deep in thought he'd forgotten the walk from his apartment to his office. Perhaps he'd bounced instead of stepped.

"But there's a problem?" Giles arched a brow, prompting Daniel to continue.

"I decided to go to my college and listen in on my substitute prof. I wanted to find out how the students were receiving his lectures. Which went well until…"

Embarrassment and humiliation swirled inside Daniel as he recalled what the students had said about him. Giles regarded him with serene patience. Confident in his abilities as Guardian and oldest brother. In contrast, Daniel felt anything but confident in himself. Rattled described him emotionally at the present moment.

"Until what?" Now both brows were arched.

"A few of the students apparently think I'm too young to be a professor who could educate them."

"You are pretty young, which by the way is very impressive to me that you've accomplished such a milestone." Giles pushed away from the wall to stand straight. "That's nothing to worry about though."

"There's more. I'm apparently seen as a pushover, too." He raked his fingers through his hair and then gripped the nape of his neck. "I'm a failure as a professor. They disrespect me and have no confidence in what I tell them. I can't be an effective teacher with that reputation. What should I do?"

"As I see it, you have two options. One is to ignore what they have to say and continue on with your job."

The obvious path forward led to continuing in his role at the college. Continue to educate himself about new findings and understandings of them. Continue his research into the origins of the earth, the strata and fossils, and the many kinds of rocks and minerals. Continue his life in Knoxville. Only, he couldn't abolish the harsh criticism of his efforts to date.

"But without their confidence in my lectures and knowledge and experience they won't trust what they're being taught." He drew in a deep breath and pushed it out. "What's the other option?"

"Give it a few years so you grow older and wiser and then find another teaching position."

Daniel stilled and stared at him. Not go back to teaching for years? That was his advice. To quit. After all the study and discussion with others who knew far more than he did. After the sacrifice and determination to achieve his goal of becoming a teacher, a professor of geology. Giles suggested he simply walk away and give up.

On the other hand, such an approach would give him time for his research. He'd have the time to explore for himself, to travel the country, perhaps even the world. Increase his knowledge so that when he did look for another position he'd have far more experience and expertise to offer. One problem: how would he survive without an income?

Maybe his brother had an answer for such a conundrum. "What would I do for money in the meantime? I'd need some place I could afford to live or significant finances if I were to travel for research."

"You may not actually need ready cash." Giles shrugged as a wry smile slipped onto his mouth. "Stay here. Rejoin the family."

"Stay?" He could only blink at him as the foreign concept careened around in his brain. "Here?"

"Cassie may have done us all the best favor possible by asking us to come." He stepped closer to Daniel as the smile faded. "I want the family to be reunited, that our mother's death might bring us together. We need each other, Daniel. I want you to stay like me and Abram. When Silas gets here, I'm going to try to persuade him as well."

Not once had he considered not going back. He'd meant to return to work in a matter of weeks. Resume his normal if boring life in Knoxville. A slight breeze carried the pleasing mix of sweet hay, earthy manure, and a hint of October's cooler temperatures mere days away. The memory of Wilma's pretty smile and sparkling eyes floated in his mind. Another reason to consider the request. But he'd never anticipated his life being flipped upside down when he mounted the slow-poke pony to answer his sister's summons. He stared at Giles for several beats, unsure how to respond.

Suddenly, a woman appeared at the far end of the aisle. Petite with dark brown hair, she wore a simple but elegant yellow dress under a dark blue cape and matching bonnet.

"Who's that?" Daniel pointed at the woman, not recognizing her.

Giles looked over his shoulder and gave the woman a smile, holding up a finger to ask her to wait where she stood.

"Haley Baker. John Baker's daughter and my next engagement for the day."

"Your engagement? You're courting her?" More surprises. His brother courting the suspected killer's daughter? What a tangled mess. "How long have you been waiting upon her? Is it serious?"

"A few weeks. I think it's becoming serious, at least I hope so. I usually go to her place but she wanted to get out of the house for a while so we decided she'd meet me here. I've got Matt putting together a little tea basket to carry up to the falls. I don't want to keep her waiting. But…I need to know." Giles peered at Daniel, searching his eyes. "What do you say? Will you stay?"

His brother seemed to be settling in for the future. Talking about courting the pretty woman at the end of the aisle who Giles had become enamored with, possibly leading to marriage. Living at the inn or perchance he'd started contemplating building his own home. A place where he could live with a wife and raise a family. Nearby to Cassie, who was also talking about marriage to Flint. Abram and Mandy also had paired up, much like he'd contemplated doing with Wilma. But stay? Forever?

"It's a stunning concept." He swallowed as Giles quirked one brow. "I'll need to think about it."

Chapter Eleven

Finally, the month of October arrived shepherding in all the fun activities of autumn, like nighttime hayrides, dunking for apples, and carving pumpkins to make Stingy Jack's lanterns. Cassie had worked over the summer in her garden to ensure she had enough pumpkins for the guests to participate in making their own fun decorations. She sat by the parlor fireplace, a merry blaze keeping any hint of chill from the room. She wielded knitting needles on soft yellow wool, the clicking soothing as she made a new shawl to keep warm in the colder months ahead. Pa had promised to be home by Allhallows Eve, only thirty days away. Soon she'd be able to seek his advice on all that had transpired in his absence..

The door swung open to admit Flint, easing into the room with a newspaper tucked under his arm and a letter in his hand. "I thought I'd find you in here."

"Back so soon from town? I thought you'd be longer." She lowered her needles to rest the knitting on her lap.

He strode toward her with measured steps. "I have some things to take care of here so I didn't take time to visit my folks."

"I'm glad you came in when you did because it just occurred to me that we should plan for some kind of party to celebrate Allhallows. I've several pumpkins growing and apples we can use for activities for the guests. I'm sure they'd enjoy putting funny or scary faces on the pumpkins."

"I'll think on it." He scanned the room before letting his gaze rest on her as he stopped in front of where she sat.

"We have time." She glanced at him, prepared to continue her sewing, only his expression gave her pause. "What?"

"A letter from Reggie." He held out the missive. "I wonder if they found Sheridan's wife yet."

"Or if Sheridan and Zander made it there." She let go of the needles to let them fall to her lap and accepted the envelope. Tearing it open, she slipped the folded pages free and skimmed her gaze over the writing. "I'll read it to you."

Sept. 22, 1821
Savannah, GA

My darling daughter,
Your letter of the 15th received with some concerning information. First, imagine my surprise when Sheridan and his son appeared at my quarters here. I'm told Flint sent word of their impending visit but I fear that letter has gone astray. Sheridan's story with regard to rediscovering his two sons brings joy to my old heart. A joy increased by having confirmed his wife does indeed work nearby. However her owner demands a significant payment to free her. We are working to raise the amount but it may take some small amount of time to do so.

I am surprised and troubled by your letter, Cassie. I know you need and want me to come home and I will soon. Just not yet as I must complete the final inspection of the furniture and arrange wagons to transport everything. With Sheridan and Zander here along with my brothers to help I do believe we will make good progress and I will shortly be on the way to you.

As for the vow Abram made. I'm afraid it cannot be broken without deadly consequences. The only way to satisfy such a spell is to adhere to the promise made. In this case, Abram has promised to go to Montgomery to your aunts' house. Once he's made his appearance as demanded, then he will be free of the spell. But not free of whatever the aunts may do in retaliation for the deception. I know you may be contemplating going instead but that will not satisfy the spell's requirements. You mustn't even think of going until I get home as you do not understand the precarious situation you'd find yourself in if you should fall under their influence. Your mother has every reason to be afraid for you. She knows her sisters far better than anyone else could.

I must end so I may have this in the mail and on its way to you. Please take care.

Love,
Your father

Flint settled onto the chair across from Cassie. "That sounds very dire."

She nibbled her bottom lip as she reread the letter. "Indeed. Abram has to go to their house but he has until after Pa comes home. But he can't go by himself. My aunts want me, not him. What might they do to him should he go in my stead?"

Think. She must find a way to satisfy the vow and not fall under her aunts' control or influence. Everything in her screamed to avoid such a dreadful state of affairs. While the witches did not appear to be evil, her ma had made very clear the risks associated with allowing them to hold any amount of sway over her witchcraft.

"Your father said not to go."

Flint looked so worried for her. Until she devised a strategy, she'd keep her own counsel. "We have time to figure out an appropriate path forward." She folded the letter and slipped it into the envelope. She must find a way to protect Abram from her aunts' intentions. Not let him go alone if at all. She studied Flint in silence for a long moment. "In the meantime, I must share Pa's letter with my brothers. They'll need to be informed in order to help with our plan."

"Plan?" Flint gripped his knees. "You have a plan?"

"We will."

Later that afternoon Cassie surveyed the group gathered around her in the parlor. Flint and her brothers perched on chairs arranged in a circle in front of the crackling fireplace. Mercy paced the painted floor boards in the center of the large room, hands clasped. Allegro had arrived as Giles and Flint were about to close the door, strong flapping wings powering him across the room to land on the back of her chair. The falcon seemed to know of her anxiety and hovered close to her.

"Now that we're all here for your so-called family meeting, sis, what's this about?" Giles wore a slight frown as he watched her from across the circle. "Let's get this done. Haley is sitting on the porch waiting for me to escort her home."

"I've received a letter from Pa. To summarize, he'll be heading home before long, hopefully with Sheridan and his wife and Zander. But the vow Abram made is unbreakable without bad things happening. So we need to find a way to satisfy the requirements of the spell but not satisfy our aunts' aims."

"Impossible." Mercy shook her head as she ambled toward the back of the parlor.

"Pa found Pansy?" Giles leaned back in his chair. "That's good."

"Yes, except they have to raise the money to pay for her freedom. That's part of the delay." Cassie sighed out the continued frustration at his delaying coming home and straightened her back. "As much as I pleaded I couldn't prompt him to return faster. So we need to deal with this situation. I'm tired of it hanging over our collective heads."

The worry and waiting had taken their toll on her emotional equilibrium. She'd relied more and more on her calming tones of voice to keep herself as well as those around her at ease. In fact, she'd made a point to sing for the customers more frequently in the hopes she'd affect her brothers as well. Nothing she'd tried seemed to quell the inner agitation. The worry for her brother's welfare and safety. She had one possible solution, but would they agree?

"What do you propose we do about it?" Daniel rested his fists on his thighs. "Abram go to them?"

"I think we both need to go." She saw no other way to satisfy both demands. Abram had to go as he promised but if she didn't go with him, then their aunts would retaliate or punish them anyway. "That's the only option."

"There's no way to accomplish such a feat without going to their house, and nobody is going to do that unless I am with them." Giles scowled around the group. "Understood?"

"I agree with Giles." Mercy paused in her annoying pacing to stand near Cassie, peering down at her with concern in her eyes. "You mustn't even think about attempting such a thing. It will not turn out well."

"What else can we do?" Give her another way, any other way, and she'd snatch it like the last hot biscuit on a cold winter's morning.

She'd lain awake staring at the knotholes in the ceiling boards more nights than she could count. Analyzing the exact words of the spellbound vow and their possible interpretations. Abram had committed Aunt Hope's phrasing to memory and subsequently so had she. "Will you swear on the Book you will join our trinity after your father and brothers have returned to the inn?" Swearing on the Book of Shadows could only mean that any of the spells inside of its covers could be used to exact vengeance for breaking the vow. While she didn't know what those spells might involve, she could imagine they spanned quite a range from innocuous to revenge. Joining the trinity meant staying in Montgomery with the sisters. The only wiggle room in the sentence was exactly when the deadline arrived for keeping the promise.

"Your father will know what to do. You must wait for him to resolve this dilemma." Mercy folded her arms, drifting up from the floor with strain evident in the set of her jaw. "Be patient."

"How can I? I'm afraid Aunt Hope is not the patient sort. I should go to her and explain that I do not want to be part of their little club. Abram was only trying to help me but it all got entangled." Allegro opened his wings to balance as her emotions soared to frustration and dismay.

"I tangled it up, so I should go to them and explain." Abram jumped to his feet, a simmering anger flowing from his core into Cassie. "I'll fix this."

"Nobody is going anywhere." Giles also pushed to his feet to glare at the group. "Let's give it some more thought and just sit tight. For now, I'm going to take Haley home."

He was giving up on her suggestion. She stared at Giles as he pivoted to leave the room. Fine. She didn't need his help. She sent out waves of confidence toward her oldest brother so he wouldn't detect her underlying uncertainty and turned around. She only needed her other two brothers. She willed them to linger and encouraged all the others to depart. Pushing her suggestion from her core in a silent plea.

Flint stood up as Giles started toward the door. He regarded Cassie for a moment and then indicated Giles' disappearing figure with his head. "I agree. Listen to him and just be patient. We'll figure something out. I've got to get to the dining room but I'll see you in a while to sing, right?"

She inhaled and let it out slowly as she nodded. Her efforts paid off quickly. "Of course."

Without another word, he pivoted and strode toward the door. Mercy shifted side to side and started to shimmer. Allegro folded his wings and settled on the back of the chair. Daniel leaned back in his seat, eyeing Cassie as if he could tell she didn't agree with Giles or their mother.

"As I'm no longer needed here, I guess I'll be going as well." Mercy bestowed a gentle smile on Cassie as the ghost began to dissipate. "You know we love you and only want what is best for you, my dear. Have faith and patience."

Cassie held her tongue but returned the smile, encouraging her ma to go until the haint had vanished. Then she let out the breath she'd been holding and pinned her determined gaze on Daniel and Abram. "We need to go. You, me, and Abram."

"The three of us?" Daniel leaned forward in his seat as his eyes widened. "What are you thinking?"

"If we can't break the promise without a penalty, perhaps I can use my magic to persuade our aunts they don't really want me in their trinity after all. Then they'll forgive the vow and I'll be free and Abram won't be harmed. But we need to try before Pa comes home because once he does then Abram is in danger if he doesn't comply."

Abram sat back down in his chair and rubbed a hand over his face. "What a tangled web we have woven. But how can we go when Giles has forbidden anyone to do so?"

"Simple. We don't tell him." Giles would be very, very

angry at the deception but he'd not given her any other choice. A wave of guilt flowed through her but she must fix the situation. "Daniel can take us there and back before anyone even knows we're gone. We'll be there and back easy as pie."

"You want me to bounce the three of us there?" He pursed his lips for a moment and then shook his head. "I don't know where 'there' is though.

"Let me worry about that. I know how to find out." Ma would tell her if she asked discreetly about the specific house where the sisters lived. The description, location, even the atmosphere if she phrased her questions carefully and used a bit of encouragement in her tone. "Then we need to figure out when. But one thing is for certain: we're going to end this matter once and for all."

A pleasant stroll up the hill to the falls brought Daniel and Wilma to a charming spot for an early evening picnic. He'd latched onto Wilma's suggestion to share a picnic after Giles had mentioned the picnic tea he'd arranged for his girl. Perhaps a little romantic outing would help set the mood and open a window to let him test her reception to him. They'd passed several others on the trail but fortunately none had claimed the grassy knoll next to the burbling river.

Daniel had one important topic he needed to discuss with her before the morrow when he'd transport his brother and sister to face their aunts. He'd floated the idea with Flint who suggested he proceed with all due caution, not to rush into sharing everything at once. He'd reiterated her detestation of any hint of lies or fabrications. He shook out the colorful quilt and let it float down over the ground. Wilma set the picnic basket on the corner and then they both sat down.

"What a nice evening for this." Wilma opened the basket and began pulling out its contents.

"It won't be much longer before we wouldn't be as comfortable, what with winter right around the corner." He accepted a plate and set it on the blanket. "Besides I thought it might give us a chance to become better acquainted without so many others around."

"I'm glad you thought of it." She unwrapped a bowl and lifted some roasted pheasant pieces onto his plate. She inhaled appreciatively. "Matt has outdone himself. We must be sure to thank him properly when we go back."

Daniel took a healthy bite of tender fowl and savored the blend of seasonings. "He really has a gift."

Placing a slice of meat on her plate, Wilma peeked at him. "I've asked him to give me some pointers."

"Oh, why is that?" He chomped on another bite as he studied her blushing cheeks.

She focused on her food for a long moment and then met his gaze. "So I can be the best cook possible for my husband one day."

His hand froze midway to his mouth. Naturally, a young woman must consider her future as a wife and mother. Why did the thought of her marrying someone else put ice shards in his very soul? Whoa. What had happened? Sure, he'd had a flash of longing to marry her, but it was likely a passing fancy. He'd expected a brief visit and then to resume his normal life, not thoughts of inadequacy and now marriage. He had more to do, to see, before he tied himself down with a wife and family. Despite Giles point-blank asking him if he'd stay, he still hadn't made the momentous decision. Yet. But the woman sitting on the pretty quilt beside him possessed every endearing and intriguing quality of the perfect wife. Intelligent, caring, capable, educated. Why wouldn't he want to fall in love with her?

"You're very wise to look to your future in such a fine way." He finished the journey to his mouth to take another bite, to help keep him from saying something even more ridiculous. How stuffy he sounded!

"Tell me more about yourself, Daniel. How are you enjoying seeing your sister again, for example? I understand it's been quite a few years."

"It's been…an education in many ways." He finished his pheasant and wiped his fingers on a napkin. "I've learned a lot about my family and myself."

How much of what he discovered should he share with her? If he had any hope of wooing her he needed to discover how she reacted to his true self let alone the rest of his family. Without revealing too much. Flint would skin him like a rabbit if he impaired the inn's reputation in any way. If she held opposition to all things magic and supernatural, then they had no future. Which would make his decision much easier to make by removing the temptation she presented. He swallowed a sigh as he regarded her entire person. She represented more than mere temptation. No, she would accept him and his family. He hoped.

"What have you learned?" She peeped into the basket and smiled as she drew a covered plate out of its depths and unfolded the cloth to reveal slices of cake. "Ooh, carrot tea cake. My favorite."

He leaned closer to examine the slices bursting with bits of carrot, raisins, and nuts. "I wonder if he used the same recipe served to our esteemed first president."

She cocked her head to one side as she peered at him. "I hadn't heard he'd been given such a treat. Was it a special occasion or did he enjoy it more frequently? After all, with his reputation and wealth it wouldn't be unusual for him to indulge in delights more often."

"I don't know about frequency, but President Washington did have a sweet tooth. I read this is the kind of cake that was served at the Fraunces Tavern in New York, in honor of British Evacuation Day in 1783. I'd deem that a special occasion." He snared a slice of cake and took a large bite of the treat. "I feel honored Matt would have gone to the trouble for us."

"It was very thoughtful." She nibbled a bite and chewed it quickly. "So, what about you? What did you learn?"

He snatched another bite to give him time to consider his reply, swallowing and wiping his mouth before venturing his answer. Her reaction to the barest mention of the revelations would say much about any possible future they might share. "I found out I can do a few things I wasn't aware of."

He hesitated. Unsure how much to share but desperate to know her feelings toward him and his family. After having discovered the shocking truth, he'd slowly grown accustomed to the idea of being able to manipulate time in one way or another. The ability was so new, in fact, he'd never faced having to tell a girl he was interested in about being so very different. He cleared his throat and braced his hands on his thighs.

"Like what?" She nibbled on the tea cake as she calmly regarded him.

"What would you say if I told you I can actually bounce, you know, move to another place?" Holding his breath, he inspected her features, looking for disbelief or, worse, fear.

"You did that by coming here." She smiled as she took another small bite. "So did I."

"Not by horse or carriage or on foot." He studied the slight frown forming on her brows. Perhaps he should explain more. If only he could anticipate how she'd receive the truth of his reality. He truly had to know. "I mean, I can will myself to be in another place. Another town even."

She firmed her lips and blinked slowly. "You can?"

He could only nod at the sarcasm and doubt dripping from her tone, afraid to say more until she had a moment to process the claim.

"I know Flint can apparently talk to ghosts, or so the gossips say. But to…what did you call it?"

"Bounce." The single word popped out of his mouth with a hint of desperation clinging to it. She resisted believing him. What if she threw him over and ended everything between them? The idea set his heart racing.

"You can physically bounce from where you are now to anywhere else?"

"Yes." He'd keep the bigger part of that ability—to anywhen—to himself for the moment. "I just learned how to do so."

"What would I say? To such tales?" Her words scorched the air around them. She scrabbled to her feet and stepped away, glaring at him. "It's not possible so why are you telling me lies? I can't abide someone who does so."

"I'm not lying." He jumped up to face her alarm, very much aware of the thin thread stretching between them, threatening to break. "Wilma, please. Calm down. I won't hurt you."

"You already have by playing me for a fool. I thought we… Never mind." She swiped at her eyes and then started shoving dishes into the basket. She straightened and whirled around to glare at him again. "I'm going back to the inn."

"No, please. Let me explain." He reached out for her but she yanked away and marched down the trail. He scrambled to hastily finish collecting their picnic and blanket and then hurried after her.

His heart broke along with the thread of their budding relationship as he trudged down the trail. He hadn't realized how much her attention and acceptance of him meant to his sanguinity, his hope and confidence in a future with her. She'd never accept him now. She thought he lied to her when he'd attempted to tell her the truth about who and what he was. No future could exist for them. None. He apparently had no future at the college, either. Indeed, his future looked quite bleak and very unclear.

Only one thing remained certain. On the morrow he'd be bouncing himself, Cassie, and Abram to face their aunts to try and put an end to their threat. Then maybe, just maybe, he could figure out what he'd do next.

Chapter Twelve

$\mathcal{A}$ cheery splash of early morning sun warmed the painted floor boards in the parlor. Cassie paced from the front window to the center of the room, aware of the two pairs of eyes trained on her progress. Abram and Daniel stood a couple of feet apart, solemn expressions with a hint of worry aimed her way. She sensed the mix of anxiety and yet determination flowing from them, bolstering her own confidence but doing nothing to ease her fears.

"Are you ready, Daniel?" She halted in front of them so they formed a triangle. "Do I need to describe the house again?"

"No, I've got it. A big old monstrosity three stories tall, three miles out on the highway leading to the city, surrounded by looming oak and pecan trees. Situated near a swamp and set back from the highway to avoid stray visitors." Daniel cocked his head to one side. "Ma didn't mind telling you about her sisters' house?"

The truth wasn't exciting after all her angst over seeking out the desired description without eliciting concern from her mother. She'd gone up to the attic and called her ma for another lesson in using her magic. Ma had been happy with her progress as she learned how to create a stronger and more protective sacred circle. Cassie asked her about where Ma had grown up and she'd described the big old house outside of Montgomery. The place she'd fled after her mother's death removed the last layer of protection Mercy had from the demands of her father and sisters.

Cassie half-shrugged. "I simply asked out of curiosity and she went on and on about how terrible a place it is and why. Not only does it scare her but she claims it's haunted as well. Like ghosts should worry her."

Abram chuckled before sobering. "Maybe not but speaking of Ma, we should do this before she notices and comes to investigate."

"Right." Daniel lifted his elbows away from his sides. "Take hold, then, and we'll get this over with."

His arm felt like warm steel beneath her hand when she fell in beside him. Abram took hold of his other arm while Daniel prepared himself for the bounce to what her ma had described as a spooky monstrosity. She crossed the fingers on her other hand and closed her eyes as Daniel snapped his fingers twice. She'd never bounced before so it was a new experience. Some whirring began, filling her head and soul with sound and trepidation. This had to work. She pictured herself telling Flint of severing the vow, of removing one of the issues facing them. A dizzying rush and pounding echoed through her and then just as suddenly stopped.

"All right, we're here. I think."

She opened her eyes to stare at her aunts' house. She swallowed the rising panic inside. She had to go in there? Reaching out with her senses, she took the temperature of the place. A foreboding swept into her and took up residence. Doric columns flanked the maw of a dark double front door, rows of murky windows across the weathered wood front provided no clue of who—or what—might live within its ivy covered walls. Somehow the house exuded an evil atmosphere in the very materials comprising its structure. The surrounding monstrous trees shielded it from prying eyes, creating a barrier while deterring passersby from daring to approach. Deterring her from daring to approach, too.

"I don't know about this…" Abram stared at the building, his fear escalating and nearly knocking Cassie down.

She raised her protective barrier. She understood exactly how he felt. Still, they'd come on a mission in which they must not fail. Summoning her courage, she squared her shoulders. "We're here so let's go."

She marched up the leaf-strewn path leading to the front door and knocked before she could second-guess her actions. Abram and Daniel stood behind her, their company comforting. With good luck, their presence would prove a sound defense.

The door creaked open slowly to reveal Aunt Faith, a switch in one hand. She startled when she realized who stood on the front porch and then frowned when she spotted her brothers. "Well, well, well. I didn't expect to see you so soon. And definitely not standing out there. Come in." She opened the door wider and gestured for them to enter like a cat welcoming a mouse.

The interior of the house was more disturbing than the exterior had presaged. It was spotless but full. Why did she have such a sense of the place, as though it had eaten too much? As she followed her aunt into the living room, she surveyed its contents. It was cluttered with strange statues of animals and eclectic objects on every flat surface. A jar of murky liquid held a small brain of some poor animal. More small statues of gargoyles and animals rested on top of stacks of papers or books. A fire burned in the small fireplace, snapping and popping with red, blue, and green sparks like miniature firework displays. A black cat with a swirl of white on its chest sat on the back of a rose-patterned sofa, its yellow eyes following her every move. An unsettled and suspicious feeling filled her, making her want to flee instead of meekly trail after her aunt. No wonder her mother wanted nothing to do with the place. She raised her emotional barrier higher as a shudder rocked her shoulders.

Cassie longed for Allegro's protection with his sharp eyes and talons but he was far away. She lifted her chin and wished for the confidence of her wand left behind as she prepared for whatever might come next. Ma said she could use her powers without the wand since it merely helped to focus her already impressive powers. She'd be fine. Besides, her brothers would protect her if necessary. "Where's Aunt Hope? I need to speak with you both."

"Actually, I need to speak to her first," Abram interjected.

"Abram, no." Cassie turned to shush her brother but she feared it would serve no purpose if he was so unwavering in wanting to take the blame and the consequences.

Faith paused to spin slowly around to assess the threesome with pursed lips. "Now what might you be about, young man?"

Abram tensed but maintained a stoic expression. "If you'd be so kind as to get your sister, we'll have our say and then be on our way."

Faith cackled and brandished the switch like a fencing sword. "We'll see. Come." She spun around and hurried toward the back of the room, the cat jumping down and trotting after her.

The cat must be Faith's familiar, there to do her bidding. What would her aunt bid the cat to do though? Cassie glanced at her brothers, fear in her throat, before heading toward the open door at the rear of the room, a flickering red light dancing on the wall in the next room.

"Sister, look who has finally come to us." Faith swept through the door and stepped to one side, ushering in Cassie and her brothers.

The kitchen didn't look anything like the work space at the inn. An immense fireplace hosted a sizeable fire with a large cauldron steaming over the flames. Metal hooks and rods were magically holding an array of smaller pots hanging near or over the fire. Hundreds of bunches of herbs and bulbs of garlic and other drying plants dangled from the ceiling around the large room. Hope stood at a large stained and scarred work table at the left, a multitude of various sizes of bottles and containers aligned at the back.

Hope smiled slowly as she stopped stirring the contents of a bowl and laid the wooden spoon on the table. "Cassandra, what a lovely surprise." She wiped her hands on the red apron she wore over her dark green nearly black dress as she strode toward the visitors. "I'm so very glad you've kept your word and come. But why have your brothers accompanied you?"

The moment had arrived to make her case but her well thought-out defense fled her mind. "We've come to explain."

"Indeed? What might you need to explain?" Hope's welcoming smile turned into something feral. "Continue."

"I—"

"It's my fault." Abram stepped forward to stand in front of Cassie. "I made the vow to you, not my sister."

Cassie grabbed his arm, not wanting him to take all the blame for their predicament. "It's not entirely his fault. It's more ours."

Faith humphed from behind Cassie, drawing her attention. The black cat licked its lips as if preparing for a delectable meal. "You didn't come to join us, did you, little lady?"

Cassie gulped back the bile in the back of her throat at the venom in Faith's tone and the warning in the cat's eyes. "Not exactly."

Hope glared at her, sparks firing in her narrowed eyes. "Then what is this about?"

Abram shielded Cassie, while Daniel flanked her other side. "I made the vow while I was in her form."

"You're a shifter? You imbecile. How dare you trick us!" Hope raised her arms, wind rushing through the pungent kitchen. "You'll pay."

Cassie shoved herself in front of Abram and shielded him with her body. She pushed acceptance toward her aunts with every magical fiber of her being. "No! He's kept his word and came to you even earlier than promised. Now the spell must be satisfied."

"Only if I say so…" Hope flared her wand, preparing to focus its power at Abram. "And don't ever use your powers against me again."

"Now, now, sister, calm down. I believe she may be partially correct. He has done what he promised to do." Faith moved around to stand by Hope, shaking her head, as the cat snarled softly. "He may be off the hook, but you, my dear Cassandra, are most definitely not."

"I am not sure I follow…" Hope squinted at Faith who merely canted her head in answer, silently communicating her reasoning. "Oh, I see. Yes, I believe you're right."

Ice flowed into her veins as she gaped at her aunts. She sensed their feeling of ultimate victory no matter what arguments she may pose. Hope lowered her arms as a sneer crept onto her lips. What had Cassie missed in her calculations? Something important and diabolical. She swallowed around the knot of fear before addressing her aunts. "Why?"

Hope cackled loud and harsh as she lifted her chin. "Because of the second part of the promise. You'll join us *after* your father and brother return from their trip."

"But I'm here now, so that should be enough."

"You're here too soon. There is still time for you to keep the pledge to unite with us. You have time to willingly comply with our request and unite our powers to become the strongest witches in the country." Faith leaned forward to examine Cassie's expression. "Unless Reginald has already returned home?"

"N-no." Her last hope dissolved in the face of the nuance she'd missed. They'd essentially extended the deadline to after her pa returned and not before as she'd interpreted. Still, the misstep didn't change her mind. "But I don't want to join your silly club."

"Silly club? Silly?" Hope raised her arms again, a whirlwind whipping up to spin a tornado of fury around the room. "How dare you demean our power?"

"You'll join us, Cassandra, or you'll die." Faith slowly lifted her arms to add her magical power to the growing storm in the kitchen. "What say you?"

Cassie could barely think let alone respond with the whirlwind whipping around her.

"Say no." Abram shifted into Cassie's form and switched places with her, mimicking her stance and expressions. "Now they won't know which of us is the real Cassie."

"Abram, no! Don't put yourself in danger." Fear for her brothers swelled inside, growing the knot in her throat. She'd miscalculated the entire endeavor.

"Too late." Abram held onto her as the wind increased.

The cat leapt toward the trio while the two angry witches chanted a spell to turn the vortex into a roaring maelstrom.

Cassie struggled against the onslaught of rushing wind, fighting to stay on her feet as her brothers guarded her. The cat hissed from the outside of the tornado, loud and menacing despite the sound and fury before her.

"We have to go. Grab on!" Daniel shouted into the maelstrom. "Hurry!"

She clutched his arm as Abram grabbed the other. Daniel clenched his jaw and snapped his fingers.

"You won't escape us! We'll have you yet!"

Hope screamed at her, the sound echoing in her brain as the whirring carried them away from the creepy house and the dangerous witches back to the family parlor. When the sound stopped, she gasped and bent over to hug her waist, tears flowing at how wretchedly they'd failed. Abram and Daniel steadied themselves and then each placed a hand on her shoulders.

"That didn't go quite like I thought." Abram's voice trembled.

"Worse than I thought." Cassie sobbed into her hands as she straightened, dashing a hand at the flow of salty tears on her cheeks. "I'm so sorry."

With a "klee" and flapping of wings Allegro flew through the open window into the parlor. He took one lap and then aimed for Cassie, Abram and Daniel relinquishing their hold on her shoulders so the falcon could take his position. The bird seemed to examine her with a sharp eye before rubbing his head against hers, his relief flowing into her. She stroked his back and forced herself to stop crying to help him settle as well.

"I shouldn't have agreed to take you." Daniel scrubbed a hand through his hair. "Man, they were mad."

"The big question…" Cassie ran her fingers down Allegro's feathers, striving for inner calm, before meeting the concerned gazes of her brothers. "What will they do now?"

"You did what?" Flint stared at his love and wanted to strangle her. She'd risked her life as well as her brothers contending with the aunts. "Without telling me?"

"Don't be mad, please?" Cassie huddled in her favorite chair by the fire in the parlor, Allegro perched on the back of the chair keeping a watchful eye on the small group gathered. "I'm shaken enough without having to face your wrath as well."

Flint crossed the painted floorboards—ones he desperately wanted to cover with a fine carpet—and flopped onto the chair opposite her. He glanced up at Giles, also keeping a stewing watch, before addressing her. "Then you should have told us."

"Why? You'd only try to talk me out of it." Her voice quavered from the shocking experience she'd survived.

Survival of an event which should never have occurred. Abram's description of what had transpired—the vortex of wind while the aunts screamed in rage—made him want to wrap her up and hide her away until Reggie returned to put things to rights.

He hated hearing fear echoing in her lovely voice. He'd do anything to never hear such again. "Indeed I would have stopped you any way I could think of."

"Or I would have if he had not." Giles shook his head from where he glared at her by the fireplace. "How do you expect me to do my job when you don't trust me?"

She gawped at him. "I do trust you, Giles."

"You don't. Or you would have told me instead of letting me find out by experiencing your immense fear. Which I've never felt quite so strongly before." He rubbed his jaw, the rasping of whiskers competing with the snapping flames. "You were terrified and I couldn't find you. I could sense you but you weren't here and I had no blasted idea you'd left the property."

"You could have done like you did before and just appear at her side." Flint studied Giles for a moment as the wagon wheel accident a month or so ago replayed in his mind. The wheel had shattered on their way into town, pitching them both to the road. The day he feared she'd died. His shoulders rocked at the memory. "Couldn't you?"

"That was the strange thing. I tried but I couldn't." Giles glared at Daniel. "I think because she was out of my range. I'm not like you and able to go wherever or whenever."

"I hadn't thought of that." Daniel looked down at his hands in his lap. "We might really have been in serious trouble."

Abram huffed from his position by the dining room table. "We were already in serious trouble in case you didn't notice."

"Yes, you were." Mercy shimmered into the room in front of Cassie, scowling at her. "How dare you trick me? I didn't realize why you were asking about that awful place. I warned you about going there."

"I agree with you, Mercy." Flint's innards roiled with distress at what might have happened. "She most definitely shouldn't have risked such a precarious and dangerous thing."

"But we had to try to put an end to the spell." Abram stood and walked over to stand beside Cassie. "I had to do something to fix what I did wrong."

"But not that. Don't you understand the huge risk you took?" Mercy shifted side to side, worry in her every move and expression. "You were all reckless."

"So we all agree we shouldn't have but we did." Cassie raked her gaze around the gathering, Allegro rubbing his neck against hers to comfort and calm her agitation. "I'm afraid they're going to come here and force me to go with them now."

"That's not going to happen." Giles pushed away from the fireplace to cross his arms. "We won't let them."

"I'll do whatever I can, sweetheart, but there's not much I can do against magic." Damnation. That admission hurt. Flint suppressed the disgust lingering in his very soul. He had a flintlock pistol and knew how to use it but what good was it against a magic tornado? Being helpless did not fit right. "Giles, let me know what you want me to do and I'll do it."

"Thanks, Flint." Giles held up a hand to quiet the buzz of conversation. "I think it's important to recognize that however ill-advised their actions, they did free Abram from the spell." Giles tapped his index finger on his elbow as he looked at each in turn. "At least he's safe and able to help with the rest of the defense."

"A defense we have no idea how to build since we don't know what attack we may face." Flint's heart hurt as he slid his gaze around the group. "I'll do whatever I can, but the fact remains her safety is in all of your hands."

Which only meant Flint was expendable and useless. He should probably break it off with her instead of hanging around embarrassing himself in front of her family. The very thought made his core ache but he must face the truth of the situation. His love for her wasn't enough. He simply wasn't good enough to be her husband and Reggie would confirm as much upon his homecoming. Time to prepare his heart for the moment of truth.

"I think I need a drink. Anyone else?" Giles rubbed his jaw again, agitation pulsing in his neck. "Daniel?"

Flint waited for Giles to include him, wanting to share with the other men their concerns and try to devise a plan for moving forward. He didn't want to presume but he did hope the brothers would desire his company during their distress.

Daniel heaved a sigh as he got to his feet. "Definitely. Come on, Abram. It's about time we brothers had a chance to share a drink together."

Abram merely nodded as he followed Daniel and Giles out of the parlor.

Flint watched them vanish through the door with a sinking in his gut. The lack of an invitation to join them settled into Flint's mind like an unexpected snowfall on a cold winter's day. They hadn't purposely not invited him, but simply wanted to have some time together. Understandable. Still. Flint glanced at Cassie. "Perhaps you should go on upstairs, sweetheart. You look worn out."

"I think you're right. Good night." She pushed to her unsteady feet, gave him a quick kiss while Allegro spread his wings to balance, then made her way across the room to the stairs leading up to her bedchamber.

"That girl. One day she'll find herself in real trouble because of her recklessness. I'm going." Mercy shook her head slowly as she shimmered and vanished.

Flint stood alone in the parlor for a moment, staring at the closed door. While he longed for some male companionship, he couldn't in good conscience join the brothers for their drink together. He'd be shoehorning himself into their company, where he obviously didn't fit. Instead, he sauntered to the stairs and slowly climbed them to sit alone in his own room. Some things never changed.

The warm glow of the pair of oil lanterns on either end of the bar barely dented the shadows in the silent dining room. Daniel had never been in such a large room shrouded in darkness. Every time he'd been in the room it had been bustling with guests and waiters all talking and laughing. The quiet eeriness seeped into his bone marrow. He shifted his chair to face the arched doorway as Giles slipped behind the bar.

"What will it be? Rum? Whiskey? Rye?" Giles examined the shelf displaying the various liquors in ornately designed bottles.

"Whiskey." Abram took a seat beside Daniel, resting his elbows on the bar. "Neat."

"Same here." Daniel leaned back in his chair. "It's been too long since we had any time together. Though I'm sorry it's because of Ma's death and everything that followed."

"Cassie has brought us back together. A good thing coming from a bad one." Giles poured three glasses of whiskey, leaving the bottle uncapped on the bar. He handed them out and took a sip of his, a steady regard on Daniel.

"The silver lining." Daniel nodded as he sampled the beverage. "We needed one after all that's transpired since we were younger."

"If only we'd had some clue as to why our parents forced us out." Abram sniffed the aroma of the whiskey before filling his mouth.

Giles looked at each of them with sadness in his eyes. "I wish things had been done differently all the way around."

"Meaning?" His older brother seemed to be harboring some secrets of his own. Daniel regarded the closed expression blanketing his brother's countenance.

"Nothing. We can't change the past only learn from it." Although Giles looked at him, he wasn't seeing him but some memory causing his sadness.

Abram clinked glasses with Giles. "Very true."

"Not even the recent past." A knot of dismay rested just beneath Daniel's crossed arms. Replaying the day's events in his mind didn't help remove the feeling. "I am sorry, Giles. I didn't mean to cause more trouble. We thought we were fixing things."

"I'm sure and yet…" Giles heaved a sigh, expanding his massive chest, and let the breath out slowly. "Cassie can be quite impetuous and naïve. One of the reasons we all need to look out for her. She's barely eighteen years old, for goodness sake."

"Old enough to marry." Abram slowly spun his glass on the bar, the lamp light glinting off the agitated fluid.

"Then her husband would look to her welfare." Giles hefted his glass, glancing at Abram and then Daniel. "Flint will do his best but like he said, he doesn't possess magical abilities like we do."

"Not everyone appreciates our abilities." Daniel stared into the amber liquid. Wilma's denial and anger echoed in his mind. He lifted his gaze to see Giles studying him with a lifted brow. Oops. Now his brother would ply him with questions until he shared what he meant. "What?"

"Who didn't appreciate yours?" Giles asked, a knowing look settling into place.

Nothing would come of trying to avoid responding. Not when Giles had his determined look aimed at him. He hadn't seen it in a long time, but it still possessed the power to pull a confession or revelation from him.

He sighed again. "I told Wilma and she's not speaking to me now."

"You told Flint's sister you can timeskip?" Abram stared at him, eyes wide and jaw tense. "What did she say?"

"I only told her about being able to bounce. But she accused me of being a liar and she won't tolerate deception of any sort." Daniel drew in a long breath and eased it back out again. "She didn't believe me."

"It is hard to believe, isn't it?" Giles swallowed a mouthful of whiskey and set the glass down. "Give her time."

Daniel rolled his eyes at his older brother. "That was a terrible joke."

Giles guffawed and lifted his glass in a toasting gesture. "You're right. It is a terrible joke. But it's still true. She needs time to think about the fact you've never lied to her before. You haven't, have you?"

"I don't lie." Daniel huffed at him, his ire rising inside at the very idea. "Ever."

"Ignore him." Abram waved off Daniel's affront. "He doesn't always think before he opens his trap."

"So what do I do to convince her to believe me?" Daniel

glanced between the other two men, searching for answers to his dilemma. "Demonstrate it?"

"Your ability isn't a parlor trick." Giles pressed his palms on the wood surface. "She needs to know you and your integrity so she'll believe what you tell her as the truth she seeks."

"Easy to say but since she's not seeing me let alone speaking to me, it won't be easy to accomplish."

"You're a smart man." Abram patted him on the shoulder several times. "You'll find a way."

"Sure I will." Daniel tossed back the rest of his whiskey and let it burn its way down his throat. "Somehow."

Early the next morning, Daniel carried the forgotten picnic basket into the kitchen. He pushed through the door with his back and then pivoted on one foot to survey the bustling room. He rarely ventured inside its warmth from the ever-present cooking fires and aromas of bread baking and bacon sizzling. Matt glanced up at him from where he carefully filleted several fish at the large scarred table in the center of the room, a woman busily peeling and chopping vegetables at a sideboard. Another woman—he really needed to learn their names—folded linens at a table at the back while Mandy glared at him where she worked kneading bread dough.

"Good morning, everyone." He hefted the basket in his hands. "Sorry I forgot to return this the other evening. Wilma and I enjoyed the meal very much."

At least what they'd eaten before their argument. Their breakup? No telling where they stood now that she had more of an idea of his true nature. Not that he'd had the chance to tell her about the rest of the family and their history. That tale may be too much for her to hear and accept. Giles had suggested he find a way to let her know about his honesty and integrity. To do that, he'd need to find a way to talk with her. If she'd let him.

"You've all been pretty busy from what Flint's told me." Matt sliced a fish open to reveal the bones. He deftly removed them and dumped them into a nearby bucket of other scraps Daniel assumed were destined for the hogs. "Just set it down and I'll have Myrtle take care of it next."

The woman—no, Myrtle—smiled and nodded at him, her hands efficiently continuing their work. Daniel put the basket on the floor by the table just as he heard a commotion from the entrance hall. He spun around to stare at the closed door for a moment, trying to determine the cause of the disturbance. Sounded like an angry woman. A chill crawled through him. He recognized the voice.

He raced out of the kitchen without another word to the occupants, intent on reaching the new arrival. The scene before him increased his flying feet to bring him to the center of the entrance hall as Hope and Faith faced off with Giles and Flint. Young Julian stood aside several paces, his expression a study in perplexity and anxiety. The poor kid didn't fathom everything happening around him but of course he most likely had been shadowing Giles.

"Where is she?" Hope flared her black cloak as she jerked left then right. "We've come to talk to her about her familial duty."

"Cassandra doesn't know everything she must in order to do the right thing." Faith tried to sidle around Giles but he blocked her progress. "We'll find her eventually. Let me pass."

"You've nothing to say to Cassandra." Giles puffed up his chest making himself even larger and more dangerous. "You may as well go back to wherever you came from."

Flint stepped right to prevent Hope from darting around the other side, his hand on his pistol. "She's already told you her feelings on the matter. I would suggest you don't press your luck."

Daniel stopped beside Giles, providing another layer of protection against the angry sisters. "You didn't listen to her. She doesn't want to be part of your proposed trinity."

Hope glared at him, her arms akimbo. "We've waited a very long time for another chance to satisfy our father's greatest desire. Now take me to her. She must join with us. It's the only way."

"You cannot force her to go with you. You know that." Flint held out both hands to either side of him, a visual barrier to their attempts to move past the three men. "Leave her be."

"She told you as much yesterday." Daniel splayed his hands as he searched the angry expressions of the two witches. They must stop acting so selfish and pay attention to the reality they faced. "You've no right to insist. Why won't you accept her desires?"

Hope clutched her cloak and drew it closed around her. "She must do what is best for the family and not hold herself so above us she cannot see her destiny. We are here to help her see."

The question remained what exactly did she need to see? What had happened in the past to make these two witches so intent on having his sister unite with them? Against the rest of the family. Despite everything they'd been told, they continued to clamor for Cassie's willingness to be with them.

"It sounds to me," Julian said, easing closer to the group, "they simply want to have a conversation with Miss Fairhope. What's the harm in such discourse?"

"The young man understands our intent." Faith smiled at Julian with approval. "He's far wiser than the rest of you."

Daniel shot the boy a quelling look, making him step back again. He had no dog in the fight so he needed to stay out of the conversation. Although an idea popped into his brain at the suggestion of a civil discussion. If he could get all parties to agree to certain rules. He addressed the two women. "If all you truly want is to talk with her, we can arrange that." He held up a cautionary finger. "But that is all you may do. No trying to kidnap her or force her to go with you. We will prevent such an attempt. Is that clear?"

He'd be sure to listen intently to whatever they had to tell Cassie. Surely they would reveal more about their motives behind the repeated demands of her compliance with their not-so-gentle requests. Then he'd have the information he needed to put the rest of his new plan into play.

Hope released her grip on her cloak and raised her chin. "I will not need to resort to forceful measures once I've explained the situation and the prodigious opportunity she has before her."

"Are you sure about this?" Giles shot a stern look at Daniel. "I don't like it."

Daniel nodded as an idea continued to evolve in his mind. "We will all be there with her to ensure her safety. We'll make it work."

"I don't see the point. She's made her decision." Flint pressed his lips together as he faced the witches. "But if you think it's safe, and it's only a conversation, then let's get this over with."

What had they stirred up by going to the witches' lair? Daniel had many questions swirling through his mind. His questioning their core reasons had prompted a startling idea. Perhaps if he knew more about what created their desire and demand for Cassie to be part of their trinity, then he could go back in time and fix it. Change the course of history so they wouldn't be so desperate for her union with them. But only if he truly understood what occurred in the past. For that, a probing conversation was necessary.

"Meet me in the parlor in five minutes." Daniel drew in a breath and let it out. "I'll go inform Cassie."

Chapter Thirteen

*H*er peaceful concentration shattered. Reverberations of the previous day's terror flared inside. Allegro flapped his wings from his perch on an adjoining chair back. They'd come for her. Her aunts. She raised her barrier against the anger and determination flowing from the witches. Her sewing fell from her hand as she stared at the door to the covered passage between the residence and the public side. She gasped when it opened and then relaxed a tad when Daniel strode through and left it open behind him. They would follow. As inevitably as the sun would set..

"Cassie." Daniel paced closer, standing a few feet in front of her. "Are you all right?"

Allegro flapped his wings again and then flew to settle on her shoulder. She searched Daniel's eyes for answers to unspoken questions. "What is happening?"

"They only want to have a conversation with you. They'll be here in a few minutes, but I wanted to warn you. Give you a chance to prepare yourself." He sat on the chair nearby to bring himself down to eye level. "Just a conversation and we'll all be here with you. You won't be alone with them."

"What is there to talk about?" She'd made it abundantly clear how she felt on the primary subject they had raised in the past. "I don't want to be with them."

"I know but they can tell us more about the history so I can go back and change it so they don't need you." He raked a hand through his hair and glanced over his shoulder. "Just hear them out and we'll see what we learn. Ask questions about what they really want and why. Can you do that for me?"

She opened her mouth to reply and snapped it shut again as Giles led the rest of the family into the parlor. She gave him a short nod while Allegro spread his wings, effectively keeping everyone a respectful distance from her. They arrayed themselves on seats around the room, Hope and Faith relegated to the chairs near the back of the room while Flint and Giles took those closest to her. Daniel and Abram occupied the chairs between the others. No one smiled or spoke until everyone was seated, watching her. The temperature in the room chilled with the clash of emotions. Good thing she'd already raised her barrier or she'd be overcome by the mix of fear, hope, worry, and resolve. Also a healthy dose of doubt from Flint. She rested her gaze on her beau, but he looked away to scan the others.

She addressed her aunts from across the room, comforted by the presence of her brothers and intended. "You wanted to speak to me?"

Hope lifted her chin and attempted a smile which failed to convince anyone she had pure intentions. "Yes, my dear, we do. You see, we realized after your…brief visit yesterday you simply are unaware of your own destiny." She waved a hand in the air. "It's your mother's neglect that's truly at fault but we won't go into her many failures."

"Do not disparage my mother if you want me to listen any further." Cassie stroked Allegro's head instead of glaring at her aunt. No need to antagonize them any more than necessary.

"Well, anyway…" Hope brushed aside her objection with a flick of her wrist. "As you already know, we need for you to do your duty to our family in order to realize your true fate. It's what your grandfather wanted more than life itself, although as you also are aware he had wanted your mother to be in our trinity. But since she refused, leaving us without the ability to form the powerful triad Father envisioned, we were forced to wait. In the interim, of course, our poor father was murdered because he didn't have the power he needed to defeat another warlock and his trinity of power."

"Wait, my grandfather was murdered?" Cassie peered at her aunt, ice forming in her veins. So many family members murdered. "Why?"

Faith sighed melodramatically. "He dared to try to defend our territory but the other warlock and his sons were far more powerful. We lost half our territory in the power grab. All because of your mother."

"My Ma?" The chill swept through her core so she wrapped her arms around her waist.

Hope nodded slowly as her eyes turned cold and hard. "It's because of her both of our parents are dead. She can never atone for her guilt."

"Do not listen to them!" Mercy shouted as she shimmered into the room, glowering at her sisters. "I did not have any part in either of their deaths."

Everyone jumped back at her sudden and explosive appearance in the room. Allegro cried out once and flapped his wings. Cassie soothed his agitation and then focused on her mother.

"Ma, tell me what happened."

"I have done nothing against my sisters. Believe me." Mercy shimmered as she hovered a few inches from the floor. "I've only worked to protect others from their wiles."

"You were so afraid of our influence you hid your children's powers from us. That led to Reginald doing nothing to prevent my son from drowning at the swimming lake." Hope shook her head slowly, threateningly. "Your fear makes you responsible for his death."

"No. That's not true." Mercy fairly glittered in distress from the accusation. "I had nothing to do with your son's poor judgement."

"She lies and she knows it." Faith scowled at Mercy. "You're even lying to yourself."

"These two would have everyone believe they are pure as newly fallen snowflakes. If they hadn't been so keen on having their own way, we wouldn't have needed to take drastic precautions." She pointed at them, shaking her finger at each in turn. "They are far from innocent bystanders. They could have helped our father defend the Covington witches' territory but they chose not to. Leaving him to face the greedy warlock and his equally greedy sons on his own. One against three warlocks? They are to blame for his death, not me."

Hope shot to her feet, glaring at Mercy. "How dare you? You were not even there. How would you know anything about it?"

"I have my contacts. Just because I moved away does not mean I did not keep an eye on events around you." Mercy shifted side to side, never taking her eyes from her sisters. "You both should be ashamed of yourselves."

Mercy solidified and stalked toward Hope. She shoved her down into her chair and leaned over her, her finger shaking in the other witch's astonished face. "And now you're trying to drag my daughter into your mess? I won't have it. Depart and take your obsession with you!"

Faith jumped to her feet and grabbed Mercy's shoulders, pulling her away from Hope's face. "I'd kill you if you weren't already dead, you wicked woman!"

"Stop it!" Cassie cried out, clutching the arms of her chair, afraid they'd start fighting with magic at any moment. "Please, stop!"

The three sisters struggled, grunting and slapping for another minute while Giles stood but hesitated to enter the cat fight playing out in the parlor. She didn't blame him.

She had to do something to stop them. Humming, she crafted a rough calming spell on the fly. Hopefully, it would work. She used whatever came to mind for the attempt. "Lavender and indigo, poppy petals and eagle feathers, combine your essences to quiet and shield." Blast. Not good enough since the women still clawed and slapped at each other. She'd have to work on her wording.

Allegro launched from Cassie's shoulder, taking charge by swooping in to separate the women. His wings beat them apart amidst cries of pain as his talons scraped across their exposed skin. Then Giles and Daniel each wrestled Hope and Faith away from the fray. Cassie moved in front of Mercy, who shimmered and drifted back, but maintained a glare at each of her sisters. Cassie rubbed a hand to her forehead as Allegro resumed his protective perch on her shoulder.

"Stop acting like children." Cassie looked to each of the embattled witches. "That will not convince me you're serious about any of this."

Hope aimed a stern look at Daniel until he released her. Then she rolled her shoulders before addressing Cassie. "I thought I told you to never use your magic on me again. Pathetic as it was. The only way this can all be made right is for you to willingly join forces with us. Then we can reclaim what is rightfully ours using our combined powers and will." She sneered at her as she swept her gaze head to toe.

"Maybe then you'd learn how to actually use your magic."

"My life is here, not with you." Cassie reached out to sense the feelings in the room, finding a mingled sense of doubt and belief emanating from the gathered group. She addressed her aunts with her own resolve flowing from inside. "You should leave."

"No, my dear." Hope shot a quizzical sidelong glance at Faith who nodded once, lips pressed together in a mutinous expression. Then she met Cassie's startled gaze. "We're not going anywhere until you agree to our demands."

Giles hurried to stand in front of Cassie, assuming a protective stance. "Do not threaten her or you'll answer to me."

"Oh, Giles, do not fear. I have no intention of harming my niece. How absurd." Hope pulled out her wand, eyes glittering. "Not yet anyway."

"Don't you dare even think about hurting her." Mercy whooshed forward before Cassie could react, hovering in front of Hope as she scowled at her. "She's not going anywhere with you."

"Fine. Have it your way. Flint, be a dear and make up our room and we'll just settle in until we get what we came for." Faith approached Mercy with a feral smile on her lips. The black cat suddenly appeared at her side, glittering yellow eyes fixed on Cassie. "We're nothing if not persistent."

"And determined, do not forget that characteristic." Hope smirked at Cassie. "Of course, if you'll simply do what familial duty requires, then we can end all this pretense and drama and move on."

They were moving in? Faith's familiar with its knowing and threatening stare, too. How had things gone from bad to horrific? Were they telling the truth about the cause of her grandfather's death or was her ma? What if she did join with them long enough to reclaim the lost territory? Maybe they'd leave her alone. Allegro bumped her with his head.

Even he sensed her confusion and tried unsuccessfully to calm her. She needed air.

Dismayed and bewildered by the conflicting demands, Cassie spun around to meet Flint's wide-eyed gaze. "Do as she says. Make up a room for them."

"But…"

"I need time to think." She splayed her hands and then clasped them together. "I'm going outside."

She brushed past Abram and hurried through the door, Allegro taking flight in front of her as she ran away from the conflict. Let them stew about her reaction on their own. She needed to escape, go outside in the morning sunlight and fresh breeze. She raced to the gazebo and flopped down in her favorite spot, breathing hard, hoping against hope they'd leave her alone if only for a few minutes of peace and quiet. Who was right about the cause of her grandparents' deaths? Of her cousin's? Was it her ma or her aunts or someone else entirely? How would she ever know the truth? Another question for her pa to answer when he came home. Soon, with good fortune.

"Well, that was unexpected." At least Daniel had the information he needed even if it upset his sister.

"I guess I'll take care of that room for you." Flint rubbed his jaw with a sigh.

"Thank you, Flint." Hope smirked at the innkeeper before addressing Mercy. "You may leave now."

"I'm not going anywhere as long as you two are here threatening my daughter." Mercy shimmered as she rose higher in the air. "I'll be watching you both."

"That's all you'll be doing." Faith briefly cackled at Mercy before shooing her away. "You needn't fret. We'll be on our very best behavior."

The threat in her tone made the hair on the back of Daniel's neck come to attention. The idea that Hope and Faith were moving in meant he needed to have an urgent conversation with Wilma. She must understand the situation evolving around her. If she'd talk to him. He caught Giles' eye with a lift of his chin, knowing he would keep order among the remaining folks. "I will see you later this afternoon for dinner." He bid farewell to the tense group with a touch of two fingers to his brow and then hurried to the public side of the building. He had to find Wilma and fast.

After poking his head into various rooms he located her sitting on the front porch with a book in her hands, a tea service at her elbow on the small table. He eased closer to where she was absorbed by the novel, head slightly bowed and lips barely moving as she read. A small smile found its way onto his lips at the sight.

"Wilma, may I join you?" He swept a hand toward the other chair. "Just for a minute."

She lifted her head and gripped the book. "I'm not sure it's a very good idea."

"I must speak with you." He quelled the hesitation in his soul. "Please?"

She briefly pressed her lips together to form a flat line. "I can't very well refuse given your family owns the inn." She gestured to the chair. "Have a seat."

He settled onto the hard surface and rested his forearms on the table separating them. "I have something important to relay to you but first you must understand how sorry I am that I upset you. Such was never my intention."

"Then why did you tell me an outright lie?" She closed the book and placed it on the table. "I thought you had more integrity."

"I fear you have abused my reputation with your assumption of my dishonesty." He clasped his hands together, interlocking his fingers. "I swear to you I do not lie. Ever."

"I do not mean to disparage you or your reputation." She searched his eyes for a long moment and then sighed. "I'm told you're a decent man, an educated and honorable one. But it's simply not possible to move from one place to another based on your will."

"It is for me. Honestly." He bumped his joined hands once on the table. "Trust me, it was a surprise to me as well. I did not know I had the capability until I arrived here."

"How is it possible?" She laid a hand on the book, fingers tantalizingly close to his.

He glanced at her hand, tempted to take it into one of his. Too soon by far for such a move. Her inquiring regard sought an honest answer. "I don't know how it's possible except to say it's magic."

Wilma simply stared at him for a long moment before shaking her head. "That's what people say when they don't fathom how something has occurred. But if you can do as you say, then you must surely know the mechanism."

"I do not know, honestly." He shrugged slightly with a rueful expression. "I don't know how I'm able to recall everything I read, either, but I can."

His unique ability to remember the books and articles and papers he'd read made it possible for him to surpass others in his education. Which all led to him being declared a genius and able to quickly advance through his studies and become a professor at a surprisingly young age. Which also led to his students not trusting him to teach them. Some gifts seemed to be a double-edged sword.

"I see." She lifted the silver tea pot and poured steaming liquid into a waiting cup. "Anything else you want to share? Can you fly, too?"

"No, that's not one of my abilities." If only. He'd love to have such a gift. "However, I do have a special pocket watch that also enables me to do something even more daring."

"What?"

"Timeskip from one time to another, past and present. I'm not certain about the future. I haven't tried that direction yet."

"You're seriously trying my credulity." She blinked quickly for a moment. "You're telling me the truth? You'd swear it on a bible?"

"Yes, ma'am. I am indeed being as honest as I know how." Slowly, she nodded at him, accepting what he said to her. Good. "But there's more you need to know."

"More?" The single word emerged with a squeak.

"You see, my entire family is magical. We're all blessed with special abilities." He searched her eyes, waiting until he saw what he needed to see. "Exactly. Giles is our Guardian, for instance. He has superhuman strength and a special connection to my sister."

"What do you mean by a special connection?" Her quizzical expression made him want to smile but he maintained a serene countenance so as not to upset her.

"He knows when she needs him. He can tell when she's afraid, for instance."

"And Abram?" Her eyes widened as she took in everything he revealed. "What's his?"

"He's a shapeshifter. He can become any living creature."

Her lovely lips fell open as she stared at him. "You're toying with me."

Daniel grinned at her astonishment. "No, I'm telling you the truth. But you must promise to keep it to yourself. Flint is concerned if word gets out, people won't continue to support the business."

"Then why tell me at all?" She tilted her head slightly, waiting.

"That's the important part I need to tell you." He reached for her hand, hovering his over hers until she accepted his silent invitation. The warmth of her hand in his gave him courage to press on. "Did you see the two women who arrived a little while ago?"

"In the expensive coach? Yes."

"They are my aunts, also very powerful witches, who have come here to try to persuade Cassie to go with them."

"What is it they want from her?" Wilma's gaze sharpened.

"She has the ability to influence others using her voice." He moistened his dry lips by pressing them together. "It's a unique and powerful ability."

"Where do they wish to take her?"

"To their home south of here." He studied her intent expression. "But it's not the where so much as the why, and more importantly what that means for you."

"Me?" Shock echoed in her voice. "What could they possibly want with me?"

"They want Cassie to willingly join them and they've chosen to move in until and unless she'll agree." He squeezed her fingers. "Which means we don't know exactly what kind of magic may be swirling about in the coming days. I needed you to be aware and prepared as much as Flint is. Just in case."

"Good, I'm glad Flint knows about all of this, though I wish he would have told me." She shook her head once with regret. "He knows I don't like it when he acts as if I am still a child and can't take care of myself." She studied him for a moment. "You're afraid I'll be mixed up in whatever comes next?"

He nodded at her, glad she'd readily picked up on his concern. "I promise to protect you just as much as I will protect my sister. I care about you."

She considered him in silence. "Thank you for telling me all of this. I appreciate your honesty and apologize for not believing in you enough to trust you wouldn't lie to me. It's a relief knowing I can because I care about you as well."

"All we need to do now is manage to convince my aunts to go home without achieving their very fixed aims." He shot her a rueful grin as he considered the daunting concept. "That's all."

Chapter Fourteen

The afternoon rush had the dining room near to overflowing. Every table had at least two people, with many of them full. Flint hustled to fill the drink orders while Isaac and Lawrence tended to the rest of the customer needs and wants. Cassie sang at the piano, her sweet voice entertaining and engaging, while Allegro perched nearby on the oak blanket stand Abram had dug up for him from somewhere in the inn. The guests had accepted the bird as Cassie's pet and having him on the stand enabled Cassie to more easily play the piano. Flint wiped the counter with a cloth and then hung it in place behind the bar. He paused to survey the guests, keeping his expression clear and welcoming with an effort. It didn't help that the aunts sat at a table close to Cassie, the dratted cat on a chair beside them. Nor did it help that John had brought his wife, Tabitha, and daughter, Haley, for dinner, adding to Flint's discomfort on Cassie's behalf. Why did John observe her so often and so closely?

Giles ambled into the room, threw a glance at the Bakers' table, and made his way straight to the bar. "Hey, Flint, can I have an ale, please?"

Flint snared a tankard from the shelf beneath the bar and filled it with frothy amber liquid. He set it on the counter in front of Giles. "You look uneasy. What's happened?"

"Nothing." Giles quaffed the ale in several gulps and plunked the tankard down. "Yet."

A thrill of anticipatory fear shook his shoulders, the same sensation he experienced when he feared future pain by a bee sting. "Do you know something you're not telling me?"

Giles met his gaze with a twinkle in his eyes. "Yes. Today is the day. Wish me luck."

"Good luck?" Flint spoke to Giles' back as the powerful man strolled over to where Haley sat with her parents at a table halfway between the bar and the doorway.

"Mr. and Mrs. Baker, may I join you?" Giles asked, one hand resting on the back of the chair next to Haley.

"Of course." John indicated several empty chairs across the table from Haley.

Flint transferred the empty tankard to the sideboard ready to be taken back to the kitchen. Then he wiped down the mahogany surface while listening to the conversations in the room. Especially the one making John scowl.

Giles pulled out the chair and sat beside Haley, a gentle smile on his lips as he spoke. "Miss Haley, how do you fare on this fine afternoon?"

"I am well, thank you kindly." Haley's expression contained more than a friendly attitude. "And you?"

"My state remains to be seen." Giles glanced at her parents and then held out a hand to Haley, who quickly placed hers in his open palm. "Miss Haley Baker, you and I have become good friends over the past weeks. But I'd like it if we were more than just friends. In fact, I have no doubt but that I have grown to admire and love you with all my heart. Haley, darling, will you marry me?"

"Marry you?" Haley pressed a hand to her throat as she smiled at him. "Yes. Oh, yes!"

"Hold on there, son." John banged his fist on the table. "This is the first I've heard of this."

"John, please." Tabitha laid a hand on John's wrist. "Don't make a scene."

"He's the one making the scene!" John pointed at Giles with a shaking finger. "I don't allow it."

Alarmed, Flint hurried from behind the bar to stride over to the table, afraid John might resort to physical violence given his appearance. "Is everything all right?"

"No, it is not." John leapt to his feet, the chair crashing to the floor behind him. "That man has defied propriety by proposing to my daughter without my permission."

John's face had turned dark red and his entire body trembled as he stood beside Flint. He needed to calm down before he had an apoplexy and died in the middle of the dining room. Definitely not good for business. Flint caught Cassie's eye and indicated John with a tilt of his head. She glanced at the man and then switched to a comforting church hymn. Flint turned back to John.

"John, please sit down. You need to regulate yourself." Tabitha tapped the table in front of where she sat.

"Yes, do, Father." Haley clung to Giles' hand, a loving expression on her face. "We'll soon have a wedding to plan, Mother."

John snatched up the chair and settled it in place and then flopped onto the hard seat with a groan. "You can't possibly think I will permit you to wed this man. I know next to nothing about him."

Flint walked around to stand by Giles so he could look John in the eyes. "You know his father and mother, and of course his sister Cassie."

"He ran a successful importation and exportation exchange on the Gulf coast from what I've heard." Haley glanced at Giles and then looked at her mother. "He's a gentle yet powerful man, one who cares deeply for his family."

"And for you." Giles squeezed Haley's fingers with his large hand. He aimed his gaze at John. "I take care of those I love. You have nothing to fear with me as your daughter's husband. I promise you that."

"Please, Father, give us your blessing." Haley sobered as she regarded her father with wide eyes.

Flint held his breath, seeing the uncertainty and defensiveness in John's features. Giles had indeed taken a huge risk in asking for Haley's hand in such a public setting, and without first clearing the way with her parents. Patience apparently was not his strong suit. The idea of Giles and Haley uniting to start a family of their own despite the concerns over her father's role in the murders may prove troubling. More concerning was John's reaction to the whole affair. Flint had never seen him pound the table nor upset his chair before. What more might he do?

"You have my blessing, darling." Tabitha folded her hands in her lap as she nodded to her daughter. "You will have a fine life together. I can tell you're well suited."

"How do you know that?" John sucked in air as he laid both palms on either side of his plate, glancing between his wife and his daughter. Finally, his shoulders lowered to a normal position. "Well, if your mother thinks it will work out then I suppose I must go along whether I like it or not."

"Thank you, sir." Giles gravely inclined his head with respect to his future father-in-law.

"Don't make me regret my decision. I shall hold you to your word that you will care for her as a proper husband ought. I'll be keeping an eye on you." John drummed his fingers on the table twice before picking up his fork. "Let's eat. Our dinners are growing cold."

"Will you want anything more, Mr. Baker?" Flint asked, preparing to head back to the bar. "I can send one of the waiters."

With the drama at an end, Flint had other tasks to see to.

He met Giles' happy grin with one of his own. Another satisfactory match between one of Cassie's brothers and a pretty girl. Did that mean Daniel would end up with his own match? A ripple of unease scurried down his spine. His sister. He glanced over to where Wilma and Julian were in a friendly conversation with Daniel and Abram. Daniel beside Wilma. So she was talking to him again, eh? They acted with appropriate restraint and etiquette, but he'd keep an eye on them to gauge the temperature of their desires toward each other. His parents would expect no less of him.

"Yes, please ask one of them to come by." John speared a bite of ham and popped it into his mouth. "And please bring me a whiskey."

Flint nodded once, and turned to find Isaac or Lawrence. Relief for Giles battled in his chest with the worry about his sister as he went back to work. A fleeting glance in Wilma's direction confirmed his concern. What were they about?

The crowded dining room meant an abundance of emotions swirling about. Cassie had raised her inner barrier earlier but it only dimmed the sensations flowing into her. She played a light-hearted song with syncopation and flourishes, injecting happiness and contentment into the lyrics. Still, John Baker stewed over his daughter's engagement. She added a thread of acceptance into her voice as she sang the last refrain and ended the song. Taking a short break between songs, she scanned the expectant faces around her.

Sterling Nelson sauntered into the dining room, barely glancing at her where she sat at the square piano before joining a group of men at a table near the back of the room. Soon the four were in deep conversation using low voices. Whatever they discussed, they obviously didn't want others to hear.

She began the next song, the weight of Aunt Hope's gaze heavy on her shoulders. She sensed her aunts' expectations as well as a general feeling of contentment in the room. Infusing her voice with patience, she sang the soothing tones of the piece. Aunt Faith leaned close to Hope and said something which put a strange gleam in her eyes. Hope nodded once and then smirked at Cassie as she pointed two fingers at the ceiling and then made a slight flick with them.

Her inner barrier dissolved and drained away, leaving her empty, disconnected to the emotions in the room. Panic swept through her at the strangeness of the sensation. Hope and Faith smiled smugly at her, the cat studying her with bright yellow eyes. What had her aunt done to her? In a flash she knew. Bound her powers. Retaliation for her previous attempts to influence them. Anger, white hot, flared inside. How dare she try to manipulate her in the same manner as her mother had done? Deprived her of her gifts to suit their own aims. A demonstration of Hope's power over Cassie. One witch should never treat another in such a heinous manner. She wouldn't give them the satisfaction of interrupting her performance no matter what they did. But as soon as she finished the song, she'd have a word with them.

Mercy shimmered into view at the arched doorway, a scowl plain on her features as she glided toward Hope and Faith. Cassie kept singing but shot a warning look at her mother. She shouldn't be in the dining room at all. Especially not when so many guests were present.

"Stop it." Mercy halted beside her sisters' table. "Give them back to her. Now."

"If she won't use her powers for our benefit, then maybe she shouldn't have them." Faith snickered at Mercy. "Just proving a point."

"Keep this little demonstration in mind, sister dear." Hope arched a brow as she flicked her fingers toward Cassie again. "We're not leaving until she agrees. But she won't have her powers if she doesn't."

Surprise, fear, curiosity crashed through Cassie before she could protect herself as her powers returned in an assault of emotions. She gasped and scrambled to raise her barrier against the onslaught. She swept her gaze across the room, glad to see most were paying her mother and aunts no attention. Only a few seemed to have noticed anything amiss. She added acceptance and an ability to ignore anything strange into her singing, increasing her volume to encourage the guests to hear and comply with her wishes.

Mercy glared at her sisters before she glanced at Cassie with a slight lift of her chin. Then she shimmered again and vanished.

Cassie finished her song and then asked Allegro to stay on the quilt stand. He bobbed his head, but spread his wings as if to say he'd be at her side if she needed him. She sent him a silent thanks and then started toward Flint to request a cider to soothe her parched throat. She had nothing to say to her aunts until her anger dissipated. Having her familiar nearby kept her calm despite the antics of her aunts and the black cat. They'd watched her like they feared she'd escape and then dared to inflict such a punishment upon her. If only she had some way of striking back. Best to steer clear until she figured out a way to protect herself from another inappropriate act.

"Miss Fairhope, may I have a word?" John flagged her down with a lift of a hand as she passed his table.

"Of course." She glanced at Haley and Giles, their supreme happiness filling her. "Congratulations on your engagement."

"Thank you." Haley stood and hugged Cassie. "I'm so glad we'll be sisters. We have so much in common."

Cassie cast a quick look at John to gauge his reaction. His raised brows and parted lips suggested he didn't follow his daughter's meaning, which was good. The fewer people who knew of the magic and ghosts surrounding the inn the better. Her ma's recent appearance did nothing to help. "Yes, we do. Especially loving my brother."

"Very true." Haley released her and sat back down with a tender glance at Giles.

Cassie turned her attention to John. "What did you want, sir?"

"I noticed your aunts have returned. What brings them back so soon?"

Why did he care and how much of the tense exchange had he witnessed? She refrained from looking at her aunts, instead studying John while she reached out to ascertain his motives. She sensed curiosity but not from John. She concentrated more and soon pinpointed the source. She swept her gaze to the back of the room and met the steady regard of Sterling. Then he broke the eye contact to resume his conversation but his curiosity continued. John, on the other hand, probed for answers for mixed and muddled reasons. Her guard went up and Giles tensed in his seat.

"Oh, they merely happened to be passing by on their way back home and stopped in for a few days." Pretending she was pleased with their decision was for his benefit. However, disbelief ricocheted through him and into her. "I'm sure they'll be gone by the next time you visit us."

"I see. Your father wrote me that he plans to be home in a matter of weeks, definitely before the festivities of Allhallows Eve are upon us." He peered at her more closely. "It's a pity he won't be here to enjoy their company since they're from so very far away."

"Indeed. I do wish he were already home." She let her gaze drift to Hope and Faith, sitting by the piano but looking at her. She raised her barrier further against the avarice aimed her way.

"It won't be much longer." John lifted his glass of whiskey and sipped. "I have missed his company and will relish having the opportunity to share with him all that has transpired in his absence."

She blinked at his comment, sliding her gaze to Flint and back again. "I'm sure Flint has been keeping him informed with his weekly letters to him."

John shrugged lightly, a sly smirk on his lips. "But did he relay everything?"

Disbelief, mistrust, doubt all flooded into her from him. "Flint is an honest and decent man. I am positive he has reported faithfully to my father."

"Are you questioning Flint's sincerity, Mr. Baker?" Giles rested his massive hands on the table. "I cannot allow you to denigrate him since he is practically family."

"We will find out once your father returns." John lifted his glass in salute. "Until then, here's to your engagement to my daughter. May you truly have a wonderful life together."

Tabitha lifted her glass while Giles merely regarded him with dark, questioning eyes. Cassie sensed he didn't trust John any more than she did at the moment. John obviously didn't trust those around him, either. The question was, why?

The situation at the Fury Falls Inn has grown to unacceptable levels. I cannot believe the number of witches present in the room. I can feel their evil intentions, in particular the two crones seated by the piano. Why have they really returned? And brought a black cat. How obvious of them. What did they want? While the young witch claimed her falcon a pet, I know it's her familiar, there to do her bidding. Then to see that woman suddenly appear. Where did she come from? She resembled the young witch.

Could it be? Mrs. Fairhope. But she lies buried out behind the inn. No. Her haint. That's how she came and went so quickly. Not only witches but ghosts have invaded. I must continue to do what is right for our community by having my compatriots work to remove the danger. I simply need to persuade them around to my way of thinking and before long the witches will be gone and take the ghosts with them. The time has come to begin the real effort to make our area safe.

Chapter Fifteen

He had an idea of how to proceed but he needed specifics. Daniel went in search of his aunts, the best source of answers he could imagine. He found them seated at a cloth-covered table with a silver coffee service on a tray between them. Despite the light rain, they seemed content to enjoy their morning beverage with a view of the foothills.

"Good morning, Aunt Hope, Aunt Faith." He paused before them, reluctant to linger any longer than strictly useful. Especially with his aunt's familiar glaring at him from his perch on the porch railing. "May I speak with you?"

Hope arched a brow at him but nodded. "Did you want some coffee, too?"

"No, thank you. Answers. That's all I'm here for." He leaned against a pole supporting the porch roof.

Faith sipped from her cup and then set it down. "What kinds of questions do you have?"

He took a breath to give him time to gather his thoughts. All of the animosity between the three sisters became exacerbated with the death of his cousin George. That much seemed clear. How did one probe for answers on such a touchy subject? Without making the situation worse.

"I remember the day when George died at the swimming lake, Aunt Hope, but I didn't see what happened. I only know that Pa carried his body all the way to the house."

"As I understand it, George and Giles were using that old rope swing. Giles was the older of the two." Hope gripped her cup more tightly as her lips pressed together. "He should have saved my boy."

"He wanted to. I don't know what stopped him." Daniel hadn't been able to determine much from what Giles had related. Perhaps his own guilt prevented him from digging too deeply into the memories of the long ago day.

"I'm unaware of anything preventing him from helping his cousin. Even your parents' attempt to hide his power shouldn't have kept him from going in to help." Hope set her cup down on the saucer with a clank. "I will never forgive him."

"George's death changed the entire family in ways we'd never imagined." Faith lifted her cup to hold in both hands, as though seeking its warmth. "He was such a good boy."

"What day did he die?" Obviously, it was summer since they were swimming, but which day precisely? With luck they'd remember the exact day and time.

"It was a scorching hot afternoon in 1808." Hope's gaze turned inward as she relived the day. "August fifteenth to be exact. I'll never forget it. I'd been putting up strawberry jam and brewing up some simples from rose petals and carnations. Lordy, it was hot. But I was falling behind in getting everything preserved. So I stayed home when George and Giles and the other kids all went down the road to swim and cool off. George drowned and apparently nobody even noticed his struggle."

"I'm so sorry. I wasn't even aware until it was too late." Imagine telling a young mother about her child's death. Definitely not a job anyone would want.

"Your mother came and told me about the accident at the lake." Hope gazed at him, tears making her eyes glitter. "She was hysterical. I've never seen her so upset. But her grief was nothing compared to mine. My precious son." She swiped at her eyes, and then drew in a shaky breath. "That was a long time ago now but it feels like yesterday."

"Do you think knowing more about his death will help Cassie see her own purpose?" Faith asked. "Will you talk with her?"

"I don't have that kind of influence over her." Nor would he try to convince her to join forces with them. Instead, he wanted to change the past to make the present better for everyone. "I doubt she'll change her mind. You must realize as much by now."

Hope studied him for a long moment and then reached to pour another cup of coffee. "I am not leaving here without her agreeing to come with us. She will be in the Covington coven and our trinity of power. She has no other choice."

The gleam in his aunts' eyes did not bode well for any of them. The only way to change the present and future was to fix the events of the past. If he didn't at least try, then Cassie was doomed.

The passing shower cooled his heated skin as Flint trotted down the front porch steps to the crushed stone carriageway. Beau and Pickles, the chocolate and black Labrador retrievers, loped over for a quick pat. He stopped to rub their heads, savoring the moment of tranquility to calm the agitation stewing inside. His musings left him worried and fretful. He needed to locate Giles and determine if he was imagining things. With a last rub on the furry heads, he resumed striding toward the barn where he hoped to find the big man.

The interior proved far dimmer than usual with the cloud cover so he paused to let his eyes adjust, scanning the rows of stalls in search of Giles. Whistling from the back left stall beckoned him to approach the sweet tune. Horses rustled in their stalls as he passed them, an inquisitive nose here and there poking over a stall door. The orange barn cat watched him from atop one stall wall, poised to run if threatened. Giles whistled while he worked with his dapple gray gelding, rubbing him down with a rag.

"Hey, got a minute?" Flint folded his arms on top of the wall.

"Sure." Giles shifted to pat the horse's forehead and then came out of the stall.

"It's about our guests." Flint pivoted in place as the other man emerged, eager for his opinion. "I've been thinking about the gentlemen who come to the inn."

"Anyone in particular?" Giles folded the rag in thirds. "Or all of them?"

"Two in particular. Sterling Nelson and John Baker. They seem to be frequenting the dining room far more often than in previous months."

"Yeah, I've noticed as much. I guess Matt's cooking is better than we've given him credit for."

Flint tilted his head with a jerky twist. "I think there's something more going on, but I don't know what. Or rather, I fear I do know. What do you think?"

"Sterling has been having his meetings at the inn for convenience, or so I understand. I've spoken to a few of the men and they all live out this way. According to them, he is being considerate by insisting on doing most of the traveling for these gatherings." He shrugged lightly, shifting the rag into his other hand. "It's good for business, right?"

The money flowing through the inn's coffers made possible all of the improvements he'd been working on over the last months. He had a few more to complete and some thoughts on future ideas. Having the large number of men frequently sharing a meal while they discussed their business had been a boon to his efforts. They had spread the word to their friends and colleagues which yielded ever more people visiting, staying the night and enjoying the waters, or popping in for a quick, delicious meal.

"Yes, I'm sure Mr. Fairhope will be pleased with the increased revenue. But what exactly are those men meeting about?" The vagueness of the snippets of their discussions intrigued as much as worried Flint. "All I know is they want to deal with some troublesome women."

"Women. So you think they're referring to witches?" Giles crossed his arms over his chest. "I thought John was our main suspect with regard to the murders."

Flint ran a hand over his head and gripped his nape. "True. He's been engaging with them as well. He may be coming more often because Reggie told him to keep an eye on things. I know Cassie has told her father about…" He glanced over his shoulder to make sure they were still alone. "About all the murders, the magic, and the hauntings. So he may be concerned."

Giles dropped his arms to his sides then turned to toss the rag onto a nearby bale of straw. "Haley said he still has late night dealings of some kind. If only we knew for certain. Maybe we should follow him?"

What an idea. In the middle of the night venture out and see where the man had business? Nothing good would come of being out in the dark when a murderer remained on the loose. They might find themselves on the wrong end of a knife or pistol. If John were to discover they suspected him of killing helpless women and he was innocent of such behavior, the fallout with Reginald Fairhope would be significant. Reggie trusted John implicitly.

"You want to spy on your future father-in-law and your father's friend?"

"When you say it like that… I guess not." Giles splayed his hands for a second. "You know, John may also suspect Cassie is a witch, especially now that her familiar has claimed her."

"I know. She's been trying to influence the audience into calling Allegro a pet but I'm not sure it's working with John." Thankfully the man hadn't mentioned Mercy's brief surprise visit. With good fortune he hadn't noticed. "He does seem to find the falcon upsetting."

"The stand Abram found seems to help with most people accepting the bird in the room. At least I don't see shocked expressions any longer."

"Do you think we should tell the deputy or the sheriff about our concerns? Leave it up to the law to handle?" Flint ran his hand over his head again. A throbbing began at the base of his skull, low and insistent. Great, just what he needed.

"I would if I had one shred of evidence or an eyewitness we could actually present to him." Giles shook his head slowly, glanced away and back. "Isabella was only somewhat helpful."

"At least I'm not imagining John and Sterling's increased presence." Flint gripped his nape again, applying counter pressure on the headache. "I suppose we just need to keep an ear open to see if we can figure out what exactly the group is planning."

"I'll see what I can find out. Give me some time to ask around." Giles grabbed the rag off the straw and paused. "In the meantime, I'll walk the perimeter."

"All right. I'm going to ride into town for the mail." Flint returned the nod of parting with Giles and then strode to the tack room to begin saddling his horse. Perhaps doing something mundane would also ease the pressure in his head, but he rather doubted such would work. Not with the vast array of worries pressing down on him.

Twisting the stem of the pocket watch, Daniel steeled his nerve. He must try. If all went well, he'd be back before dinner. Alone in his bedchamber, he aligned the last tick mark and pressed the button. A whoosh and a buzz sounded and then moments later he found himself outside of the aunts' home near Montgomery. But the landscape looked different than when he'd stood on the road the last time with Abram and Cassie. The trees stood a tad smaller and much less threatening. The road was a narrow dirt path instead of the wider avenue of the present day. It worked. He started down the road in the direction of the lake, one of the fondest memories he held from being a boy. If he timed it right, maybe he'd arrive before George even thought about jumping into the water. He quickened his pace, urgency fueling his strides.

A little while later he spied in the distance several weeping willows draping their long fronds toward the ground. Or more accurately, the lake and its life-giving water. He scanned the road ahead of him, looking out for any of his family who might recognize him. Of course, his older self didn't look like his seven-year-old self. He'd just pretend to be a passerby if he encountered anyone suspicious of him. His steps faltered as it occurred to him he might actually see his brothers and parents and maybe even little five-year-old Cassie. He hadn't seen his parents, alive anyway, in many years. He hadn't walked this street of memories in even more years.

As he approached the lake, he could hear the sound of boys calling and splashing in the water. He was too late to prevent the boys from swimming, but not too late to prevent George drowning. He kept to the side of the road until he could see the blue water glistening in the sunlight. Then he ambled closer, taking his time while he judged the situation.

Abram and Silas were splashing around on the far side along with Daniel's little boy self, waiting for their turns. Giles swam back to shore after using the rope swing to splash into the center of the lake. The best way ever to cool off on a hot summer day. He'd loved to climb up the tree and then swing out and drop into the lake as a boy. On the shore, George waited with the rope swing in hand for Giles to clear the way for his own splash into the water. Daniel's father sat on a folding camp chair he'd brought out with him to supervise the boys. If Daniel hurried, he could stop what Aunt Hope told him would transpire. He'd been so self-absorbed that day he'd not paid any attention to the next few minutes. Didn't know what had happened until after his cousin died.

He marched toward the boy but then George grabbed hold of the rope with both hands. He hesitated for a split second, too short a period for Daniel to do more than reach out an impotent hand, before jumping up and swinging forward, twisting in the air to dive into the lake head first. Oh no! They never went head first, always feet first. The lake wasn't deep enough for diving. What was he thinking?

Daniel ran toward the lake while young Giles hesitated a moment on the shore before he started back into the water. George surfaced, floating face down in the water. Suddenly, their father raced to Giles and grabbed his shoulders, forcing him back to shore. Giles argued, struggled to wrench free to no avail. Shock and bitterness filled him as he watched his father lead Giles away from the floating body, all the while surveying the area for onlookers. Daniel ducked behind a weeping willow so his father wouldn't see him, peering through delicate flowing branches as the two argued for a minute. Then his father went in and lifted the boy's body out of the water and carried it to shore, calling to the others to get out of the water, and on toward their home.

He collapsed against the tree trunk as the scene replayed through his mind and his memories. His father had restrained Giles from helping George. Actually fought with him so he couldn't even try to aid his cousin. Why? Perhaps the boy was already dead and Pa didn't want young Giles to see. But still Giles had reacted to his Guardian instinct to go in and do something to assist. His father stopped him. Did nothing to help until it was obviously too late to save him. Pa was complicit in the boy's death.

He'd failed in his aim of preventing the death and thus mending the broken family's relationship. No wonder Aunt Hope blamed Giles for George's death but she should also blame his father. If Daniel told her that truth, how much more rancor would there exist between her and his father? The family at large? Should he try again? Go back farther in time and do something to keep them all out of the lake? Confused and upset, he shivered in the summer heat. Better to go back to his present time and consult Giles on his thoughts as to what Daniel had witnessed for himself. He made the necessary adjustments to the pocket watch and pushed the button, determined to have a pointed conversation with someone who surely still carried a sense of guilt for his inaction.

<h1 style="text-align:center">Chapter Sixteen</h1>

The afternoon sunshine filtered through the trees, dappling the grass and fallen leaves scattered across the front yard. Cassie had retreated to the gazebo with the letter Flint had thrust at her. He'd returned from a quick trip into town to pick up the mail and newspapers and then dashed inside to his office to handle some paperwork. She enjoyed spending a few minutes alone in the confines of the gazebo, even if she'd been forced by her promise to Flint to bring young Teddy with her as her guard. The whole idea seemed rather silly, truth be told. What could the boy possibly do to protect her against her powerful aunts? Or a killer for that matter? If nothing else, he could bear witness to what happened so the others would know what had become of her. Cheery thought. Nonetheless, Teddy sat off to one side, reading the book she'd given to him.

Since his father was locked up in jail awaiting trial for his role in Mercy's death, she'd taken the nine-year-old under her motherly wing. The work he performed around the place helped him become more useful and resourceful. He'd filled out in the couple of months he'd lived at the inn. He'd probably grown an inch or two, shooting up with the better nutrition he found in the kitchen. Even his shock of brown hair seemed glossier and in need of a good trim. She had ensured his safety, kept him fed, and out of trouble. The one thing she didn't feel qualified to do was to teach him. Yet the boy needed schooling in order to grow into a good citizen, one who could provide for himself and a family. Perhaps Flint could help her inquire about a tutor or possibly a local school. She wouldn't allow him to attend any overnight schools, not until he matured enough. If he even wanted to go.

"Teddy, can I ask you a question?" She waited for him to lift his head and peer at her curiously with his green eyes.

"Sure." He held the book open, balanced on one palm.

"Would you like to attend school?"

"Me? Oh, yes, please." He grinned at her as he sat up straighter. "My pa told me I couldn't 'cause we ain't got no money. But if'n I could, I have so many questions in want of answers."

His glee shone from every pore of his being. The lad really was eager for the chance to learn new things. "Then I will talk with Flint about options for you. Keep reading for now to prepare for the day when we find the right situation for you."

"Thank you, miss." With a flash of a smile, he returned to reading the text.

He endeared himself to her with his willingness despite all of the adversity he'd faced in his young life. Essentially abandoned by his father, left to scavenge for food to survive. With loving attention, the boy blossomed right before her eyes. Perhaps his future would be bright.

Speaking of futures, she glanced at the envelope in her hand. From her brother Silas. She could tell without even opening it. She could sense the care with which he'd written to her through the paper she held. Her senses seemed to sharpen and become more refined with each passing day. Growing more powerful and more confident in her power as a result. Time to find out what Silas had to say. She opened the letter and scanned its contents.

Sept. 28, 1821
Louisville, Kentucky

Dear Cassie,

My deepest apologies for not answering your letter earlier. I am sorry to hear about our mother's death and our father's absence. With luck he will arrive before I do, but we both know he can be somewhat selfish at times. I've been on assignment in Kentucky for the last couple of months but am now free to head south. Did you know that I have a job for a Boston paper as a travel writer? I journey about, writing articles that show what other travelers will find in various places. You'll probably not recall how fond I am of writing and language in general since you were so young when I struck out on my own. But I should follow this letter in a day or two. I know how very much you need me and so am pleased to finally be able to come to you.

See you soon, sis.
Fondly,
Silas Fairhope

She refolded the letter and plopped it onto her lap, taking in the hustle and bustle of the inn's afternoon guests and diners arriving for dinner. So he was finally on his way. The last of her estranged brothers coming as she'd asked months before. She reached out with her senses to test whether she could feel his approach. Closed her eyes to concentrate harder but didn't sense him. He was probably too far away yet for her to make contact.

He was correct in that she didn't remember his love of language and writing. How interesting that he'd become a professional writer and traveling as well. He must have many stories to tell of his adventures. Perhaps he could help her write some songs to sing. Or better yet, spells. She'd ask him once he showed up.

She had several other questions for him, and of course many things to tell him, when he arrived. What was his special ability? Had it manifested to him yet or would he be surprised to learn he possessed a gift? But even more importantly, how did he know she needed him? Did he surmise from her letter or did he know something she didn't about the future? She looked at the envelope in her lap. A few more days and she'd have answers.

The longer he pondered what he'd witnessed, the angrier he became. Daniel stormed into Flint's office after Abram had told him where to find their oldest brother. Flint sat behind his desk, a lined ledger open in front of him, with Giles in the chair facing him, one calf crossed over his other thigh. So cool and calm it made Daniel angrier, if that were even possible.

"What's the matter?" Flint laid down his pencil as a frown dipped his brows. "What's happened?"

"A lot happened I was entirely unaware of. Why didn't you tell me the whole truth?" Daniel pressed his palms on the edge of the desk, peering at Giles.

"About?" Giles tapped his leg with one hand.

His nonchalance further fueled Daniel's ire. "I saw you and our father let George die."

Giles stilled his hand and lowered his foot to the floor. "What do you mean?"

"He went back." Flint fisted his hands on the desk. "You timeskipped back to the day when your cousin died, didn't you? Without telling anyone."

"I did." Daniel pounded the desk with a hand. "I wanted to fix things. But I saw Pa stop you from helping George. I couldn't believe it."

Giles drew in a long breath and let it out slowly. "I had forgotten until recently. Put it out of my mind how he'd interfered. But, Daniel, it was for the best."

Daniel gaped at his brother. "For the best? George *died*. You and Pa did nothing. How was that for the best?"

"I think Mercy was right to not tell you guys about your powers, to bind them actually." Flint sat back in his chair, glancing between the pair of men. "I don't always agree with your mother but on that point I do. Especially knowing her sisters."

"I'm confused." Daniel spun away and paced in front of the lone window with quick, angry strides. He dragged a hand through his hair hoping motion would help to settle the anxious feeling stirring his gut. Something he could control. Unlike his emotions.

"You can't go back and change everything to make it better." Giles pushed to his feet to stand in front of Daniel, effectively stopping his marching to and fro. "You'd have actually made things worse. I can't imagine what our grandfather would have done, would have made us do, knowing of our powers."

"But we'd all be together instead of scattered across the country deprived of knowing the truth of our lives." Couldn't he see how being divided had torn apart the family? "Family is everything, or should be. Except ours split apart and you're fine with that?"

"Don't put words in my mouth." Giles folded his arms over his chest and glared at Daniel. "I know we've found ourselves in a strange and dangerous situation. But it doesn't mean I would change the past to defeat what our parents accomplished."

"What on earth are you talking about?" They'd sent their sons off on their own to make their own way as best they could but kept Cassie close. She at least had their support, their love, their protection. Did they fathom how difficult his life had been? If Daniel hadn't met a concerned man who turned out to be a professor and took him under his wing, helping him with an education and a job, he didn't know where he would have ended up. "What exactly did they accomplish?"

Giles shrugged with a brief splay of his hands. "They kept us safe from the clutches of those who wanted to control us, to use our powers for their own aims. Our aunts and our grandfather would have used our caring nature against us, to convince us their desires should be ours. Now that we're grown, we can make choices for ourselves based on our moral compass instead of theirs."

"But…" His logic made some sense but did a young boy have to die in the process? "Why did Pa stop you from helping George? How did that fit into this protecting us scheme?"

"Ma told me he stopped me because he knew I had already started demonstrating my strength as being unusual for a boy my age and size. He was afraid to expose my powers to the others. That's when they decided to bind our powers and not tell us about them. So we'd grow up like normal kids."

"Even though you're anything but normal." Flint picked up his pencil and tapped it on the page of numbers. "I mean that with all due respect."

"Noted." Giles chuckled as he resumed his seat and studied Daniel for a moment. "Now that our powers are our own, so too our choices. While you have the option to travel through time, I hope you don't choose to do so to try to save George again. What's done is done and we have to live with the consequences of those actions."

The impulse remained strong, to play God and correct past mistakes, but damnation his brother was right.

"Changing the past isn't the right choice. Witnessing it is fine to understand it, but not to interfere with the choices others have made."

"You are wise beyond your years." Flint fiddled with the pencil as he regarded Daniel. "I applaud your decision."

Although he may have made the right decision, he still harbored a sense of guilt from not being able to save his cousin. To not stop the tragedy, the grief of the boy's parents, the separation of the family. If only it all could have been avoided they'd have had a closer relationship with the rest of their relatives.

"How did you handle the guilt, Giles?"

"I'm still working on that." Giles gripped his knees as he leaned forward. "I hope one day I can make amends to his mother but I have no idea how."

"Aunt Hope hasn't forgiven you or our parents in thirteen years." Daniel rolled his shoulders to ease the tension. "I wouldn't hold your breath."

"This whole dust up about Cassie uniting with them is not going to end well." Flint dropped the pencil on the desk and stood. "We need to stay close to her, be there for her."

"That's why I came to the inn." Daniel had risked everything to come as she had requested. His job. His apartment. His friends. "That's why we all came, right?"

"Once Silas arrives we'll all be together for the first time in years." Giles stood and headed toward the door. "I have a feeling he'll get here before too long, or at least Cassie now does. I'll go set up a space for him in my room."

"I gave her a letter from him today so you're probably correct. Right now, I've got to check on Mandy. I need to relieve her of the kitchen work soon or she may quit." Flint motioned to the open door Giles had already passed through. "After you."

Daniel nodded and strode to the door, taking the hint that the conversation was over. Maybe Wilma would like to take a walk with him or simply talk. Help him calm down after his upsetting day. Finding her would be worth the effort in either case.

Chapter Seventeen

The evening rush was dwindling down as the guests returned to their rooms and the others departed for home. Flint breathed a sigh of relief. It had been a busy few hours. Cassie lingered at the piano, playing softly and singing some gentle tunes while Allegro supervised from his perch. Encouraging everyone to relax and grow sleepy, no doubt. Hope and Faith had taken up their usual seats at a table near the piano, pretending to be merely listening to Cassie's performance, but more likely impatiently waiting for her to change her mind. At least the cat had found somewhere else to nap. Wilma and Julian sat with Daniel and Abram at another table, and Giles had gone out to do his twice daily perimeter walk. Not that he ever found any trouble but it did seem to make him feel better. Perhaps just getting outside helped.

Wilma caught his eye and then stood to hurry over to him by the bar. "I'm going to stay a few more days but Julian is ready to go home. If that's all right with you?"

"I thought you'd both go home together. What changed?" But he knew. Daniel. They'd been nearly inseparable except for when Daniel had timeskipped. Always holding hands, whispering, taking walks.

Her cheeks turned pink but she met his gaze with a steady look. "I am having a good time and have made some new friends I want to spend more time with. There is no reason for you to look at me with such an expression."

"I'm simply surprised." Her quirked brow indicated her disbelief in his claim but he'd stick by it. "I had assumed you were only staying for a couple of days and you've been here for weeks instead."

"Do you want me to leave?" Her eyes glistened as she blinked slowly.

Damnation. Now he'd upset her. "Not at all. I merely thought Mother would be missing you."

"I'll send her a note along with Julian, explaining everything." She waved away his weak excuse for a reason for her to leave. "She won't mind."

Flint accepted his sister's embrace, meeting Cassie's amused grin over her head. When Wilma pushed away, he couldn't help noticing how lovely she appeared, all glowing and happy. He couldn't blame Daniel for his interest, and in fact his attentions may have led to the luster surrounding Wilma's very being.

"Go on then." He smiled at her to soften the resistance he'd demonstrated upon her unforeseen decision. Only, it wasn't so much surprising as concerning to him to see his little sister in a relationship. He couldn't very well dislike Cassie's brother though, not without being accused of being hypocritical. Daniel was a decent man, educated, and cared for his sister. Flint could see how much in his expression, in his deference to her opinion bnd preferences, and in his attention to her.

"Thank you, Flint." She made her way back to the table and gracefully slid onto her seat beside Daniel.

Her beau. Give it time and they'd be planning a wedding. Speaking of which, his other sister's wedding would be soon. And when might he and Cassie be wed? If her father agreed to their engagement, which he probably wouldn't since Flint had no special powers like the rest of them. His thoughts continued to spiral downward each time he contemplated actually marrying Cassie. He longed for the day, but feared it would never be allowed to arrive.

He felt the weight of someone staring at him. Surveying the room he espied the aunts glowering at him. What had he done now? He swallowed as he tried to sort out what they might expect. Cassie got up from the piano bench and headed toward him, a quizzical smile on her lips. Allegro shifted on his perch, spreading his wings as if preparing to take flight, before folding them neatly. The falcon seemed to understand Cassie without her having to say a word. Did her powers apply to animals as well? Was that new? He felt even more useless to her.

"What's the matter?" She tapped a hand on his upper arm. "You look positively distressed." She canted her head to one side. "You are upset about something. What's going on?"

"Wilma and Daniel." He'd keep those thoughts to himself. But he could admit to his concern about his sister. As the words left his mouth, though, he realized how silly he was being. Why wouldn't Daniel fall in love with his beautiful and talented sister? Indeed, Flint would probably be insulted if the other hadn't recognized her worth. "She's staying because of him."

"Good. They look well together." Cassie slid her gaze to observe the pair in question. "I like knowing Wilma will be my sister, possibly twice over."

He peered into Cassie's captivating eyes, a hint of dismay at the previous line of thought flickering in his soul. "I'm glad to hear so. I do hope your father doesn't object to me as your husband."

"I see no reason for him to object." She eased closer and lifted her lips toward his, lightly pressing a kiss and holding it for a moment. "I know he trusts you or he wouldn't have left you in charge."

Running the inn was a very different animal to marrying his daughter. The qualifications were very different, indeed. "I suppose we will find out in the next few weeks when he finally comes home."

"While I have a minute, I wanted to ask you about Teddy's schooling. He would really like to learn." She smiled at the memory of the boy's joy at the mere prospect. "But is there a school nearby? I wouldn't want him to have to go too far away so I can keep an eye on his progress."

He hesitated, considering her question. "I do not believe there are any publicly funded schools in the area. Not that I am aware of, at any rate. We'd need to either find a private grammar school, which would be unlikely, or a tutor, which may prove too expensive."

"Then how should we ensure he receives a proper education?"

"I will need to think on that." Another problem to solve. Add it to the growing list in his head. "I'll let you know what I figure out as soon as I do."

"Thank you. I know how anxious he is to begin his studies." She gave him a quick kiss and a smile. "I'm doing what I can, but I think he'll need more than I know."

"At least you're providing him with a start." Movement at the arched doorway drew his attention.

Mandy appeared, paused to scan the room, and then headed toward him. The look on her face suggested she was not happy. But he already knew as much after his earlier conversation with her. She was about to walk away and leave him high and dry without the kitchen help Matt needed. He must find someone else to work in the kitchen so she could return to working in the dining room. He'd rather have both men and women waiting tables than to lose her help altogether. Besides, Abram would never let him hear the end of it.

"The deputy is here and he wants to talk to you." Mandy huffed as she glared at him. "I'm not your secretary but I could be if you didn't keep me out of sight in the kitchen."

He had no need of a secretary. Or did he? He hadn't thought of such a role for her but it was something to consider. He could teach her how to place orders and receive them, maybe even turn over the reservation ledgers to a competent secretary. Such a position would not satisfy her desire to interact with the guests. So perhaps she could act as hostess in the dining room, seating the guests so she could be involved with them but not waiting on them. A thought worth investigating further. After he found out why the deputy called at the inn.

"Where is Deputy Parker?" he asked, glancing toward the doorway.

"He stopped to chat with Abram for a moment but he'll be in shortly, I would imagine." She glanced over her shoulder and then back to Flint and Cassie. "I do hope you take me seriously about finding me another job here. I will not work in the kitchen much longer before I'll walk out and not look back."

Flint raised a hand in pledge. "I promise to find someone else as quickly as possible."

But who could he tap to help in the kitchen? The advertisement he'd placed in the paper didn't yield any applicants. Mayhap he could ask John to lend him a slave for a time until he could hire someone else. No, Cassie wouldn't approve of such a maneuver. She had become quite an abolitionist in her own right. He'd ask Haley if she knew of anyone since she'd sent Mandy his way to begin with. Maybe the Marple sisters had a friend they could suggest.

Barney sauntered into the room and headed straight to Flint, holding out a hand to shake with him in greeting.

"How are things going here? Everyone safe? There's been another killing not far from here and I wanted to make sure you're fine."

"Another? How awful. Thankfully, it's been fairly quiet here." Flint released the man's hand and flicked a glance at Hope and Faith and then back to Barney. How much should he tell him, or even hint at, about the presence of the aunts and his suspicions of the shadowy group of men? "We're fine."

"Ha. That's not exactly true, now is it, Flint?" Mandy huffed and shook her head. "There's more going on here than he's letting on, sir."

"Mandy…" Cassie shook her head at the other girl.

Barney glanced between the two and then lifted a brow at Flint. "Something I should know about?"

Yes, but he couldn't prove anything nor provide a shred of evidence as to their suspicions. "No, not a thing."

Mandy smirked. "I've been working here long enough to know he's not being forthcoming with you."

"How do you mean, miss?" Barney inspected her belligerent expression. "What's going on?"

What was the girl doing? Did she intend to tell the deputy about the presence of magic, witches, ghosts, everything? The gleam in her eyes spoke volumes. She did, a form of blackmail to make sure she got her way. What could he do to stop her revealing far too much to the good deputy?

"She's just joking with you. What she means is that she has a new job around here, as my…hostess, so she won't be waiting tables any longer." Flint shot her a quelling look, one laced with hope she'd go along with his offer. "You know I'd tell you if…something was actually wrong. But look around and you'll see everybody is fine."

"Yes, everything is fine now that I have my new job all lined up." Mandy tossed her head, a victorious grin on her lips.

"Congratulations on your new position, miss." Barney surveyed the remaining people in the room, lingering on the carefully averted faces of Hope and Faith for several uncomfortable moments. He returned his gaze to meet Flint's somewhat frantic one, frantic lest Mandy said anything more blatant about magic and ghosts. "See that you do tell me if something is bothering you or if you have any problems. I wouldn't want things to get out of hand around here."

Flint nodded, buying a moment to swallow the knot of panic in his throat. A close call. One he hoped to avoid ever facing again. "Without fail."

The next morning, Cassie decided to defy Flint's orders and spend some time actually alone in the gazebo, reading. It had been weeks since she'd done so, and nothing untoward had occurred in the interim to suggest it was any more dangerous than before. She'd set Teddy to reading a new book on geography, with the task of listing any unfamiliar words for them to discuss later. She may not be the smartest person, but she could help him learn new words and subjects. In the meantime, she had a book of poetry to devour. She closed the front door behind her and started toward the steps.

"Cassie, wait."

She hesitated in the middle of the front porch, tucking the slim book under one arm, as Flint dismounted from his buckskin paint horse. Leading Buck by the reins, he advanced toward her as she trotted down the steps to the crushed carriageway. In the late morning drizzle, his hat and the shoulders of his coat glistened with rain. Despite the dampness, he still looked handsome and eager to see her.

"Did you need something?" Cassie stood in front of him, admiring his twinkling eyes and easy grin.

"I have a letter from your father for you." He fished in an inner pocket of his coat and pulled out a slightly crumpled envelope to hand to her. "I'd like to find out what he has to say but I'm running behind this morning. Tell me later?"

"I will. Go on." She tucked the letter inside the cover of the book and then glanced at the gazebo before smiling at him. "I'm going over there to read what he has to say. I'll see you in a while."

With a distracted nod, Flint turned to lead Buck to the barn. Good, he made no comment on her choice of reading place. Cassie dashed through the light rain across the yard to the relative safety of the gazebo. She had time before she needed to return to work. Time to find out more about her pa's plans. She clutched the book to her chest and sent up a prayer he was on his way home. The cloudy sky hid any hint of sunshine, creating a scene dreary and mystical. Allegro swooped from the sky and lit on the bench beside her, an inquisitive eye aimed at her.

"Good morning." She stroked his head and then he sidled closer to hop onto her shoulder and rub her neck with the top of his head. "I'm glad you're here. Let's find out what Pa has to say."

She pulled the envelope from its protected spot in the book. She opened the envelope and withdrew several pages of cream stationery. She glanced at the falcon as she chewed her lower lip for a moment. Taking a fortifying breath, she unfolded the paper.

Monday morning, Oct. 1
Savannah, GA

My dear Cassie,
I write with joy that we have secured freedom for Pansy Drake at last! She and Sheridan as well as Zander are all thrilled to be reunited as a family. Naturally, Mrs. Drake is

anxious to return to see Matt as soon as possible. We're making the final preparations to return home, getting the proper documentation in order and finding wagons and oxen to pull them. Please tell Flint to continue doing the fine job that Mr. Baker reports he's been doing until I come home. I have missed you and the inn these few months that I've been gone. However, the furniture is now ready and meets my demands despite my brother Beck's attempts to sway my aims.

Can you please ensure there will be sleeping places for everyone traveling with me? All told I believe I'll have six in my party. I, of course, already have my bedchamber, although it will be very different to occupy it without my wife beside me. Sheridan has his as well, which he'll share with his wife. Zander also has a spot, but the other two will need some place to lay their heads.

We will be leaving here in a few days so will be home by Allhallows as I've said all along. The Fates are working in our favor for a change it would seem.

I know you're anxious for my return and will do all I can to expedite our journey. Fare thee well, my dear.

Love,

Your father

"Hallelujah!" Cassie lowered her hands until the pages rested on her lap. Allegro spread his wings and leapt into the air to dart around the gazebo. What had startled him? He circled the interior several times as she resumed perusing the letter in her hands. "He's on his way." The clock was now ticking as to when she must face the deadline of joining her aunts.

Suddenly someone grabbed her from behind, an arm around her neck pulling her backward. She clawed at the muscular limb as she fought for air, her book landing on the floor with a thump. The beat of falcon wings sounded above her as Allegro tried to scare her attacker away. Only the pressure on her throat increased as a flash of steel appeared to her left. She froze at the sight of the gleaming blade.

"Witch." The deep, harsh voice grated in her ear. "After you die, there will be one less of you creatures."

The witch killer. Oh good lord. Spots swam before her eyes as she struggled to drag in air. She was going to die. In her favorite spot on the entire property. Alone and unaided, she'd fall victim to the very thing she'd feared might happen. If she hadn't been so independent it wouldn't have ended in such a manner. Her strength seeped from her the longer he pressed his arm against her throat. She struggled until she had nothing left.

Something bright and hot whizzed past her and the man grunted in pain. He released her just as suddenly as he'd grabbed her, the sound of his booted steps receding behind her as he ran away. Allegro swooped after him to ensure he kept running. She clasped her sore throat, relieved he hadn't been able to carry out his threat. Tears streamed down her cheeks as she forced her eyes open, spluttering and coughing, and spotted Aunt Hope hurrying up the steps to stand in front of her.

"Are you all right?" Hope sank onto the seat beside her. "Who was that?"

"I-I do not know. I didn't see him nor recognize his voice."

"He was dressed all in black with a mask covering everything but his eyes. Why was he attacking you?" Deep concern echoed in Hope's tone as she inspected Cassie for any sign of injury.

Cassie swiped at her wet eyes with shaking fingers. "I think he's the man who has been killing witches."

Flint had every reason to insist she be supervised. She should have trusted his judgement instead of ignoring his request and breaking her promise. Doing so nearly cost her life. Her body shook from the close call and from her own stupidity.

Hope reached down to retrieve the book and letter, handing both to her. "Well, whoever he is he won't get a second chance. I was unaware your life was in danger from some witch hunter, my dear. All the more reason for Faith and I to remain here until he's caught."

"Did you… did you stop him?" Cassie searched her aunt's angry expression. "He sounded hurt."

"I merely aimed a small lightning bolt at him." She narrowed her eyes. "If I'd known who he was, he wouldn't have walked away."

"Thank you for coming to my rescue." Allegro returned and landed on her shoulder, rubbing his head against her neck in sympathy and comfort. "He meant to kill me."

"So it appeared. Why were you out here alone?" Hope frowned at her. "Especially knowing of a killer on the loose."

"I came out to read this book of poems. I've sat out here so many times without anything untoward occurring I thought I'd be fine." She blinked as she tried to calm her racing heart. Tried to stop the shaking rattling the paper in her hands. "At least, my pa writes that he is coming home at long last."

"Ah." Hope eyed the falcon poised in a protective posture on her shoulder. "Does he come to you often?"

"My pa?"

"No, silly, your familiar." Hope shook her head. "Do try to be serious."

Her tone suggested annoyance and something else. Cassie squinted as she tried to separate the threads of intent tangled in her aunt's suddenly haughty voice. Anticipation. Determination. A hint of fear. And…what? She could almost grasp the elusive intent but it slipped away. She shook off her musings to answer her aunt's question.

"Yes, he's been visiting me every day." She stroked the soft feathered head. "He's very smart, too."

"Naturally. Your familiar knows you and how to support you." Hope tilted her head to one side. "If you follow your destiny and join me and Faith, then you'll learn far more about how to interact properly with your familiar, how to use its talents and skills to the greatest effect."

There it was. The real reason for the unexpected if timely visit from her aunt. "I've told you I'm not interested."

"Come, come. You have far too much potential to waste away out here." Hope tsked at her. "My sister has not done you any favors by keeping you in the dark for so long. You should be far more able to work your magic. To be able to defend yourself from such a mundane attack. Together, we'll hone your skills and explore the extent of your talents until you're one of the most powerful witches in the world."

Tempted. So tempted. To be able to honestly protect herself from ever facing such a terrifying experience. But why was she tempted to find out the extent of her talents with the help of her aunts? She'd always been able to resist knowing the perils of accepting such an invitation. Everyone had warned her against allowing Hope and Faith to persuade her to their way of thinking. Still, if Cassie indeed knew more about her abilities and felt more confident in how to use them effectively, what more would she be able to do? Would she be able to identify the killer and stop that threat? Catch him in the act? Then all the women in the area would be safe. She'd feel proud of herself. Something she hadn't felt in a long time.

"Well, don't just sit there staring at me. Answer me." Hope leaned forward to gauge her reaction. "Won't you join us? Discover your true potential and live your destiny?"

The anticipation in her aunt's expression nearly made Cassie relent and accept. The temptation to satisfy her curiosity about everything magical sifted through her. Tickling her inquisitiveness in ways she'd never experienced.

A movement behind her aunt caught her eye. Flint passing the window in his office. If she left, he'd be devastated. She wouldn't be able to live with herself having hurt him. She wouldn't realize her dream of marrying him. Pain flashed through her heart at the thought.

Her resolve strengthened, making her sit up straighter and meet her aunt's gaze. "I cannot."

Hope jumped to her feet, her long dark skirts and black cloak swirling around her ankles. "You obstinate, selfish, childish witch. When will you realize you cannot deny your destiny? I can't force you to see reality and make you come with us because that would weaken your powers, and your heart and soul would not be in your witchcraft in any case. But you will eventually unite with us. You must. In the meantime, you will have two more people looking out for your safety. After all, I can't have anything *untoward* happen to you, now can I?"

Cassie stood up slowly while Allegro spread his wings behind her head. "If you cannot force me to comply, then you must accept I have chosen my path. My own destiny. You may as well pack your bags and go home. Alone."

"Bah!" Hope swung away to stare at the inn, gleaming in the light rain falling around them. She spun back to glare at Cassie. "We shall not leave without you. It is your destiny."

Cassie raised her chin, Allegro tensing beside her. "I believe you are destined to be disappointed."

"We shall see." Hope gathered her cloak with her fists and stormed down the steps and across the yard to the inn.

After her aunt disappeared inside, Cassie finally let her held breath out into the air. She'd come close to succumbing to her aunt's persuasive tones and words. Ah, that was the elusive intent she'd sensed. Hope was employing magic on her to try to convince her to agree. What other methods had her aunt attempted to persuade her without Cassie realizing what she was about?

She needed to speak to Flint about her aunt but also about the number of people traveling with her father on his journey home. Then it struck her what her pa hadn't said in his letter. Why hadn't he identified the two additional travelers? Why did he create yet another secret in the family?

Chapter Eighteen

The new arrangement suited much better. Flint had shifted a few of the tables toward the back of the room to allow a space for dancing by the piano. Several couples had taken to the floor and enjoyed stepping to the sound of Cassie's sweet music as she played and sang a lively jig, Allegro keeping a watchful eye on the folks in the room. Daniel and Wilma, grinning and laughing, fumbled their way through the quick steps. Despite his earlier misgivings, they made a nice couple. Cassie was right to encourage them to become better acquainted. Honestly, his sister had chosen well.

He let his gaze rest on Cassie for several measures of her song. She'd nearly died. If the very aunt who most threatened her composure and future hadn't stepped in and saved her. The stark thought rattled around in his brain. Why had she broken her promise to him? Gone out to the gazebo alone. He mentally kicked himself for ignoring her earlier intent to do so, but he'd been in a hurry to resolve an issue with an order he'd placed. Never again. He'd see to it.

The afternoon rush hadn't quite begun but still many people occupied chairs at several tables. He'd been surprised by Cassie's news from her father. Very glad to learn Sheridan's wife was finally free and reunited with her husband and son. He needed to tell Matt yet, since he hadn't had a moment to do so. Which meant more people coming who needed a place to sleep. In addition to the increased number of overnight guests of the inn. After all, only so many people could share one bed and those must be of the same sex to maintain propriety. He could only think of one solution: add on to the inn. Another major improvement to plan and supervise.

He turned from scanning the room to stride back to the bar where Giles sat alone. Ever since Julian had left, the big man seemed depressed by no longer having a shadow to talk to whenever he wanted. "Can I get you something?"

"I want that killer." He drummed his fingers slowly on the mahogany surface. "But I suppose an ale will have to be enough for the moment."

Flint poured the beverage, eyeing his friend's sad countenance, and slid him the tankard. "Missing Julian, aren't you."

Giles swallowed a gulp of ale and then set it down. "I'm surprised to admit I am.

"You can always go visit him in town." Flint snatched the towel off the rail behind the bar and wiped down the counter. "I'm sure he'd be pleased if you did."

The relationship between fathers and sons, at its most fundamental level the same as instructor to student, could be tense. Between mentor and youth, more open and honest discussion tended to occur. The youth sought the advice of the mentor unlike the father giving advice whether the son asked for it or not. No wonder Giles missed having the boy around.

"After we settle things here. I won't leave Cassie unsupervised again." Giles took another gulp as he regarded Flint. "You look like you've got something on your mind."

"Your father is on his way home, which is good." Flint draped the towel over the rail and then rested his hands on the bar. "But he's bringing not only Sheridan's wife but two others."

"All right. What's the problem?"

"He didn't say whether those two are related or even of the same sex and thus would want to share a room, or if they are not husband and wife but some other combination."

"Meaning?" Giles grabbed hold of the tankard.

"I don't know where they're going to sleep." He'd wrestled with possibilities but not found an acceptable arrangement. But one idea kept surfacing. "I'm thinking I may need to add on to the inn in order to accommodate everyone. But I don't know exactly how much time I have until they arrive."

"It will take several weeks to travel all the way out here from the coast." Giles glanced away and then back to Flint. "Somebody's anxious to talk to you it seems."

Matt hesitated at the arched doorway to the dining room and then hurried over to the bar. "Mandy told me you have news of my mother but she wouldn't tell me what it was."

The girl couldn't seem to mind her own business. First, she almost tipped Barney off about the haunting and the witchcraft. Then she prods Matt with a hint about the news from Reggie. He stifled an annoyed sigh. It wasn't Matt's fault he was irritated with the chit's actions. Not the least of which was forcing him to assign her a new job, one made up at the last minute. What would she do as a hostess? It wasn't like they were throwing a ball or party. He mentally shook his head. He'd have to sort that mess out later.

"Cassie had a letter from her father saying they're bringing your mother home with them." Flint grinned at the slowly spreading shock and then joy on Matt's face. "She's free and anxious to see you."

"Oh my good sweet Lord!" Matt grabbed the edge of the wood counter so hard his knuckles lightened. "They did it."

Giles patted him on the back with a massive hand. "Wonderful news."

Flint saw Cassie watching the excitement playing across Matt's features and nodded to her. She must have sensed Matt's joy from her expression. The aunts sat at their usual table, close enough to Cassie to make their presence unavoidable. Surely they knew their mission was futile. Cassie told him earlier about Hope's attempt to sway her decision in their favor. And the witch's new purpose for staying: to protect Cassie. Maybe he should have a word with them. He might be able to finally convince them to leave her alone. Worth a try anyway.

Matt pushed away from the bar, a smile glued to his face. "Thank you for that, Flint. I'll go back to work now." He whistled along with Cassie's singing as he left the room.

"That's one happy son right there." Giles took a drink and then held the tankard between his hands. "I'm happy for him. For all of them. You know, since Haley agreed to marry me, I'll need to build a house for her somewhere around these parts. I imagine Abram will want to do likewise."

Flint looked sharply at Giles. "I hadn't thought of that. But now? With all that is happening?"

"No, not yet." Giles drained his ale and set the empty vessel in the center of the bar. "Not until things calm down and Cassie's no longer in any danger. I want to stay close."

"Good." He let out a breath as relief flowed through him. The big man's presence gave him much needed reassurance. Until the two main dangers ended, he hoped he'd stay. Flint stared at the aunts and then made a decision. "I'll be back in a minute."

"Where you going?"

"To speak with your aunts." Flint moved out from behind the bar and strode over to where Hope and Faith kept close watch on Cassie. The suspicious black cat narrowed its eyes from where it sat on a chair beside Faith as he neared. He stopped by their table and then sat down in a chair. "Ladies, might I have a word with you?"

He used the term loosely as their actions to date had been anything but ladylike. Instead of being polite and demure, they acted stubborn, pushy, even willful. Might he add aggressive in a way more manly than feminine, which was no compliment. If he approached them from a logical standpoint they wouldn't listen. He'd try tapping into their emotions.

"You may." Faith sat back in her chair to regard him down her sharp nose. "What did you want to talk about?"

"Cassie has no intention of accepting your offer. And I'm glad because if she did then our relationship would become very difficult to maintain. We intend to marry after her father returns." Their expressions didn't change, serene and confident. He must make them see why they couldn't and shouldn't succeed. "If she were to accept your offer, she'd have to end our engagement. You wouldn't want to spoil our chances for a happy marriage, now would you?"

"You do not enter into the equation. Surely you must know we simply do not care about any other future she may have thought she had." Hope arched one brow in disdain of his claim to Cassie's affections. "The trinity is her destiny. So you do not interest me in any way as you do not add to her attractions but distract her and diminish them. Once we've caught the witch hunter, then we will take her home with us. You may go." She turned her attention back to watching Cassie, dismissing him.

"But—"

"You cannot dissuade us from pursuing our niece and her potential powers when she finally sees the light." Faith shooed him with one hand. The cat arched its back as it emitted a low growl. "Go tend the bar and leave us to our endeavors to enlighten her."

"I will leave you alone but it is you who will fail." He slowly stood, praying with all his might he would continue to be right, and made his way back to the bar. Glad to put distance between himself and the blasted cat. He stood beside Giles for a long moment without saying a word.

"What happened?" Giles spun sideways to address him.

"I failed to convince them to leave Cassie alone. They're more determined than ever to have their way." He raked a hand through his hair as he searched Giles' eyes. "I'm afraid of what they may attempt next. I wish your father was here. I feel sure he'd know how to handle them."

"Why are your aunts staring at Cassie?" Wilma asked Daniel while they came together during the intricate steps of the quadrille.

He enjoyed conversing with her in snippets as they moved through the steps of a figures. She hadn't reacted well at first to his earlier revelations although she did accept what he'd said as truth. "They want Cassie to willingly go with them, to join their trinity of witches."

Wilma briefly met his eyes as she turned, preparing to continue to the next series of steps. "But why are they so determined?"

She needed to know the truth. He had an important question to ask her, but only if she understood what she'd be getting into if she said yes. He grabbed her hand and guided her to the side of the dance floor. He released her hand, aware of the looks from others in the room. "The truth?"

"Is it related to what you told me earlier?"

He indicated for her to follow him and he led her to the side of the room, far enough away to have a private conversation. "Entirely."

"Then tell me. I've thought about what you said and none of that matters to me. I like you and want to spend time with you."

"I like you, too." Relief flowed down his back. "My aunts are powerful witches and they want Cassie to join her powers with theirs to become even stronger. But she doesn't want to work with them because of the kind of magic they practice."

"So why do they stay here instead of going home?"

"They insist she'll change her mind." He pivoted so his back was to his aunts and the room at large. "Wilma, may I ask you a question?"

The moment had arrived for him to find out the answer to one burning question.

"Of course." She gazed up at him with her soft eyes, lips parted in anticipation.

"Wilma, I am very glad to have met you and become acquainted with your fine qualities, your gentle yet stubborn self." What a lovely young woman stood before him. "I have quite fallen in love with you. Will you marry me?"

He'd finally summoned the courage and asked her. He'd been contemplating doing so for a week, but doubt and uncertainty prevented him. Knowing she accepted his truth changed everything. Her answer could change everything else.

She blinked up at him as her mouth fell open. "Marry you?"

"I can't stop thinking about you, of wanting to spend the rest of my life getting to know everything about you." Her divine eyes and blushing cheeks suggested she considered his question. If only the answer he longed for would emerge from her tantalizing lips. "So will you consent to be my wife?"

"You're a fine, intelligent, caring man, Daniel Fairhope." She searched his eyes for several frantic beats of his heart and then nodded. "I would be proud to be your wife."

Joy and relief tornadoed through his chest. His future, his world, opened up with her sweet words. She said yes. They had many other decisions to make to plan the path to their future. How long of an engagement being the first question on his mind. His brain whirred with the many tasks before him, to relocate his belongings from college to the inn, to build or buy a house for them to start a family in. But first, he must do one thing.

"I should probably seek your brother's approval before we declare our engagement." He glanced over to where Flint conversed with Giles at the bar. "To make it proper."

"After, we should tell my parents the news." She smiled up at him, her joy sparkling in her eyes. "You'll get to meet them and my sister, too."

He considered her suggestion for a moment before shaking his head. "I look forward to doing so, but we'll need to wait until my father arrives and we resolve the standoff with my aunts." He tucked one hand around his elbow. "Come, let's talk to Flint."

"I understand why we need to wait, but I'm anxious for you to meet them all." She stayed close to him as they strolled toward the bar. "I'd like to stay and help if he will let me."

"That's very kind of you, sweetheart." He stopped at Flint's side and waited until the two men stopped their conversation to look at him. "Flint, I would like your blessing as Wilma's brother on our engagement. She has accepted my offer of marriage."

Flint's jaw tensed as he slid his astonished gaze to Wilma. "You have?"

She smiled at her brother. "I have."

"Love is most definitely in the air around here." Giles thumped a hand on the counter as he shook his head. "Congratulations to you both."

"I haven't given my blessing." Flint propped his hands on his hips, the slight frown shifting into a broad smile. "Now I am though. Congratulations!"

Daniel accepted Flint's brief handshake as Wilma laughed. Maybe things would all sort themselves out soon so he could marry the beautiful woman at his side and be happy. He glanced over his shoulder at Cassie's smile and then the suspicious looks from his aunts. He turned away from Hope and Faith's stares, his heart sinking. Maybe not quite yet, though.

Chapter Nineteen

$\mathcal{F}$lint rapped on the bar with the back of his hand. "I'm calling this meeting to order.

After speaking to Giles the previous afternoon, Flint had spent time in his office drawing up plans for the proposed addition. He strove to design a pleasing addition which would complement the existing structure. Only with time a factor, he'd had to resort to building with lumber instead of stone, but he'd add a façade resembling stone to the foundation to blend the new with the old. Matching the windows and roof proved far easier, with a respectable result he hoped his boss would approve. Now he needed to organize the crew to build his dream.

"All official like, hm?" Giles huffed as he leaned back in his chair to smirk at Flint.

"Indeed. I need all of your help to add on to the inn before your father returns." He scanned the three brothers' faces and then flicked a glance at the customers seated at nearby tables, listening in with interest. "We only have a few weeks to add on four new bedrooms on the north end. Will you help me?"

"Of course we will." Abram tugged on his waistcoat as he looked at Daniel and Giles. "What do you need us to do?"

"Do you know how to build a building or house?" Flint prayed they had some experience but on the surface they didn't appear to have had such an opportunity to learn hands-on building techniques. "It's not something we've talked about, so please don't worry if you do not have such skills."

"I've built things before, so I can show them what they need to do." Giles crossed his arms as he glanced at his brothers. "We'll need to make a plan and then order supplies."

"I've sketched out what I have in mind but I'd appreciate your thoughts." After all, Flint hadn't ever designed a building even though he'd pored over architecture magazines for years. Now that he had designed the addition he could add a new tool to his toolbox. Assuming everything worked out as he envisioned.

Isaac hurried in with a large tray of plates and bowls and carried it past the group at the bar with barely a glance. He placed it on a table near the group of men meeting at the back of the room, John and Sterling both presiding over the concerning gathering. As Flint watched for a moment, he saw Isaac lean down between John and Sterling and say something before handing out the various steaming dishes. But what? Probably checking on their satisfaction with the food and service. What else could it be? Mentally shrugging away his suspicions, Flint addressed the Fairhope brothers.

"I'll put together the supply order after we're through here and see about buying the lumber and nails, window glass, shingles, and such."

"Why don't you hire a few of the neighborhood men to help so we move this project right along?" Abram asked. "Promise them free meals or something in addition to paying them as an incentive?"

"A fine idea." Daniel glanced away to where Wilma and Mandy sat chatting with Cassie over a cold cider. "The sooner we get this done the better, I'd say."

"I'll put out the word." Flint followed his gaze, making eye contact with Cassie. She smiled softly at him for a moment and then stood to walk across the room toward him. Her every movement pleased him and he longed to be able to say confidently she belonged to him. At least her heart. If only he felt worthy of being her husband, it would make waiting for her father's longed-for but questionable blessing easier. Even the aunts dismissed him as worthless in their machinations and intentions. The aunts in question occupied their usual places, sweet glares aimed his way.

Cassie stopped beside him but didn't reach out to him. "Everything all right over here?"

Flint nodded. "We're planning the addition to the inn."

"As I thought." She swept her gaze across her brothers' faces and then smiled at him. "I've had an idea."

"What's that?"

"With Pa and everyone on the way home in time for Allhallows Eve, why don't we plan an open house in conjunction with the party, to showcase the new addition and celebrate their homecoming along with the special day?"

"A party! I'm in." Daniel rapped the bar with his knuckles. "We can announce our engagement, too."

"All of them, I guess." Cassie looked at Flint with a knowing grin. "There really must be something in the air around here."

Reggie would be home before the celebration so hopefully Flint and Cassie would have good news to share. He studied her pretty face as she interacted with her brothers in jovial banter and all around fun. He'd be lucky to call her his wife. How he loved the sound of her name changing to Cassandra Hamilton, Mrs. Flint Hamilton to the world. If only... He stopped musing to focus on the conversation at hand.

"I'll have Isaac and Lawrence help spread the word to the customers, and let John know so he can help relay the news even farther afield." His girl really did have great ideas. Life with her would be interesting. "I will tell Matt and he can start planning the menu."

"Have you found Mandy's replacement yet?" Cassie arched her brows at him. "I imagine we'll have a crowd and Matt won't be able to handle the preparations with only Meg and Myrtle to help. I mean, I can help some but we'll want entertainment and dancing, too."

"I'd rather you not work in the kitchen for that event. I think I might have someone interested but I'm not sure." Myrtle had suggested a young widow looking for work to put food on the table for her three children but he hadn't spoken to her yet. In the meantime, perhaps it would be wise to have some insurance. "I'll put another ad in the paper when I go into town to order everything we need."

"Mandy seems to enjoy working as hostess." Cassie peered up at him, a knowing look in her eyes. "You were smart to give her the position."

After careful consideration, Flint had spoken to her about what her duties would be as hostess. Mainly, to greet and welcome the guests and ensure they had a place to sit. Then assign which waiter would serve which tables. She could mingle with the guests to ask if they needed anything but she must keep an eye on the front to handle new arrivals in a timely manner. The additional attention each customer would receive as a result should make them feel special and encourage their repeat business.

"We'll see how it works out, but I hope so." Flint addressed the small group gathered at the bar. "Any questions?"

"We have our orders." Giles stood up and pushed away from the bar. "Let's take a look at that layout, Flint."

"It's in my office." Flint led the way out of the dining room and into the future of the Fury Falls Inn's new addition. He mentally crossed his fingers that his boss would approve. Of both the changes to the inn and of him as son-in-law.

How dare they plot their mischief in plain view in a public place? I try not to stare at them, gathered at the bar, laughing and smiling as if they haven't a care in the world. If only Cassie had died as intended. If it weren't for the older creature, she wouldn't be breathing. And Flint Hamilton is thick as thieves with the witches surrounding him. Why does he need to add on to the inn? To harbor more witches most likely. More like the hateful, conniving pair of crones at the table by the piano with their black cat. They seemed to threaten the young witch in some way but I couldn't quite gather specifics.

Isaac approached the table with a tray and set it down. I motioned him over. He bent down beside me to hear my request. "Find out what you can about what they are planning. It can't be good and we must be prepared to defend our community without another failure. Understood?"

"Yes sir. I'll let you know what I find out." Isaac straightened and started passing out our food.

I am glad I thought to have a couple of my own men planted here at the inn to keep me informed. We'll succeed yet in ridding the region of evil witches and those worrisome ghosts, too. Mark my words.

"I'm amazed at how much has been accomplished in only a week." Cassie stood beside Flint in front of the inn, a short distance from the pounding of hammers on nails and cursing when someone hit a thumb.

The two-story addition of four new rooms, two up and two down with a short hall between on each floor, made the large structure even more imposing. Teddy came around the end of the new construction carrying a water bucket, offering a ladle of water to the men on the ground. The boy made her proud with how he didn't wait to be asked but found a way to contribute to the men's progress. She could only imagine what a fine man he'd become as he matured and received a formal education.

"They should finish putting the shingles on by early afternoon at the pace they're going." Flint supervised the work, to ensure the resulting building met his exacting standards, but he had also made a point to pitch in when needed. "Then the finish work inside will need to happen."

"When are the linens going to be sewn and ready?" He'd placed an order for additional sheets, towels, rugs, and blankets from a shop in town and her curiosity remained high as to how fine they'd be.

All this fuss because her pa was finally on his way home and bringing additional residents. How fortunate they'd all been to have not only located but arranged for Pansy Drake's freedom. Cassie's curiosity was also aroused by who the two mysterious others might be. Maybe family she'd not met yet. Finally knowing her father's side of the family would be a boon.

She glanced to the front porch of the inn where Hope and Faith along with her familiar sat at the little table beside the double doors, supervising her as intently as Flint did the inn's progress. If only they'd relent, realize they would never succeed in convincing her to do what they wanted her to do. Her pa would know how to handle them once he arrived and assessed the situation for himself. She hoped. But what if he didn't? A chill inched through her veins. He must.

"They should be here in another week if the roads are passable." Flint shielded his eyes with a hand as he watched the men climbing on the roof to pound the oak shake shingles onto the addition. "Then your family will be reunited."

"That is true. I'm so glad to have you in my life, Flint." She didn't look at him, aware of being watched from several directions. Giles paused in his labor on the roof to sweep the area with his intense gaze, keeping a lookout for any mischief. She shivered as she recalled the stranger's attempt to slit her throat. Knowing so many were on alert helped soothe her jitters. "No matter what happens, I'll never leave you. We'll always be together."

Flint lowered his hand to regard her with his gentle eyes. "I hope *that* is true. I plan to be with you the rest of my life if I'm permitted to do so."

"Whose permission do you need?" Asking her father's blessing wasn't permission so much as agreement with her chosen course.

"Apparently your father's, right?"

She pivoted to face him, searching his eyes for some hidden truth. Reaching out with her senses she picked up on his true feelings. Startled by his truth, she reached up to kiss him lightly on the lips. She cupped his jaw with a hand, infusing her voice with hope and love and confidence. "I love you for the man you are. Don't doubt my love for you. We're not waiting because I doubt but because I want to honor my father and try to understand my family history before we join our lives together. That's only right."

"I'm not worthy of you, Cassie." Flint's voice rang with certainty.

"Don't say that. Of course you are." She felt his deep-rooted doubt and insecurity and loved him all the more for caring so much for her happiness he despaired of measuring up to some hypothetical yardstick he'd conjured in his mind. "Pa would not have entrusted his entire business and home to your care if he couldn't rely on you. I know in my heart he will approve of our being betrothed." She kissed him again, aware of the eyes boring into her back as she exhibited such affection for him in public.

"You are far more confident of his opinion than I am." He regarded her for a beat. "What do you think he'll have to say about your brothers also finding love here?"

"I imagine he'll be happy for them as I am. I'm glad Abram and Giles are staying, even going to build homes nearby."

"Daniel may do likewise, or he may decide town life is more his speed." Flint sighed and glanced up at the house where Daniel, Abram, and Giles worked alongside several other men. "It's hard to believe my sister is betrothed but at least she's chosen well." He gazed at Cassie with a gentle lift of his lips. "Our families are becoming entwined."

"Yes, in more ways than I ever imagined…" She paused, her senses alerting to another presence approaching. She reached out farther, testing the strengthening connection. There. She could practically see through his eyes as he rode up the lane toward the inn. "Silas is nearly here. We should prepare a place for him to sleep."

Flint frowned and blinked at her. "How can you possibly know that?"

"I sense his presence drawing closer." She grinned up at him. "More help is on the way as my family continues to show up as requested."

"I wonder what kind of help he's bringing."

Silas had the same ability she did to sense another's emotions. He'd established the mental connection between them as he neared. He was content and happy and worried about what he'd find when he arrived. But he had a strong conviction that she needed him. Much hovered out of view, a resolution to their situation or perhaps some form of revolution to overthrow the status quo. How could she know the future? The family coming together would most certainly make them stronger and better.

"I don't know." She kissed Flint once more for good measure. "We'll just have to wait and see."

The End

Thanks so much for reading *Fractured Crystals*! The adventure continues, so stay tuned for more to come in this six-book series.

To find out about new releases and upcoming appearances, please sign up for my newsletter via my website at www.bettybolte.com. I send out a monthly newsletter with book news to share with my readers, upcoming events and signings, and even a few favorite recipes, puzzles, and other doings!

I'd love to hear from you! Feel free to send me an email at betty@bettybolte.com, find me on Facebook at www.facebook.com/AuthorBettyBolte, follow me on BookBub, or connect with me on Twitter @BettyBolte.

You can always find an updated list of the titles in this series, as well as all of my other books, at www.bettybolte.com.

Thanks again for reading!

Betty

About the Author

Bestselling, award-winning author Betty Bolté is known for authentic and accurately researched American historical fiction with heart and supernatural romance novels. She's been published in essays, newspaper and magazine articles, and nonfiction books but now enjoys crafting entertaining and informative fiction. She earned a Master's Degree in English in 2008, emphasizing the study of literature and storytelling, and has judged numerous writing contests for both fiction and nonfiction. Get to know her at www.bettybolte.com.